BEFORE WE LOVED

Chai Rose

Chai Rose

Before We Loved

Chai Rose

This book is a work of fiction. Names, characters, places, and events are strictly the work of the author's imagination or are used fictitiously. Any resemblance to actual events, locales, or persons, living or dead, is coincidental.

Copyright ©2016 by Chai Rose

All rights reserved. In accordance with the U.S. Copyright Act of 1976, the scanning, uploading, and electronic sharing of any part of this book without the permission of the publisher or author is piracy and theft of the author's intellectual property.

Thank you for your support of the author's rights.

Printed in the United States.

Before We Loved

∞∞∞∞∞∞

A novel by

Chai Rose

Chai Rose

Cover design by Get eDesigns

Thanks to the Blurb Bitch

Special Thanks to:
Dad and Mom, Andrea Hitchings, and Glenyse Grenier

And, of course, thank you to Phoebe and Ellie…

For my family…

Chai Rose

Part One

Chapter One - Now

Normally I'm able to charm the pants off older men – and I mean that quite literally. But my head is swimming and the rest of me is about to drown. So, I don't even try flirting with the detective. I can't remember specific details, or even exactly what happened. But the blood is live and in technicolor, right in front of my mind's eye. And he's lying on the floor with bright red blood running out of him.

He's dead. I'm pretty sure of that. And I think I killed him.

And yet, most of me doesn't care. There are far too many other things to worry about.

My hand is trembling as I shake the detective's hand. He's bald with a white goatee. If I was to sit down and sketch out what I thought a police detective would look like, he would pretty much be it.

"Are you okay?" he asks.

"Not really."

"The officer who brought you in said you remember very little about what happened tonight. Is that correct?

I nod my head. "Yes."

"Well, hopefully if we start at the beginning, it will come back to you. Okay?"

"Okay."

There's a dull pain in my head. It's beginning to throb just behind my right eye.

"Hopefully this won't take too awfully long," the detective says. "But I'm sure this isn't going to be quick either. I just want to give you the chance to tell your side of things. And don't leave out anything. Okay? Sound fair?"

I shut my eyes and see Blake standing before me. He's about to cry and I just want to hold him. I want him to hold me. But that isn't possible. He shrugs his shoulders and then turns and walks away into the darkness. I open my eyes and the detective is just sitting quietly, staring at me.

"Sorry," I whisper.

"Do you need any medical care before we begin?"

I shake my head. "I'm fine."

I was nearly killed just a couple hours ago. A man lies dead in my apartment. Blake is gone. And I left the scene before the police arrived. So, I am most certainly not fine.

"Can I get you anything before we begin?"

"No thank you. Not right now."

He sits down across from me. "Okay, why don't we get started and then maybe we can take a little coffee break in a bit. Sound good?"

I nod my head.

"Good." He flips open his notebook and pulls his cell phone from the front pocket of his shirt. "Now, I want to make it clear to you that you're not under arrest so I'm not going to read you your Miranda Rights. Do you know what Miranda Rights are?"

"Yes."

"Good. So you're not under arrest and you have no obligation to speak with me. In fact, you can leave right now. Or request an attorney. Okay?"

How can I possibly leave if my car is parked two miles away? And if I'm not under arrest then why did the officer take me out of my car and put me in the back of a police car and bring me here?

But I just nod my head. And I want to tell my story – all of it. So, maybe being here isn't such a bad thing. Maybe it will help me sort everything out and help me move forward.

But not so far forward that I get stuck. Because I can't remember everything that happened. I know Blake is gone. I know my head hurts. And I know there is a lot of blood back at my apartment. But that's about it.

"So, you know why you're here, right?"

"Yes."

"And you're willing to tell me everything that happened? You'll tell me how and why a man was killed in your apartment earlier?"

Hearing him say it makes it hard for me to swallow. My throat aches and feels as if it's about to shut. There's a flash in my mind of blood of running across the floor and eyes just staring up at me. And suddenly I can't stop seeing it.

"Ms. Sanders," the detective says.

I shake my head and close my eyes. I try to un-see the blood. And I try not to think of Blake. I seriously might lose it all. And going crazy might not be a bad option.

"Sorry," I whisper again. I open my eyes and look down at the shiny table.

He smiles; it's surprisingly warm and makes me want to trust him. I want to hug him.

"I'm going to hit record on my phone here and then we can begin."

"Okay."

He taps the screen on the phone punches in four numbers, and then hits the red button on the screen. "It's August 5th. Please state your name," he says.

"K-Katie Sanders."

"Your age?"

"Twenty-three."

"And your address?"

"One-twenty Holland Street Apartment One, Dulcet North Carolina."

"Okay, now before I ask you any questions, I thought I'd give you a chance to tell me the story of what happened today."

But suddenly I just want to tell the story of Blake and myself. I want to tell the detective that Blake and I had the most amazing love ever – like once in a lifetime, Romeo and Juliet, Kate and Jack kinda love. I don't care if I sound cheesy to him. Because our love is – I mean was – no I mean is - just that perfect and powerful.

But I know he wants to hear the whole story. And whether I get out of here, depends on me telling him everything. That includes the dark secrets, the moment I knew I was being stalked, and everything about Blake and Kendra and Neil too.

"From the beginning right?" I ask just to make sure.

He nods his head. "That would be perfect."

So I suck in a deep breath and close my eyes. I see Blake's smile with his glorious dimples popping in both his cheeks. And I see him defending us that night in the parking lot of that bar in DeRuyter. He was so confident and tough and just plain hot.

That was the night we met. And that's when it all started.

I open my eyes and look at the detective.

Then I begin.

Chapter Two - Then

I hate to admit it, but I was a slut. Or maybe I still am. (Can a slut lose such a label?) I never wanted to be. What girl does? But that's exactly what I am. So, I'm no better than her. Let's get that straight from the start. And I'm probably worse in every other way. Except I can stop drinking after a few beers and she can't. I don't have to drink every day, and she does. I don't *have* to get drunk. But my sister does. So, anyway, that's what I was thinking as I swung open the door and walked into the bar: I'm no better than her.

It was a huge place with a long bar at the front and a stage on the back deck. The place was over half full so I didn't see her right away. I walked all the way to the back and then around past the bathrooms. I was just starting to think maybe she'd already left, but then she found me. I heard her screaming before I saw her.

"Katie!"

I turned and Kendra was hugging me before I even laid eyes on her. She smelled of pot and beer. But I didn't care. It felt great to hold my sister – absolutely wonderful. I hadn't seen her since she left for rehab and that was over six weeks ago. I hadn't spoken to her in almost three weeks. When I held her I knew she was safe for at least a few seconds, so I could stop the worrying. But only for a few seconds.

"Have a shot with me!" she yelled and then she started for the bar.

I grabbed her hand and pulled her back. "Hang on," I told her. "Let me look at you a second."

She faced me, smiled, and rolled her eyes. "I'm still just Kendra. Always have been, always will be."

"You cut your hair," I said. I reached up and placed my hand on the side of her head. "It looks good," I lied.

Kendra always had the most gorgeous, long red hair. It was the kind of red hair that *always* got compliments from strangers. The color, the body, the way it naturally hung on her – it was all so perfect. But now it was cropped short to her head.

"Do you like it?"

"I do," I lied again.

"Marty told me to try it. He wanted something different."

"Marty?"

"Yeah, my boyfriend. He's here, you have to meet him. But first a shot!" she yelled.

She pulled me to the bar and we ordered two shots of whiskey and three beers. Kendra raised her shot glass toward me, I clinked mine against it, and down the hatch it went. Then I grabbed my bottle of beer and followed her as we snaked our way back toward where Marty was sitting.

What the hell was I doing drinking with my alcoholic sister? Our mom sent me there to get her – to rescue her, really – and here I was downing shots with her and drinking beers. But our relationship was always complicated. And saving an alcoholic from herself – and some stupid guy she met at rehab – is not an easy task. So I had to do what felt right. And all too often, with Kendra, that had to include drinking with her.

I was the one who brought Kendra to rehab a little over two months ago. It was her fourth try at it. But she promised this time she was going to make it work.

"I'm twenty-four years old now and my life is passing me by. It's time for me to grow-up and stop all the bullshit," she told me early one morning.

So, I dropped her off for the ninety-day inpatient stint that could have turned into a longer stay followed by a halfway house. But, sixty-two days into her stay, she decided to leave with some guy and she fell off the map for a couple weeks. Nobody heard from her and we didn't know if she was dead or alive.

Of course our mother was beside herself. No matter how many times Kendra screwed up, my mom stayed just as invested in her and continued to worry herself sick. I mean, Kendra stole from my mom the first time when she was fifteen and hasn't ever really stopped. When she was eighteen she took my mom's car and crashed it into a light pole in the Walmart parking lot. Her BAC was .27 – more than three times over the legal limit to drive. That's the first time Kendra went to rehab.

She was sober for over a year but then she fell off the wagon hard. She moved in with some guy who was a couple years older than her. He lived with his grandparents and had a nasty heroin addiction to go with his own alcoholism.

That was probably the hardest time in our relationship. Kendra and I were always inseparable. But during that time, we didn't speak for probably a year or more. Then one night, while I was at college, I got a call from her telling me she was about to kill herself. Her boyfriend was dead. He got a bad batch of heroin and died with a big stupid smile on his face. Kendra said she'd never seen him looking so happy. And she wanted to go like that too.

So, my roommate drove me two hours to where Kendra was and we brought her back to our dorm room. She stayed with us for two nights. But then she nearly burned down a frat house during a party, and wound-up back in rehab after serving three months in the County Correctional Facility.

After all that, she stayed sober for a while. She even got a job at a fast food restaurant making donuts and serving coffee. She went to AA meetings and saw a counselor every other week. For a short while, I thought she really might make it. But it was a hollow hope. And I knew that even as I chose to embrace the feeling. Because when I looked into her eyes, and really listened to her voice, I could still see and hear her pain. And soon she did fall down again.

Kendra once told me that every time she walked into a store she could feel a warm hum coming from the beer coolers. She could go into a store for the very first time and know exactly where the beer was. Staying sober, she said, was not a case of simply not drinking. It was ignoring that hum that always lived inside her and grew louder when alcohol was near and the nights turned dark and cold. Eventually, the hum grew too loud again. She started drinking again and spent four days on a bender that ended with her in the in hospital with a BAC of .47. She should have died. But she didn't. So, I brought her to rehab again.

Our dad was an alcoholic. Mom always said he drank because of the horrible things he'd seen as a police officer. I'm sure he did see lots of horrible things. Who am I to say he should have been stronger or tougher or had more love in him? I don't blame him for the drinking or for treating my mom like shit for the first seven years of my life.

My bedroom and Kendra's bedroom were right next to each other at the end of the hall in our old house. So, our closets were connected, separated by only a thin wall. When my dad used to get really drunk (and usually fight with my mom too) Kendra and I would sit in our closets and talk for hours until dad finally settled down. Kendra used to tell me the stupidest, funniest jokes I'd ever heard. She was less than two years older than me, but in those moments, she seemed like an adult. She gave me comfort. And she always cheered me up when I was crying and wishing my family was normal.

But, like I said, I don't blame my dad for being a cop for fifteen years before getting fired. And I don't blame him for drinking or for being a jerk when he was drunk. But I do blame him for leaving when I was eight years old. And I do blame him for walking out and never coming back. He just left one Saturday before breakfast – without even saying *so-long* - and never came back. I have no idea where he went or where he is even now, but I hope he's dead or completely alone and miserable. I know that's a horrible way to feel. I know that. And I do feel bad for feeling this way. So, I guess I do still love the asshole. I guess.

When Kendra left rehab the last time I was more worried than usual. I just had a feeling that she was dead. Nobody heard a word from her for so long. All the rehab facility could tell us was that she left with some other guy. They wouldn't even tell us who she left with and where she might have gone. So, my mom and I called the police but they had no interest in trying to help locate a twenty-four-year-old alcoholic who had a criminal record. So, we just waited and prayed and hoped.

Unfortunately, I found myself finding more and more comfort in Neil.

So when my mom called me and said Kendra had just called her from a pay phone outside a bar in DeRuyter – a town about thirty miles east of Dulcet – I went right after her. Thankfully my car started right up and the drive only took me just over a half hour.

I followed Kendra outside onto the deck and over to a table where an overweight man sat holding a cigarette in one hand and a beer in the other. He smiled up big and wide at me. I couldn't help but see his resemblance to Jabba the Hutt.

"My love, this is my other love, my sister Katie."

He shoved the cigarette between his lips and shot a huge, fat hand toward me. "Damn, I guess beauty runs in the family. Nice to meet ya sweetheart. What's yer name?"

"Katie." I said shaking his hand. It was sickeningly warm and sweaty, like he'd been holding it down his pants for the last hour or so. "And you're Marty?"

"I am Marty," he said slow and proud. Then he took the cigarette out of his mouth and arrogantly blew circles into the air. I waved my hand to break them up before they reached me.

"So how long you guys been together?"

"I'm not sure," Kendra said. She sat on his right knee and he bounced her up and down like a father would do to his little girl. She looked over her shoulder at him. "Do you know?"

"I don't have a clue," he laughed. "All depends what yer definition of *together* is. We've been living together for over two weeks now. But we were a thing back in the hospital before that."

"The hospital?" I asked.

"That's what he calls rehab. He doesn't like the word *rehab*," Kendra said throwing up air quotes with her fingers.

"And where are you living?"

"We're staying with friends," Marty said before Kendra could answer herself. He took a long pull from his beer, wiped his mouth with his fingers, and then jammed the cigarette back into his mouth.

"And where might that be?"

"With friends" Marty repeated, this time his voice was lower and laced with something that seemed to be making an attempt at authority.

I raised my eyebrows and took a swig of my own beer. I listened to Marty tell stories of his time with the Marines (the assholes kicked him out for going AWOL one little time to go to his brother's bachelor party). And he talked about all the *good times* with his friends (the time they threw an empty wine bottle off a balcony and broke a car's windshield eight stories below and the time they kicked an entire biker gang's ass because they accidentally walked into the wrong bar).

I nursed my beer along, knowing I was going to be driving home at the end of the night, hopefully with Kendra in the car too. So, before I was even halfway finished with beer number one, Kendra and Marty were already ready for another.

"Your turn to get me another round," Marty said to Kendra.

"But I just got the last one."

He pushed her off his lap and slapped her on the ass. "Well, as long as I'm buying the beer, yer fetching the beer. Off you go."

And as soon as Kendra went back inside, Marty started right in with the disgusting comments.

"So your sister's hair down below matches the hair on her head. How about you? You a natural blond or do you bleach yer hair?"

"That's a question many have wondered but few have found the answer," I answered as nonchalantly as I could manage. "You can keep wondering. Seems like your plates already pretty full."

He laughed, or more like roared. "Oh there is plenty of room on my plate – especially for sisters. And the size of my table will amaze and delight you. Believe me."

"Your table?" I asked. I slammed back a swallow of my beer and banged the bottle back down onto the table. "You mean like your bed is really big and comfortable?"

"My bed?" he laughed. "What the hell are you talking about? I'm talking about my junk. My crank. My dick."

I'd met a lot of guys like him. He wasn't special. Unfortunately, my sister, when she was actively drinking, always seemed to find the biggest assholes on the planet. So, I was pretty much prepared to deal with him.

I leaned forward and grinned at him. "If that's what you meant then you should have said your utensil is huge or something like that. Not a freaking table. That makes no sense."

He looked confused.

"The metaphor was like a meal," I explained to him like he was a five-year-old. "You know, who you're dating or who your screwing is a plate? So saying your utensil is big would make more sense than your table."

"But it's got good wood," he answered. "And you make it hard like a table." Then he roared with laughter, so loud that everyone on the deck turned to look at him.

I almost threw up in my mouth. The vomit got up past my chest and burned in the bottom of my throat. I rolled my eyes and leaned back in my chair.

"Yeah, okay," I smiled. "I'll take your word for it thanks. But if that's the route you want to go then I'm sure a TV tray would probably be closer to the truth than a whole table. Or maybe just an airplane tray. You know, one of those little, fragile things that fold down from the back of the seat."

He sneered at me and opened his mouth to speak but Kendra was back with another three beers. She put one down in front of me, one in front of Marty, and then the third in the spot between me and Marty. She started to sit in the chair beside the two of us but Marty grabbed her by the waist and planted her back down on his knee.

"Your sister was just flirting with me."

"She was?" Kendra asked, feigning shock and surprise.

I shook my head. "Nope. Not me," I said.

He laughed his big booming laugh and Kendra looked at me and rolled her eyes. Then she mouthed two words to me that I couldn't help but understand.

Help.

Me.

I frowned at her and took another drink from my bottle of beer. Kendra nodded ever so slightly and shifted her gaze toward the door. I didn't need any more signs.

"You know what?" I said. "I really have to pee."

"Me too," Kendra said quickly.

I grabbed her by the hand and pulled her off of Marty. "Then let's go."

"Be right back," Kendra said to Marty. She leaned down and kissed him on the cheek. As she tried to straighten up, Marty grabbed the back of her head and kissed her hard on the mouth.

"Don't be long," he told her. And then he gave her one more slap, this time on her right thigh. Kendra winced in pain and limped as she took her first couple steps toward the door.

Once we got back into the bar, I threw my arm around her shoulder. "Tell me you hate that asshole," I whispered in her ear.

Kendra laughed, tripped over the leg of a chair, and stumbled into a table. She caught herself before she fell over an old man who was eating a plate of nachos. I helped her regain her balance and then we both went to the bathroom. I shut and locked the door.

"Come home with me right now."

Kendra smiled at me. "Come home with you? No way. We're drinking, having a good time. Come on let's do another shot. But first let me pee."

She pulled down her pants and that's when I saw the welts. They were covering her thighs. But Kendra didn't notice me looking at her. She bent down and flinched as she sat down on the toilet seat.

"Holy crap, Kendra. What happened to your legs?"

"What?" She looked surprised at first but then she glanced down. "Oh this?" she asked pointing with her index finger. "This is nothing."

"It doesn't look like nothing."

"It really isn't anything. I can barely feel it. Really it's not as bad as it looks." When she finished and was starting to pull her pants up, I stopped her. I grabbed her by the arm and turned her to the right so I could see her backside. It too was covered in bruises and welts.

"Holy shit, did he do this to you?"

"Stop looking at me you perv," Kendra giggled. She finished pulling up her pants and fastened them. "I'm fine. I really am."

"Marty did that to you?"

"Yeah, but he just jokes around. It's fine. It really is."

"He jokes around? That doesn't look like a joke. What did he hit you with?"

She bent over the sink and washed her hands. "He used his hands or a belt or a book or whatever. But he's usually just joking or else I said or did something stupid. You know I-." her voice trailed off.

I considered walking out to the deck and breaking a beer bottle over that bastard's head. Then I might just jab the broken bottleneck into that prick's prick that he liked to brag about.

But he was a big dude and I didn't know anyone else in the bar. Attacking him wouldn't be a good idea. No, the better plan was to get Kendra the hell out of there.

I grabbed her by the hands and looked her hard in the eyes. "Kendra. This isn't okay. Come home with me. You know you want to. You just asked for my help."

"Yeah but I didn't mean I wanted to leave. I just needed to get away from him for a couple minutes. He creeps me out sometimes.

That's all. I can't leave him." She looked at me with pleading eyes. "I seriously can't go."

"Are you scared of him? Did he threaten you?"

She looked down at the floor. Then she pulled me toward the door. "Let's do another shot. Come on." She was beginning to giggle and bouncing up and down. At that moment, this was not my sister. This was the alcoholic.

"Kendra," I said flatly, "we're leaving. I'm taking you home."

"But I want to drink," she said. She tipped her head to the side and pursed her lips, making a pouty face.

I looked around the bathroom trying to think. Someone outside rapped loudly on the door. "Hurry up in there! I'm gonna pee my pants!"

"Kendra, come with me, please?"

"Come drink with me first," Kendra said. She unlocked the door and put her hand on the door knob.

I put my hand on top of hers. "We'll get a six pack on the way home and drink at Mom's and sit up and talk all night. It will be just the old days."

Kendra's face lit up. "Make it a whole case and I'll do it."

"Half a case."

Yes, I was negotiating with an alcoholic about how much beer we were going to buy. But, again, until you lived with an alcoholic, don't judge.

"Done," Kendra smiled. She grabbed my hand and shook it.

Then we both walked out of the bathroom, across the bar, and out the front door. And there was Marty standing with his arms crossed, resting on his big belly.

"You girls going somewhere?"

"We just need to talk about some girl stuff," I said quickly. "You know; I'm having boy trouble. And I need my sister's advice."

How the hell did he even know we were about to leave? It was slightly surprising but not totally. From my experience, when Kendra was drinking she would forget her own name and not have the sense to do what was right for her. But she developed a sharp sixth sense that helped protect her addiction. When it came to drinking, her intuition was astounding. Apparently Marty's was too.

"Go back in the bar, now," he growled at Kendra. He jabbed a finger into my chest. "And you get the hell out of here."

Kendra turned to walk back into the bar but I grabbed her wrist. "Yeah, she's coming with me. Go screw yourself."

But as I tried to walk past him, he reached out and stopped me. He grabbed me hard on the right breast and then threw me back into the side of bar. I was more shocked than anything else. He was so strong. Granted, I only weighed about one hundred and twenty pounds, but with just one arm, he threw me like I was a ragdoll.

Kendra looked at me, looked at Marty, and then looked at me again. I looked back at her. This wasn't good and it was about to get much worse. This asshole might have thought the fear of his beating made Kendra loyal to him. Or maybe he thought the addiction they shared formed a bond between them. But he was wrong. Despite everything, Kendra and I made a pact a long time ago that we'd always have each other's back. This time was no different.

The two of us were no match for Marty. But we'd sure give him one hell of a fight.

Kendra took a run at him with her arms flying in all directions. Loud smacks like machine gun fire drowned out the noises of the bar as Kendra connected with his face and arms. But he ended her attack by swinging his right fist around and connecting with the side of her face. It sounded like a slab of beef hitting against cement. Kendra tumbled into the side of a car and fell down onto her side.

I thought to run back inside and scream for help. But I didn't know anyone in there and maybe he did. Maybe they'd help me or maybe they wouldn't.

So I reached for my back pocket, to grab my cell phone. But Marty went at Kendra again and I couldn't take the time to make the call. I ran and jumped on his back. I wrapped my left arm around his neck and tried to dig his eyes out with my right hand. Marty spun around twice as I scratched away chunks of his face. Then he grabbed a handful of my hair, bent down at the waist, and slung me off. I hit the gravel driveway and skidded for several feet.

I rolled onto my back, expecting to see Marty coming at me or attacking Kendra. But all I saw was *him*. He was standing over me with the overhead light casting light that shimmered all around him.

He looked like an angel.

I got to my feet and stood beside Kendra, directly behind the man who stood between us and Marty. I doubted this guy could protect us. He was a lot taller than Marty but much skinnier. Not skinny like scrawny – more athletic skinny – but still, there wasn't enough meat on his bones to compete with Marty, even though the guy was at least six inches taller. I wrapped my arm around Kendra's waist and held my breath. I didn't want to see some random guy get his ass kicked on our account. But I was thankful he was trying to help.

"You need to go back inside," the man was saying to Marty.

"I suggest you stay out of this friend before I kick yer ass too. I'm just protecting what's mine."

"I'm not your friend, believe me. I'm not friends with cowards who fight women. And I'm not going anywhere." Then he half turned back toward us and grinned. "I'm Blake Newman, by the way. Nice to meet you ladies."

Who the hell was this guy? He was way too calm and charming. Didn't he know he was about to fight?

Marty was dumbfounded. "That's my girl and this is not yer fight," he said pointing first at Kendra and then at Blake.

"See, I don't know a whole lot but I do know we don't own people. So, she's not your girl. And as a lawyer, I can tell you she has the right to leave if she wants and it's a criminal offense if you stop her. See that camera up there," he said pointing to the corner of the building. "That will be a great piece of evidence in court."

Marty turned and looked up at the camera. He shook his head. "You ain't no lawyer."

Blake shrugged his shoulders. "Yes, I am actually." He rubbed his face. "I know my boyish good looks make it hard to believe I'm old enough to be an attorney, but I am. And I know the law, and you, my never friend, are breaking it right now."

Marty cracked a smile and started to turn back toward the bar. But he quickly reversed his course and went at Blake. There were two flashes as Blake jabbed Marty's nose. His fists were so fast that the overhead light barely allowed them to be seen. Marty staggered back holding his hand against his face.

"See, that's called self-defense. The camera saw it and so did all these people," Blake gestured toward the small crowd that had formed just outside the door. "But I'm glad you came at me so I could hit you. You deserve to get your ass kicked, you slimy son-of-a-bitch. Come at me again. Please."

Marty didn't move. He took his hand away from his nose. It was covered in blood as was his mouth and chin. "I think you broke my nose."

Marty's face was all red and his teeth were gritted. His shoulders were heaving up and down as he opened and closed his hands into fists. There were three lines clawed up the right side of his face, and four lines dug into his forehead. I looked at it with pride as adrenalin pumped through my veins. *I did that to you! You bastard! I did that!*

Then he made another run at Blake. Two more flashes, each followed by a sharp crack. And then Blake swept his right leg and kicked out Marty's knee. He went down hard.

"We can do this all night. I bet my reach is about five inches longer than yours. So, you just let me know when you're done having your ass handed to you. Okay?"

Blake was so calm. Just completely in control of the entire situation. I looked at him and then at Marty and then back at Blake again. Marty was a monster compared to Blake. About twice his weight. Yet, Blake didn't show even one sign of fear or hesitation.

Marty got up onto all fours. Then back up onto one knee. Eventually he pulled himself back onto his feet. He stumbled back two steps and then tilted forward and then to the right and then to the left.

He reached into his pocket and pulled out his pack of cigarettes. "Maybe we can work out some type of deal here? Isn't that what lawyers do?"

"Not with people like you."

Marty tapped out a cigarette. He spat blood onto the driveway and wiped his mouth with the back of his hand. He looked Blake up and down and spit again. Then he popped the cigarette between his lips and lit it. He blew a stream of smoke into the space between him and us. We all just stood still, waiting to see if Marty had it in him to try again.

"It ain't worth it," Marty said. Then he pointed past Blake, right at me and Kendra. "I'll find you. And when I do it won't be pretty. I've killed for less."

"Goodbye," Blake said to him.

And then we all watched Marty go back into the bar. I kept one eye on the door and one eye on Blake. I half-expected Marty to come charging back out at us, maybe carrying a baseball bat or a gun. But Blake didn't seem concerned.

"Sorry about that," he said to us.

"Thank you so much," I said. I didn't know what else to say. My God he looked like a hero straight out of the movies. He was too perfect. And if I knew anything, it was to never trust perfection.

"Well, I'd invite you girls in for a drink but given the circumstances, I think it's probably best if we all leave."

"Oh good." Kendra put her arm around his waist and started walking with him. I took the lead, heading toward my car. "We were just going back to my parents to drink and we'd love for you to join us. But I call shotgun," Kendra said.

"That's not really what I meant. I meant we should all leave, but separately."

"What are you too good for us?" Kendra asked. "What are you a stuck-up snob?"

Blake chuckled and shook his head. "I just need to get home," he said softly.

I opened the passenger door and helped Kendra into her seat. "Buckle up for safety," I whispered just before I closed the door.

"Sorry, she's a little drunk."

"No apologies necessary, believe me. But I do need to go see my mom. She's been expecting me."

I nodded. Man, this guy was pretty tall. Like, not freakishly tall, but still several inches above me. And I'm almost five eight.

Blake walked with me around to the driver's side. *Don't ask me for my number. Please don't hit on me. It's been a long night and I have to meet Neil soon and I really can't deal with anymore crap. Please. Just please. Walk away.*

He opened the door for me. "You okay to drive?" he asked.

I frowned. "Yeah I had half a beer and a watered down shot. But gee Dad, thanks for asking."

He frowned. Then he smiled, and I hated the excitement that ran up my spine when he did.

"Just asking. You know, I always have to be the responsible attorney."

"I know. And you really like letting people know you're an attorney."

"Yeah, I hate how I do that," he smirked. "Promise it won't happen again."

I looked up into his eyes and stopped myself from playing with a lock of my hair.

"I'm sorry. It's just been a bit of a crazy day, ya know? And thank you again for saving us."

"Not a problem."

"Was that your sister's boyfriend?" he asked pointing behind him toward the bar.

"Yeah, sort of."

And now he's going to ask me if I have a boyfriend. And what the hell will I tell him? Do I have a boyfriend? No. I don't. Neil is not my boyfriend. Is he? Oh God, just don't hit on me. Don't you dare hit on me.

"Well you better get her home," he said taking my hand and helping me slide into the driver's seat. "Take care and drive safely."

And then, just like that, he closed the car door. He never even tried to get my number or find out anything about me.

I slid the key into the ignition and tried to start the engine. It clicked and then rumbled for a brief second and stopped. *Come on you old piece of shit. Come on!* I tried again and this time it coughed a few times and then turned over and started running.

I noticed my hand shaking as I gripped the steering wheel. What the hell had just happened? And who the hell was this Blake guy? I almost wished I'd asked him for his number. But that was silly.

I shifted the car into gear. And then I waved a hand at Blake and pulled away toward our home as Kendra sang an old Madonna song to herself.

Chapter Three - Then

Throughout my life, my counselors always told me I was only attracted to older men because of the things my father had and hadn't done. And I know that's true. I guess. But when I stop to think about it, why is anyone really attracted to someone else? Some people are born hardwired to like certain people and some people are shaped into people who are just pulled toward one type of person.

How does an abuser keep attracting a mate who will take his or her shit and not leave?

Why does my sister keep choosing these crazy losers?

Why did I sleep with three of my college professors and have a pretty deep and meaningful relationship with one of them?

He was forty-three and drove a Volvo and had a pretty wife and a little boy who played tee ball in the spring and soccer in the fall. His name was Robert Van Vorst. Dr. Van Vorst. That's what all the students called him. Hell, it's what his friends called him. But I called him Robert or Robbie (though he hated that one). Except when we were in bed together, then I called him Dr. Van Vorst too. I knew about his wife and his kid and I didn't like having an affair with him. But I couldn't stop myself. Just like I can't stop myself from seeing Neil.

It's amazing to me how quickly a relationship gets started. I remember when I was a freshman and flirting with my Psychology 101 professor. I never thought it would lead to anything and I was positive that if it started to roll down the hill of no return, I'd be able to stop it. I mean, he was a psychologist. He wouldn't be so stupid as to have a fling with an eighteen-year-old girl. Sure, he was single and only twenty-nine, but he was *my teacher*. But it happened. And it went from me staying after to help him carry tests back to his office to us being naked on his office floor in about seven minutes. I don't even remember what was said or who made the first move. It was a blur.

And that's usually how it goes. It goes from zero, to five miles an hour, and then you're doing about one hundred and fifty and loving every minute of it. And then once one of you stops loving it, you hit the brakes and you might both fumble around and pretend somehow it will work, but eventually it drops back to zero and you go your separate ways.

I have no idea what the older man might think of me afterward – *what a great kid* or maybe *wow she was a great lay* or *holy shit she was crazy*. I have no idea.

Do they miss me? Do they hate me? Do they think I'm a slut? Because for what it's worth, before I find someone else, I do miss me and I hate me. And, though it makes me incredibly sad and disappointed, I know I was a slut.

When I got back into the car at the bar, Kendra was a slobbering mess. She got about three lines into the second verse of that Madonna song and then she broke apart. She hated herself, she hated Marty, and she hated her life. Then she loved me and she loved Marty and she loved her life. Luckily she forgot all about our deal to buy more beer and spend the night drinking together. Apparently she and Marty had been drinking for almost two straight days. She passed out before I got her back to Mom's and I practically had to carry her upstairs to her old bedroom.

Mom was awake in the living room. She was so grateful that I'd found Kendra and convinced her to come home with me. Mom gave me a big hug and thanked me over and over. We talked for a few minutes and then I told her I had to get going, I had to close the bar, which was a lie. Of course, she didn't like me being a bartender with the history of alcoholism in the family and the fact that I was letting my college degree in English just waste away, but for the most part she never said anything. She had much bigger problems with Kendra.

That was just before ten and I was supposed to meet Neil at the hotel in Wilmington at eleven. It was over an hour away. So, I quickly went back to my apartment and changed into nicer clothes, sprayed a little more perfume on, and put my hair up. I texted Neil I would be about a half hour late and then I was gone.

We always had to go to Wilmington to meet because everyone in Dulcet knew Neil – Neil Anderson the successful businessman who seemed to own half of our town. He was a real estate businessman who owned dozens of properties. This included the tavern where I bartended. Neil owned the property but Buzz paid him rent and was considered the actual owner of *Take a Shot.* Honestly, I'm not exactly sure how all that works. But that's where I met Neil.

Just like the others, our relationship went from practically nothing to everything in the space of just a few minutes. Neil used to come in and sit at the end of the bar and talk to me for hours. He was funny, smart, and seemed to genuinely care about my life and my problems. He was a great listener. And yes, I knew he had a wife at home and I knew she had a couple little kids who didn't live with her. But despite knowing differently, I still believed we weren't going anywhere and if we started to, I'd be able to stop it.

But then one afternoon he asked me to take a trip to Wilmington with him. He said he had two tickets to the musical, *Dirty Dancing,* at the Wilmington Theater. His wife was out of town and he really wanted to go but couldn't go alone. I told him I didn't have anything to wear and he said that was okay. I told him I had to work and he said he'd take care of that. He told me to pack an overnight bag just in case the musical ran late and we didn't want to drive back. He said he'd make sure the room was a suite with a bedroom and a living area with a couch. He said he'd sleep on the couch, if we decided to stay. But the final decision would be up to me.

He talked to Buzz and got me the day off. Then he picked me up early in the afternoon and took me shopping for a nice dress. I picked a midnight blue V-neck spaghetti strapped evening gown. He bought it for me and then I changed into it and he took me to dinner at a French restaurant before we went to the musical. I felt like a princess the entire day and he acted like the perfect prince. Or, to be honest, he acted like the perfect king.

I didn't want the night to end so I chose to stay in Wilmington for the night. Our hotel room was ridiculously lavish. As promised, Neil pulled out the couch and gave me the bedroom off of the main living area. I purposely left my bag out by the couch. So, after we talked awhile and drank a couple glasses of wine, I retired to my room. But I walked back out to the living room a few minutes later, wearing nothing but my underwear. I told him I forgot my pajamas and when I bent down to get my bag, he grabbed me from behind and lifted me clear off my feet. He held me close and kissed me hard.

The rest is history, as they say.

Now, several months later, after the incident at the bar with Marty and Katie and some guy named Blake, I was at a hotel in Wilmington with Neil. I was waiting for room service to deliver the bacon cheeseburger I'd ordered a few minutes after I'd arrived. I was drifting off to sleep, dreaming of Kendra and the two of us fighting Marty, when a loud knock on the door knocked me from the dream. I jumped and let out a small scream. Neil was reading emails on his phone.

"It's okay," he said to me, "it's just room service."

It was my bacon cheeseburger and it smelled heavenly. Neil set the burger in front of me and I immediately took a huge bite. It tasted as good as it smelled.

"Want some?" I asked holding it up in front of his face.

"I can't eat that crap," he said pushing my arm away. "You're lucky you're so young and your metabolism is still running like a racchorse."

I took another huge bite, chewed, swallowed, and wiped my mouth with the linen napkin.

"Hey, I work out sometimes. And I like to eat a burger once in a while. So what? I don't eat it because my metabolism *runs like a racehorse*," I said mimicking his voice.

Neil laughed. Then he glanced down at my breasts and grimaced.

"How'd that happen?" he asked.

"What?" I had no idea what he was talking about. I got off the bed and looked at myself in the mirror. My right breast was the color of storm clouds. Then I remembered how Marty latched onto it just before throwing me aside earlier. "That asshole ex-boyfriend of my sister's did it." I bit on the tip of my thumb and twisted my body, looking at the breast from all possible angles. I shrugged my shoulders and got back on the bed. "Oh well, it doesn't really hurt."

"I bet it will tomorrow."

"You think so?"

"I bet." He went back to reading his emails. "Then you might wish you'd called the police."

I'd told him the story about what happened at the bar but I left out the part about Blake helping us. Neil could be really jealous sometimes and I didn't feel like fighting with him. I also liked making myself seem better than maybe I actually was. So, I told Neil that I punched Marty in the nose a couple times and the bastard backed right down.

I finished my burger while Neil stayed focused on his phone. I waited a few more minutes and sighed heavily a couple times to see if he'd noticed. When he didn't, I slipped off my bra and climbed into his lap, facing him.

"I'm feeling a little left out," I whispered. I bent over and nibbled on his earlobe. "What's got you so distracted tonight?"

"Just work stuff. I have some important decisions to make and a couple deals might be in the works. Plus, I just got a text from my wife. It seems her little bratty sons made it safely to our home."

He could and would mention his wife whenever he wanted. I wasn't allowed to get jealous. And honestly, I didn't care how much he mentioned her. I knew my role. And I knew what type of relationship I was in. Of course, Neil said the love went out of their marriage a couple years ago and that they'd be filing for divorce in the next year or two. His wife, Angela, treated him like crap (of course) and she wanted out of the marriage too. I didn't know if any of that was true, but I did appreciate him at least saying it.

Did he really dislike his wife's little kids or did he just pretend around me? I pictured him tossing a football around in a front yard with two shaggy haired boys. I pictured him sitting at a dinner table laughing with his wife at one end of the table, him sitting at the other end, and the boys sitting on each side. For some reason, in my mind they were all sitting in the Huxtable's dining room.

He looked at my bare breasts. "Have you ever thought about getting a boob job?"

I giggled, even though I didn't know if he was joking. "What?" I asked.

"Not that you need one," he replied. "You have great boobs, you know that." He set his cell phone down on the bed beside us and reached up and cupped my left breast. "And you know you're gorgeous. But the rest of you is like a perfect ten, and your breasts could be a ten too."

"Are you kidding me?"

"I'm just wondering if you've ever thought about it. I mean, I know a guy who could do it for you. Seriously, you wouldn't need to make them a lot bigger – just a little. And then you would seriously be the most beautiful person in the world."

I didn't know how to react. He seemed so serious about it. I knew he cared about me and he was probably one of the smartest people I'd ever met. The thought of getting a boob job had never crossed my mind. But maybe it should have.

I pulled at my right earlobe nervously and debated if I should slap him. I decided against it.

"Are you offering to pay for it?" I asked.

"If you wanted to do it. Sure, I'd pay for it."

I was flattered that he was willing to spend so much money on me. But I didn't need, nor did I want, to have a boob job.

"I don't think so," I shook my head.

"Okay, I'm just asking."

He was still cupping my breast as he clicked off the lamp. Then he grabbed both my wrists and pulled me down so I was flat against him. He was very fit for a forty-seven-year-old man -with six pack abs and bulging pecs. Best of all, he knew exactly how and where and when to touch me. He was an absolute magician with his fingers. And within minutes, I'd forgotten all about the boob job conversation. I was driven over the line into a world of almost unbearable pleasure.

All I cared about was being with him in that bed, it was everything to me. But soon, I'd realize it was nothing. Everything I knew was about to be rocked. My life was about to be tossed into a blender. And I had absolutely no idea then.

But the fuse had already been lit, and my world was about to explode.

Chapter Four - Then

As a little girl, I used to pray really hard that my dad would come back to us. I can see myself as a blond haired little girl lying in bed, covered by frayed blankets, with hands clasped so tight in prayer that my fingers turned white. I'd beg God to make him come back. To give him a reason to return us.

I missed him because he was my father and because I was supposed to miss him. I don't think I had any other reasons. But I still wanted him to come back so that my mom would stop crying at night and so we would stop being so poor.

The three of us shared a one-bedroom apartment and there were a couple nights a week when my mom didn't eat dinner because there wasn't enough food. Of course, she told us she just wasn't hungry and we believed her, but when I was fifteen or sixteen I figured it out and asked her what was really happening and she admitted it to me. She sacrificed so much for us. Always.

But my dad never came back despite all my prayers. And I don't know if God is real or not, but I am certain that if He exists, he doesn't care about me. He doesn't even know I exist.

Eventually my mom got a job at the bank as a part-time teller and worked her way up pretty quickly. Within about a year we could afford to eat but we still hadn't pulled ourselves up into even the lower middle class. It wasn't until mom met my eventual stepdad, Chris, that we finally had extra money.

Chris is the Chief Financial Officer for the bank and makes really good money. When he and mom married, we went from living in a seven hundred square foot apartment to living in a five bedroom, three and half bath, twenty-five hundred (give or take) square foot house in the hills that overlooked Dulcet. It was a bit of culture shock, but as a thirteen-year-old girl, I got used to it pretty quickly.

To be honest, despite how nice Chris has always been to us, and despite the fact that he's pretty rich, I never stopped praying that my dad would come back until Chris and my mom got married. That's when I finally stopped. And that's when I stopped praying completely. Not long after the marriage, Kendra, who's almost two years older than me, started drinking and getting into trouble. I guess it wasn't too long after that that I discovered boys were quite interested in me and I liked doing things to draw their attention. But I was a good girl all through high school – for the most part. It wasn't until college that I realized I liked older men. They could warm a spot inside of me that had been cold and empty my entire life.

After I left Neil at the hotel in Wilmington, I drove straight to my mom's house to see how Kendra was doing. Mom was frying eggs and bacon. I kissed her on the cheek and sat down on a stool at the large island in the middle of the kitchen. The sunlight streaming through the windows felt wonderful on my back.

"You look like crap," Mom said to me as she flipped the bacon.

"Nice to see you, too. You're not looking so great with your old lady nightgown and hair all frizzy and what not."

We both laughed.

"You know what I mean. You look tired and worried. Are you worried? You want some coffee? How about some bacon and eggs?"

"I'd love some coffee please. But I'll pass on the eggs and bacon." I patted my stomach. "I'm trying to watch my weight. I need to start eating better."

She slid a mug of coffee in front of me. "Watching your weight? That's ridiculous," she said with a frown. "You know where the cream and sugar is."

I nodded and took a slurp of the coffee. It was hot and strong and perfect.

"I just take it black now." (Neil taught me to appreciate a cup of strong black coffee. It's what he lived on when he had to work late nights.)

Mom went back to the stove and talked to me over her shoulder. "So are you worried?"

"I'm tired," I answered quickly. "I didn't get a lot of sleep."

"Well, I sure am worried. I mean, I'm glad she's back home but we both know that's not going to solve anything. We need to get her the help she needs."

"Yeah but she needs to want help."

Mom turned around and faced me. "Do you really think she wants to live like this?" she asked waving a spatula around. "Do you really think she likes dating horrible men and drinking herself to the point of near-death every day of her life?"

I could tell she was getting worked up.

"No," I replied quickly, hoping my agreement would settle her down.

"Well I can't take much more. I'm going to ask Chris if he'll pay for her to be sent somewhere far away to a better rehab – maybe in California or even Hawaii."

My stepdad didn't like to give us money. He was very generous while we were in school, but once we were out that was it. Since Kendra never went to college, her gravy train stopped when she was eighteen. Mine stopped when I graduated college. I doubted Chris would make an exception in this case. He was a firm believer in us taking responsibility for our own lives – good or bad.

"You have a place picked out?"

Mom was flipping the bacon so intently that she didn't even bother turning her head toward me.

"There's this one great place in Malibu," she said. "You go for 6-12 months and they help get you set-up with an apartment and a counselor afterward. They even help you find a job. They claim that fifty percent of their residents are still clean a year out."

Fifty percent was really good. Most rehab places had a success rate in the single digits. Anything over ten percent was considered above average. It's why some people say all rehab facilities are nothing more than revolving doors. People come and go and come and go again. Over and over. They usually come in the winter and then when the weather warms they leave rehab and spend several months drinking and partying until the summer ends. And then it's back to rehab.

But that wasn't Kendra. She wasn't playing any type of a game. She truly wanted to get better. I really believed that.

"Morning," Kendra groaned as she walked into the kitchen rubbing her head.

"Morning honey," Mom said. She walked over and gave Kendra a huge hug. "So good to have you home. Breakfast is just about ready. How are you feeling?"

"Like a truck hit me. Got any juice?"

Mom went back to the stove and kept right on cooking. "There's OJ and grape juice in the fridge."

Kendra smacked her lips and stuck out her tongue. "Anyone see that cat that took a big crap in my mouth last night?"

"Why don't you go brush your teeth," I suggested.

Kendra got herself a glass of orange juice and sat on the stool beside me.

"I'll wait until after breakfast." She took a sip of the juice and put her hand on top of mine. "Thanks for getting me last night," she said. "I think."

I didn't bother to look over at her. But I did put my other hand on top of hers.

"You're welcome. I think."

Mom served up the eggs and bacon to Kendra and herself. She put a plate in the oven to stay warm for Chris, who was out for his morning run, and then she sat down across from us. She had a million things to say about amazingly boring stuff that was happening in her life. Her aunt Gladys just had a wart removed from her back and thank goodness it's benign; the neighbor Susan just quit her job and is taking a trip to

Utah to see her sister; the other neighbor Ray is thinking about getting a new pool installed next spring. It went on and on.

"So what are we doing today?" Kendra asked me, interrupting my mom as she was telling us about the price of gas dropping three cents in the last week.

I had the day free. I didn't have to work and Neil said he was going to be busy the next week or two with his wife's family and making plans for some family reunion. He hoped to maybe see me this coming weekend but not before then.

I reached over and grabbed a piece of bacon off Kendra's plate. She slapped the back of my hand but I took it anyway. I broke it in two and popped a piece in my mouth.

"I hear there's a carnival going on over near the pier," I said. "I thought we could check that out this afternoon. Then maybe grab some dinner or just come back here and watch a movie."

"A carnival?" She shriveled up her face. "Is this what my life has come to?"

"You've always loved carnivals and fairs," mom quickly chimed in.

"Yeah. What are you too good for carnivals now?" I added. "You'll date circus freaks but won't go to one?"

Kendra looked appalled for about a second and then she laughed.

I laughed too.

It felt really good.

"Stop being a brat." I put the other piece of bacon in my mouth. Then I stood up and kissed her on the cheek. "I'll be here to get you around three." I waved my hand in front of my face. "And please brush your teeth before then."

Kendra and mom both chuckled. I walked around and kissed mom on the forehead.

"Now I'm going to go home and take a long hot shower and then catch another couple of hours of sleep. Tell Chris I say *hey*."

I left the kitchen and walked out of the house. It was a warm and sunny day with a slight breeze blowing in from the east, off the ocean. It was a perfect day for a carnival. And, though I didn't know it at the time, it was also the perfect day to begin to fall in love.

∞∞∞∞∞∞∞

It was Wednesday afternoon so the carnival wasn't overly crowded. The rides and games were set-up down near the ocean and included everything a carnival should have – a Ferris wheel, a carousel, a tilt-a-whirl, the Comet, and the Scrambler. I got so sick on the Scrambler when I was fourteen or fifteen. Some stupid boy convinced me to go on it with him. When I got off I threw-up grape soda and popcorn all over his new sneakers. Needless to say, he never spoke to me again.

Kendra was dying to ride the Ferris wheel so I went on it with her. I hated heights but I love the view from up there. It was just my luck that we stopped right at the top as new passengers got into another basket.

The ocean was absolutely gorgeous. The sun was shimmering off the water making the waves look like they were full of diamonds as they raced to the shore. Farther out, the ocean was so massive and so peaceful looking. To think of the time that passed while that very same ocean was just there. And to think of the foreign lands that same water touched. It was all so mysterious. The ocean was probably the number one reason why I was still in Dulcet. I didn't want to leave her. She was an old friend that I didn't want to wander too far from.

Kendra was looking out at the people around the carnival. I hoped she wouldn't see the bar that was about a half mile away, and that she wouldn't notice the beer tent that was even closer. But if she did, she didn't mention it.

"Thanks for getting me last night," she said to me.

"Not a problem."

"Did he hurt you?"

"Not really. My boob is all bruised and it hurt too much to wear a bra today but I'm fine."

"Your boob?" Kendra smiled. "Sure some random dude didn't do that to you in the sack?"

"Haha. Very funny." But I did laugh. It was *kinda* funny.

"Well thanks," she said again. She put her hand on my knee and squeezed. "I didn't want to be with him. He could be a little crazy. And I'm sick of all the drinking. I think I'm done with it. We looked at each for several seconds. "Really. I mean it. I think I'm done for good."

"I hope so. I really do."

A gust of wind blew against us. A tear slid from the corner of my left eye and raced down my cheek. I think it was probably the wind that caused it, but I'm not positive. We both knew she was probably lying. But she wanted it to be true, and that counted for something, right? She turned her head back to look down at the people below and tucked a lock of her hair behind her ear.

I watched her watching them as the Ferris wheel slid down another couple notches. I could see the pain in the slight twitch that pulled at her right cheek. I could feel the desperation radiating off of her. I wanted to grab her up in my arms and hug her so tight. But she didn't like long, strong hugs, and I knew it wouldn't do any good at all. Because no matter how hard I tried, I couldn't beat back the demons for her. Just like no matter how hard I prayed and wanted our dad to come back, he never did. He left us both all alone fighting against a storm. Kendra just didn't know how to find safe shelter. And I truly doubted if she'd ever figure it out.

"He was quite the sick asshole," she said after a while. "He used to hurt me pretty bad. He'd use a belt or the chain he wore around his neck or even his shoe. And he'd hit me in really weird places and laugh about it."

I grabbed her hand for all of about a half second before she pulled it away. She allowed people like Marty to touch her in all kinds of places but not her own sister.

"I'm sorry," I said to her. But you're safe now."

She looked at me. There were tears in her eyes, but it could've just been the wind.

"I kind of liked it." Her voice was like a sheet of ice. "The hitting and the pain. A part of me enjoyed it."

"No you didn't," I replied. "Maybe your messed up brain thought you liked it, but you didn't. Not you – Kendra. The alcohol has just messed everything up. And now you can get well and stay away from all that shit. All of it."

She just shook her head and didn't say anything. These were always the worst days – the days when she tried to swear off drinking. Judge me however you want, but the days when she was drinking were always easier than the ones when she was trying to pull the monkey off her back.

I was happier when she was drunk. Because something inside of me could feel that something inside of her was happy. If that makes any sense. Of course I was against her drinking because I knew it was ruining her life and eventually could kill her. And before you think I'm a completely horrible person, I was always happiest when Kendra was in rehab, and I knew she was safe, and I hoped she was getting well.

"What do you think that means?" she asked.

"What?"

"That I liked it. Does that make me crazy?"

"No," I said with as much certainty in my voice as I could manage. "It means you're confused, or your brain is. Drinking just turns everything upside down. That's all."

"Hey, isn't that the guy from last night?" Kendra asked as we slid down another couple places.

Just like that, the heaviness was gone. The pitch of her voice rose and her face brightened. She sat-up straight and pointed off into the sea of people below us.

"What?"

I had no idea who or what she was talking about.

"The guy who kicked the crap out of Marty, isn't that him?"

"How do you even remember what he looked like? And how the hell can you see that far?"

I tried to follow the line from her finger but I couldn't see any one person. I only saw a mass of humanity moving back and forth.

"Yeah he's right there. And he's with some really cute guy too. What was his name?"

"Blake," I said softly before I even realized I answered. But I couldn't see him. She was pointing at least fifty yards away from us. "What do you have like bionic eyesight or something?"

Kendra looked up at me and raised her eyebrows up and down. "Yeah, I'm a superhero in disguise. But seriously, you don't see him. He's wearing a blue shirt and the guy he's with has a red baseball cap on. Don't you see them? Right there," she said pointing. "They're walking this way."

I still didn't see them. But within less than three minutes we were at the bottom of the wheel and Kendra asked to be let off. So the attendant, a middle-aged bald man holding a cigarette in the gap where he was missing a front tooth, stopped the wheel and let us off. Kendra darted into the crowd and I tried to follow her best I could.

"Hey!" she called. "Blaine!"

"It's Blake," I corrected her.

Now I did see the back of a head that could've been his. There was a man who stood above most of the other people around him. And I remembered he was tall. But still, I was sure Kendra was mistaking. Her eyes were not that good. She couldn't recognize someone who was so far away. And she was so drunk last night the odds of her accurately remembering him were slim. Plus, if somehow it was really him, he didn't want to see us. And God knows I didn't want to see him. The whole thing was embarrassing and was best left in the past.

"Hey Blake!" she screamed as we drew within about ten yards of the two men.

People all around us turned to look. And so did the two guys we were chasing after. I thought we were about to be embarrassed for calling out to two random guys. And I hoped Kendra wouldn't make it worse by trying to strike-up a conversation with them. But when they'd fully turned around, I saw that she was right. It was him.

Blake was looking at us with his head slightly tipped to the side and a half smile on his lips. The guy he was with looked confused but smiled wide when he saw the two of us.

"Hey, we know you," Kendra said to him.

She was slightly out of breath from pushing her way through the crowd.

"The ladies from last night?" Blake asked.

Kendra wrapped her hands arms around my left arm and smiled big. "Yup, that's us."

This was going beyond embarrassing. I pulled at my ear lobe once and then bit on the tip of my thumb. My face grew warm and I knew it was turning red. I looked up at him and of course he was looking at me, probably judging me. I locked eyes with his. My heart leapt and threw off a warmth that flooded up into my head and down into my stomach.

Holy crap he's hot. How did I not notice this last night! I knew he was good looking, but not this hot!

"I'm Kendra and this is my sister Katie."

"If you don't remember, I'm Blake and this is my brother Steve."

We all shook hands and I tried not to seem impressed. When he shook my hand he smiled big and I fought hard not to smile back. I felt like a middle school girl who finally meets the Varsity quarterback she'd bene crushing on for years. But that was silly. I didn't know him and the last thing I needed was to fall for some stranger. Things were already complicated enough in my life. No, I couldn't be a stupid school girl about this.

"Katie huh?" He was still looking at me; we were still shaking hands. "I didn't remember your name from last night."

"Probably because I didn't tell it to you." My hand in his, while we were shaking, felt too good. It felt *right*. But it couldn't. It shouldn't. I pulled my hand away and nodded my head. "But thanks again for last night."

"These were the ladies who were being harassed last night," Blake said to his brother.

"We're the ones he saved," Kendra said. She was smiling way too wide at Steve.

"Well, not exactly saved," I quickly added. "I was just getting warmed up. I think I could've taken him."

"Yeah, Katie had it pretty well under control. I really just finished him off for her," Blake said. He was obviously trying to make me like him, but it wasn't going to work.

"Okay," I smiled. "We just wanted to thank you again." Kendra was still holding onto my arm so I pulled her and tried to start walking away. "It was good seeing you guys."

Kendra wouldn't budge.

"Wait a second," she said. "We should buy you guys a drink or something as a thank you."

I couldn't help but flinch at that suggestion and I think I saw Blake frown too.

But Kendra quickly corrected herself. "Or like a soda or maybe a candied apple or something."

"We just ate," Steve said patting his stomach. "But hey, Blake was just about to walk me down and show me the fishing pier. You girls are welcome to join us."

"Absolutely," Blake added.

"No, we really-," I started.

But Kendra spoke over me. "No, we'd really love to get some food with you but we'll settle for a walk."

Finally, she let go of my arm and the four of us walked off toward the pier, two by two. Steve and Kendra were in the front and Blake and I followed.

This isn't fun. I don't like walking beside him or even being near him.

I will not like this or him.

This is not fun.

"So if I came across as a cocky jerk last night, I'm sorry. I was just trying to act tough and confident. I find it helps with intimidation."

"I didn't really notice," I answered honestly.

"So what do you do, Katie? You still in school?"

"School?"

"Yeah, like college? Unless you're still in high school."

Was he trying to offend me? In a few years I might be flattered, but not now. I looked at him and the grin on his face told me he was messing with me.

"Do I look like I could be in high school?"

"It's hard to tell with girls these days. Sometimes sixteen looks like thirty."

"Are you saying I look thirty?"

He chuckled. It was a soft laugh that somehow sounded warm. It was a nice sound.

"Maybe I'm saying you look sixteen," he said.

"Sounds like you speak from experience. Get yourself into some trouble, Blake?"

He laughed. "Um, no. Nope." He shook his head. "But in my profession I've seen a few people prosecuted for such things."

"So you really are a lawyer?"

He nodded his head. "I am."

He didn't look old enough to have graduated law school. "So what are you like forty years old or something?"

He chuckled again. My gosh, I liked how it sounded.

"Ouch. That hurts." He put his hand on his chest and then into the pocket of his jeans. "Actually I'm almost twenty-five."

He didn't look that old but, then again, it was always hard for me to judge anyone's age.

"So where'd you graduate from?" I asked.

"Law school or undergrad?"

"Both."

"Undergrad at UNC and law school at Duke. How about you? Not in college? Still in college?"

I ignored his questions. "Is that even possible?" I asked.

"What?"

"To go to UNC *and* Duke? Seems like UNC would take back their degree when you decided to be a traitor."

"You'd think so. But surprisingly, plenty of people do what I did. So did you go to North Carolina then?"

He really wanted to know how old I was and if I went or was going to college. I liked not letting him know anything about me. It gave me a little bit of power - an edge on him. And I needed anything I could get. Because every time I looked over at him, I felt completely unarmed and defenseless.

"So you must have just graduated then," I said.

"A little over a year ago."

"But I thought law school was four years, no? What are you like the Doogie Howser of lawyers?"

"Doogie Howser?"

"Yeah, that kid doctor from the old eighties show," I explained. But I could see he wasn't getting it. "This kid was like a genius and was like a teenage doctor. Never mind. You're not a fan of eighties television, huh?"

"Sorry," he said. "I love movies but I'm not so big on any TV shows. Never have been. But to answer your question: Law school was three years and I started college when I sixteen about to be seventeen. I started Kindergarten a little early and then I skipped the seventh grade." He looked at me and raised just his right eyebrow. "Does that make me sort of like Dougie House-er?"

"It's Doogie not Dougie. And Howser not House-er."

The pier came into view. Steve and Kendra kept erupting in laughter. Things were obviously going very well for them. I had no idea how things were going with me and Blake. He seemed like he just might have brains and a good personality to go along with his alarmingly good looks. But I didn't really know. And I didn't really want to care whether he did or not.

"So, you live around here?" Blake asked.

"Your brother and Kendra seem to be hitting it off. Is he younger or older than you?"

"Older. I'm the youngest of three boys. Steve's a couple years older than me and then there's Alex who is going to turn thirty soon. See that's how that works."

"What works?"

"Asking questions and giving answers."

"Yeah I know how it works."

"Then why have I asked you like fifty questions and not gotten one answer?"

"If I answer that question then we'll break the streak. So, I'll just keep asking the questions."

Blake laughed again. "Can I object?"

"Hello?" I grinned. "I can't answer that either. We have to honor the streak. So, do you live around here?"

"No."

"Where you from?"

"Not here."

"Vacation here or are you here on business?"

"Yep."

Now he was screwing with me. I fought back a smile and glared at him. "Stop being a jerk."

"I'm just answering your questions. And since you won't answer my questions I'm just going to assume you're a sixteen-year-old homeless high school dropout."

"Assume away," I told him. "For what it's worth, I think your story about being a lawyer is all bullshit. Being so smart that you skipped a grade and went to UNC and Duke. It's a load of crap."

"A load of crap?"

"Is that a question? If so, then I'm not answering. But I know a line when I hear it, and all that is a line."

"Technically it'd be a whole pack of lines." His body swayed and his hip rubbed against my waist. "And it's all true. If I wanted to lie I'd make myself an astronaut or maybe a rock star."

I ignored the jolt of warmth that zipped from my waist to my chest when his body accidentally touched mine. I could not like this guy. I just couldn't. He was a lawyer and I was a bartender. He obviously had his life together and I was a mess.

I looked up at him and pushed my hair behind my ears. "Well I don't believe you."

He chuckled. "That's fine with me."

"Good."

"Excellent."

"And by the way, you're too tall."

"I can squat down while I walk if you want. But that might look strange."

"Ha ha. Very funny."

We reached the pier and kept walking in silence, listening to Steve and Kendra talk about a thousand things. Apparently they'd become the best of friends (or something more) in the space of about fifteen minutes. We walked past tourists snapping pictures on their cell phones and old men fishing off the side of the pier. We reached the end of the pier and stood against the railing, all four of us shoulder to shoulder in a line with me and Kendra in the middle.

Gorgeous blue was all around us – high, low, and on all sides. Jaegers, gulls, and terns skimmed the top of the ocean and occasionally dipped into the water. In the distance two large ships were traveling in opposite directions. The sky and the water were both so blue that it was tough to see exactly where the water ended and the heavens began.

This pier on the ocean and all the spots like it, were my slice of perfection. They were my evidence that life was worth living.

"Wow, this is pretty impressive," Blake said softly. "Gorgeous."

"Yeah, just don't try to hold my hand," I told him.

"And don't you grab my ass," he answered.

I had no choice but to smile.

But just a little.

Chapter Five -Now

The detective stands up and stretches tall with his arms extended out to his sides. He suppresses a yawn and then picks-up his notebook.

"Seems like a good time for a little break. I need a strong coffee. You want one?"

"Yes please."

"Good," he smiles warmly.

I'm still not sure if he's just acting friendly. Maybe he's the good half of the *good cop/ bad cop* duo and maybe the bad cop will show-up later, when I'm done with my story. Or maybe he's both the good and the bad cop and just waiting to bring out the bad one, once he has my trust.

He makes it halfway out the door and then turns back toward me. "You take cream and sugar?"

"No thanks. Black is perfect. Seems like it's that kind of night."

He chuckles. "You got that right. You probably don't even know how right you are."

And then he's gone. I have no idea what he meant by that last part. I don't know how right I am? I'm pretty sure I do. I have the marks on me to prove it. And I have the images too, both distinct and completely separate: Blood on my hardwood floor, running in a stream toward the bathroom, and Blake walking away from me forever.

Sometimes making love to a man is worse than killing him. Did you know that? It's absolutely true. Disheartening. But true.

The detective comes back in shaking his head. "It's one of those once in a lifetime bat-shit crazy nights Katie." He puts the coffee down in front of me. "Is it okay to call you Katie?"

"What's your first name?" I ask him.

He smiles. It does look genuine enough. But who the hell knows?

"Okay," he says. "I'll stick with Ms. Sanders." He points at my coffee. "You might want to let that sit for a minute. It's really hot, like about to burst into flames."

"So you're warning me not to spill it down the front of me?"

"Wouldn't be a good idea."

"Could be the making of a lawsuit," I say though I'm not sure why.

"Could be," is all he says in reply.

"It's the new American dream, right?"

"Oh trust me, cops know all about lawsuits. Well, you must know a little too, given who your boyfriend was."

I don't like the use of past tense. But I just smile and nod. Because if I think about what happened with Blake, it might distract me too much.

"I don't think I told you Blake was my boyfriend," I tell him.

Without thinking I take a big sip of my coffee. My tongue immediately feels like it's on fire. I swallow the coffee to save my mouth and it scorches everything from my throat all the way down to my stomach.

"I told you to be careful," the Detective says pointing back at the coffee. "And sorry if I made a presumption about him becoming your boyfriend, but I think I see where this story is going. At least part of it.'

I don't say anything. He has no idea where my story is going. And he doesn't know the first thing about me and Blake. Nobody does. It was just that special and rare. But again, I just smile, nod, and play the good girl. And then I suck air through my top teeth, trying to quench the flames that are dancing on my tongue.

"Are those bruises from tonight?" he asks pointing at my forearm.

"Yes."

"And those on your neck, too?"

"Yes."

"We'll need pictures of all of that before we're done. I'll get someone in here on our next break."

"Okay."

"Are you okay?"

"Yeah, why?"

He leans back in his chair and clasps his hands behind his head. He has two huge sweat stains darkening the armpits of his dress shirt. "You just seem awfully calm. Can I ask you something before you continue filling me in on your story?"

"Sure."

"Would you say every life is precious and worth living?"

That's the type of question Kendra used to ask me. I'd always tell her *of course every life is worth living and of course every life is precious and meant to be lived to the fullest.* I know why Kendra used to ask such things – she was looking for me to validate her life. But I have no idea why the Detective is asking me this.

"Yeah, every life is precious," I answer slowly making sure my mouth only says the safe words and not the dangerous ones that I'm thinking.

"So killing someone would be wrong, right?"

I don't like what he's hinting at. I look down at my coffee for a while, hoping he'll ask me to go on with my story. But he doesn't.

Instead he rephrases the question. "Do you think murder is ever justified?"

I know all about this. Blake taught me that if a question is abandoned by an attorney or anyone else, then it really wasn't important. But if it's twisted or turned to be asked again in a different way then it's very important, and the answer is even more significant.

I can hear Blake telling me to be careful. So, I pick up my coffee, blow on it for a few seconds, and then take a cautious sip. It's either cooled a lot in just couple minutes or my tongue is burned to the point of being numb.

Finally, I look up at the Detective and let a stream of air out of my lungs that feels like it's been there for hours.

"Do I need to request an attorney now or can I finish my story?"

The Detective grins at me. This time it's fake as hell. It looks like it belongs on a used car salesman or a politician.

"I was just wondering," he tells me. He waves a hand in the air as if brushing his questions away. "No need to answer. This isn't an interrogation. By all means, go on with your story."

I look at him for a few seconds, and he just looks back with that same piece-of-shit-buy-my-car-vote-for-me-smile.

I lick my lips, wrap my fingers around my cup of coffee, and I continue with the story.

Chapter Six - Then

From the time I graduated college, I worked at the bar every Thursday night. My shift was seven in the evening until midnight. It was usually pretty packed from about eight until eleven or so. It was mostly a beer bar with the occasional glass of wine or whiskey sour thrown in. So, it was pretty easy on the mind, but not at all on the body. I'm sure I probably speed walked about ten miles by the time my shift was over. But the tips made it all worth it. When I first started it wasn't uncommon for me to take home about three hundred dollars for just that one night. Lately, business had slowed, but Thursdays, with the great drink specials Buzz offered, were still busy enough for me to make somewhere in the neighborhood of a couple hundred bucks.

The day before, Kendra and I had stood at the pier with Steve and Blake for about ten minutes. Then I gave her the evil eye and we both left. She got Steve's number before we left. She said she really liked him and was definitely going to call him in a couple hours. I told her she was crazy. And I tried not to wish I'd gotten Blake's number.

I called my mom before my shift began and mom told me that Kendra had gone to the beach with Steve at about noon and the two of them were supposed to go out to dinner too. That wasn't surprising to me. Everything Kendra did, she did it fast and hard. Poor Steve didn't know what he was in for, but he was about to find out.

I also asked my mom if she got a chance to ask Chris about the rehab in Hawaii or California. Mom said she'd actually called the place in Malibu, California and they said they had two open beds and they could take Kendra as soon as she was ready to go. But it was an absolute no-go. Chris refused to even pay for half of it. And there was no way mom could afford it alone. I wished I had the money to pay for it or to even pay for a quarter of it, but I didn't. I was the personification of the saying *living hand to mouth*.

That Thursday was like the old Thursdays when business was hopping. It started really picking up at a little after eight and by nine it was rocking. I was bartending with Linda and Ron. They'd been working with me at the bar since I'd started. We were running our asses off behind the bar. I didn't even see Kendra walk in. It must have been after eleven when she came up and ordered three bottles of beer.

"You're kidding, right," I said to her. "You shouldn't even be in here."

"Why?"

"Because it's too much of a temptation."

"Oh pish-posh," she said to me. "Temptation-splation. Just give me a beer. Actually give me three. Please." The harder consonants slurred from her mouth.

She was really drunk. "Who are you here with? Did you come alone?"

"No," she shook her head. "I'm with Steve and Blake. They're sitting over there."

"Where?' I asked.

How could they allow her to drink? I knew I didn't like Blake. He was too good looking. He was too perfect.

Never, ever, trust perfection.

"Oh come on Katie, don't be lame," she said to me.

"You promised me you wouldn't drink anymore."

"Yeah and two nights ago you wanted to drink with me. Hell you did drink with me. What, was that just all bullshit?"

It was starting to turn into a scene. Half of me knew that. Or at least twenty-five percent of me knew it. But the other part of me was growing so angry I was starting to see red. It was an anger born out of frustration, lost hope, and betrayal. Yes, betrayal! Betrayal from Kendra (to be expected) and betrayal by Steve and Blake (not expected – they pretended to be nice guys). How the hell could they let her drink?

"Actually it was bullshit. It was bullshit to save your ass from that prick you decided to shack up with. It was bullshit to try to save you from yourself."

"I don't need saving!" Kendra yelled.

People were stopping their own conversations and tuning into ours. I couldn't allow this to turn into a scene.

"Just stop drinking, okay?"

"Never mind, Ronnie will give me a couple beers."

"I think you better go home."

"Home? I'm just getting started."

I was livid. How could Blake allow her to drink? He pretended to be such a good guy – my savior! Yeah right. He was full of shit.

"Don't serve her," I yelled to both Linda and Ron.

They both nodded their heads with understanding. They knew Kendra's story. In fact, they'd seen more than a few examples of Kendra being so drunk she couldn't walk or pronounce her own name.

I walked out from behind the bar and went straight over to the table where Blake and Steve were sitting. Blake must have seen the look in my eyes. He got to his feet and smiled nervously.

"How could you guys?" I asked sharpening each syllable and stressing every other word.

"You okay?" Blake asked me. He put his hand on my forearm but I slapped it away.

"Don't you touch me," I said jabbing a finger at his face. "Don't you dare touch me!"

"Okay." He put both his hands up at chest level, holding them away from me. "But can we just slow down a little here." He looked at Steve and shrugged his shoulders. "We don't know why you're so mad. Can you slow down?"

"For giving her alcohol. For getting her drunk. Goddamn it!"

"Oh man, she's underage? Oh shit," Steve said. Now he was on his feet too. "She told me she was twenty-five."

"She is twenty-five, asshole."

"Can we just maybe take this outside where we don't have to yell? And you can let me know what the hell is going on here? You're acting kinda crazy."

"Don't you dare call me crazy. You want to see crazy, give her a couple more beers and then you'll see crazy."

Blake moved in a step closer to me and grabbed my hand. "Listen, people are starting to watch us. Can we just go outside and talk about this? It will take just two minutes. I promise."

Shit.

Despite all my anger, when he grabbed my hand I *still* felt it. There was that attraction – that exciting comfort that scared the hell out of me but still made me want more. I pulled my hand away and looked around the bar. Almost everyone was enjoying the show I was putting on. I stepped back and turned for the door. Without saying a word, Blake followed me out.

There was a couple making out on the hood of a car and a group of four guys smoking cigarettes in the center of the parking lot. I walked several steps past the kissing couple and then spun around.

"So explain yourself."

"I don't know what to explain. I don't know why you're so upset."

The fresh air felt good but I was still ready for a fight. All my emotions that I'd bottled up for the past several months – Kendra's alcoholism, my not knowing what I was going to do with my life, my messed-up *relationship* with Neil – all of it was boiling over.

"And what the hell are you even doing here? What are you stalking me?"

"I'm with my brother."

"Yeah you make a great third wheel. You're not my type but you're an okay looking guy. It seems like you should be able to get your own date."

Blake laughed but I'm pretty sure he was hurt – stung at least. And that's exactly what I was going for. I just wanted to hurt him.

"There's a lot to be said about a third wheel," he said nonchalantly. If I'd hurt him he didn't show it.

"You mean like they're unnecessary and pointless and just make everything less fun?"

"Like they are a lot safer than two wheels and I kinda think three wheeled bikes look tough. If they're done right. And they're kinda cute, too."

He grinned at me but I wasn't about to let him do that. I wasn't just going to crumble.

"Well I don't like either of those things," I replied because I didn't know what else to say.

"Well, that would explain why you hate me."

"Seriously? Did you just say that?"

Who the hell does this guy think he is?

"Yeah, I mean I miss the mark sometimes but those are my goals – tough and a little cute."

"I don't see either." I shook my head. "Nope."

"Not even a little?" he grinned.

I squinted my eyes, like I was really studying him and thinking hard.

"Nope, not at all."

Blake shook his head. "Listen. Can you just stop with the insults for a couple minutes? Can you please tell me why you're so pissed? Please?"

I sucked in the cool night air, it felt refreshing in my lungs. I bit on the tip of my thumb and debated not telling him, but he had to know.

"She's an alcoholic," I said. "A freaking drunk. Does that mean anything to you?"

"Oh shit," Blake swore. He ran his hand through his hair and swore under his breath. "I didn't know. And I'm sure Steve didn't know either."

Honestly, I hadn't even considered that possibility. I thought everyone knew Kendra was a drunk. Wasn't it obvious? But she did still appear young and gorgeous and she seemed to have her life together. As long as you didn't look too closely. Of course it was possible Blake and Steve didn't even know. I suddenly felt like an idiot. And my mind raced for another reason to be angry with him.

"Well you should have asked!" I blurted.

"Asked what?"

"If she-." I wanted to tell him he should have asked if she was an alcoholic. But that was ridiculous. "Well, if she-. I mean. You could have asked me if there was anything about her that you should know about."

"Really?" Blake asked raising his eyebrows. He squinted and smiled just enough so that his dimples dented his cheeks.

I pulled on my earlobe and ran a shaky hand though my hair. "Yes really," I answered. I fought the urge to smile.

"You mean like give you a permission slip with some kind of a health form attached? Kinda like a packet that parents need to complete to send their kids to summer camp? By the way, has she had a physical lately? And when was her last tetanus shot?"

"You're an asshole," I said. I spun away from him and folded my arms tightly across my chest.

Blake walked around me so he was facing me again.

"Look," he said to me. "My brother just got out of a really messy relationship, and he has a tendency to move too fast with girls anyway. And he really likes Kendra. So, they went to the beach earlier and then out to dinner. They came back to the house and asked me if I wanted to come to the bar with them, they said you were bartending, so I agreed. We all had one beer and she started acting really drunk. I guess she's been drinking for hours. But we didn't know she's an alcoholic. And when she started acting really drunk we refused to buy any more beer, but she insisted. And that's when she went up to you and ordered another one."

It all made sense. Too much sense. I looked down at the ground and shook my head.

"Any idea how much she's had?" I asked.

"No idea. But I think a lot. I'm sorry Katie. And I'm sure Steve is too. We didn't know."

"Shit." I just kept shaking my head and looking down at the ground. "I'm sorry. I'm stupid and I'm sorry for yelling at you. You and Steve didn't deserve that."

"No need to apologize. I'm sorry."

I looked up at him. The moon was directly over his right shoulder, hanging plump and beautiful. I wanted to hate him. I wanted to hate the way he made me feel, the way he made me want him. But I was about a million miles from hate.

"And you came here to see me?" I asked.

"Well…" He looked up at the night sky. "Well yeah I guess-."

But his words were interrupted by a loud crash from inside the bar. The sound of breaking glass quickly followed the crash. Then there were a couple screams, a lot of yelling, and more breaking glass. Blake and I looked at each with wide eyes and took off toward the door.

We made it inside just in time to see Kendra behind the bar and Rob trying to grab a hold of her. She wiggled out of his grasp and threw an elbow at him. It landed square in in the center of his face. His head rocked back and propelled him into a bar cooler. His hand went to his mouth and he disappeared into the back of the bar. Kendra went right back to hurling empty beer bottles across the bar.

All the people were ducking behind their tables and trying to stay out of the way. Most people were laughing, really enjoying the show, but a few looked genuinely scared. They were all in Kendra's world now, and it wasn't a good place to live. Lucky for them, they were just visiting.

I'd been living there for years.

Steve was slowly making his way toward one end of the bar and Blake was moving toward the other side. Kendra saw me standing near the door and whipped a bottle toward me. It landed five feet too short, skidded past me, and bounced off the door jamb without breaking. She cocked back and fired another bottle at me. This time her aim was a lot better and I had to duck or else it would've taken off my head. The bottle shattered against the wall, prompting more screams and laughter from all over the bar.

Kendra bent down to pick-up two more bottles and that's when Steve and Blake made their move. They ran at Kendra from each side and had her before she even knew they were coming at her. Steve grabbed her under the arms and Blake grabbed her feet. Then they hustled her toward the door. I swung it open and out they went out with her. I followed close behind.

Kendra was screaming and yelling the entire time. They went across the parking lot with her and put her in the grass. "Just calm down," Steve was saying to her. "Calm down!"

But she wasn't calming down. She was kicking and throwing fists and elbows in all directions. She tried to get back to her feet but Steve held her down. He straddled her waist and held her wrists against the ground. She turned her head to try to bite his arm but she couldn't quite reach.

Then Buzz came out of nowhere with a huge bucket. He hustled over to Kendra and dumped ice all over her.

That stopped everything.

For several seconds Kendra was motionless with her mouth wide open and a mountain of ice covering her chest and stomach. She looked like she was silently screaming. It might have been funny if I didn't know how true it was.

Buzz walked past me. "Get her out of here. Have these gentlemen take her home. And then take a couple minutes to collect yourself and get back behind the bar. We're falling behind. I'll clean-up the broken glass and bottles myself."

"Thanks Buzz," I said.

"Don't thank me. This shit's starting to get old."

"I know. Sorry."

"And don't apologize. Not your fault," he called over his shoulder.

Steve lifted Kendra to her feet and began brushing the remaining ice off of her. Kendra's face crumbled and she started crying. Steve put his arms around her and held her close. She buried her head in the space where his neck met his shoulder. And they stood that way for a long time. I could see by the look on Steve's face that he didn't have a clue what the hell was going on.

Blake and I stood trying to look anywhere but at the two of them. It was too intimate of a moment to be witnessed. But I couldn't keep myself from looking. It was like witnessing a car accident, except the exact opposite.

"We'll take her home, okay?" Blake said softly to me.

"Yeah, thank you."

"I'm so sorry," Kendra said to all of us. Her head was on his shoulder and his arm was wrapped around her waist. She let go of him and gave me a hug. She smelled like stale beer. "I'm sorry Katie. I'm so sorry. I'm a total loser. Sorry."

"It's fine," I whispered to her. "It's okay." I said, even though things were pretty freaking far from fine and nothing was okay.

As Steve got her into the car, Blake walked back over to me. He was looking me right in the eyes. I glanced up at him and then looked away. Something about the expression on his face or the way he was walking, it made me want to fall into him. But that was ridiculous. I couldn't allow myself to be taken in by him.

Blake didn't say a word. He just wrapped his arms around me and held me close.

Don't touch me. Do not hug me. Just stay away from me.

Okay, but just a little hug. Just for just a minute. But don't expect me to hug you back.

Ah shit. To hell with it. Maybe I'll just let him hold me maybe for a minute and maybe I'll just hold him back.

But just for a little while.

At first I kept my arms folded over my chest as he hugged me. But it felt so good and so right. I pulled my arms out and hugged him back. The dam inside of me almost broke then. My shoulders jerked up twice and a cry nearly erupted out of me. But I fought it back. I couldn't allow myself to cry. Not there. Not then. Not around him, and certainly not while he was hugging me.

To be honest, I could have stayed that way forever. While he was holding me, it was if nothing else in the world mattered. It was almost as if my soul had been waiting my entire life to be held by him. But of course, that was ridiculous and childish. Wasn't it?

"You okay?" Blake whispered.

"Yeah," I managed to answer without losing it.

He let go of me and I let go of him. He stepped back. "We'll get her home. Is there anyone there?"

"Where?"

"At home. Her home. Your mom's home."

"Yeah my mom should be there," I nodded. "I'll call and give her the heads-up."

"Okay. Sorry again. I promise we didn't know."

"I know," I whispered.

I watched them drive away with Kendra in the backseat. She looked at me through the back window and gave a little wave. I waved back and then put my thumb to my lips. Kendra looked like a little girl who was lost and all alone.

And that was the bitch of it all: Underneath everything Kendra was still that sweet little girl who played Candyland with me on the living room floor and spent hours cheering me up through our closet walls. She was not a drunk. She was not a screw-up hell bent on ruining her life, and possibly the lives of me and mom too. No, to me she would always be that little girl who liked to play dress-up on Saturday mornings and always told me she *knew* Daddy would be back home really soon.

The feeling of loneliness hit me in the gut and I had to sit down on a cement parking curb. I couldn't take much more of it. I knew when my shift was over I'd be a mess. So, I pulled out my phone. Neil would make me feel better. If I could just sit with him for a few minutes and have him hold me. Then I'd be okay.

I punched the code into my phone, and then I tapped out Neil's number. It rang twice and rolled straight to his voicemail. I listened to his voice, picturing his face as he said the words. When he was done speaking, I waited for the beep.

"Hi. It's me Katie. Umm, sorry I'm calling so late. But I really need to talk to you. Umm, actually hopefully we can see each other. Tonight. For just like ten minutes or something. Just really quick maybe we can just drive around and talk a little. Maybe you can pick me up after my break? I don't know. But call me, okay? Soon, okay? I just really need to see you. So… yeah… call me back. And sorry again."

I hit END on my phone and then dialed mom's cell phone. It rang twice and was answered by my stepfather, Chris. He sounded tired and annoyed.

"Hello Katie, do you know what time it is?"

"Sorry." I was getting really sick of giving and hearing apologies. Such was life with Kendra when she was actively drinking. "Is my mom there?"

"Yes. Is everything okay?"

"Yeah. It's just Kendra."

"Is she okay?"

"Yeah, but she's pretty drunk."

"Shit."

"Can I talk to mom or can you let her know? A couple of friends of mine are bringing her home to you. They should be there in about five minutes."

"Here's your mother," he said.

I heard rustling and then indecipherable talking. I stood up and walked back toward the bar.

"Katie?" my mom said. "How drunk is she?"

"Pretty drunk. Like usual."

"But I thought she was going to try to make it this time," my mom said. Her voice broke on the last word and I knew she was crying.

"It's okay mom. She's fine. We'll figure it out tomorrow. Will you just keep an eye out for her? A couple friends are bringing her home right now. They'll be there is a couple minutes."

"Oh friends, huh?"

I didn't appreciate the accusatory tone in her voice when she uttered the word *friends*. "Yeah mom, friends. Friends of mine. They had nothing to do with her drinking. So be grateful they're helping. Okay?"

She exhaled into the phone making it sound like she was in the middle of wind tunnel.

"Okay, yeah. Of course we'll help her. I'll go down and wait by the door now."

"Thanks mom. Love you."

"Love you too."

I hung-up and looked to see if Neil had called me back yet. Nothing.

I walked back to the door of the bar and stopped before going in. I tapped out a quick text: *Please call me. Soon.* I sent it to his cell and then I went back into the bar to sling more drinks.

Over an hour later it was almost midnight and I still hadn't heard from Neil. No text. No call back. Absolutely nothing. What the hell was he doing? Watching a movie with his wife? Sleeping beside her in their bed? Or maybe he was working late in the office. That was my hope. Maybe he was busy and hadn't even seen his phone yet.

Things were a lot slower in the bar – once the specials ended most people left. A lot of them had jobs to get to in the morning, one more shift before they got to the weekend. My shift was about to end in about an hour and I couldn't wait any longer. I told Linda and Ron I'd be back in a few minutes and I went back outside to call Neil.

Outside it was absolutely perfect. The temperature was in the mid-sixties and the sky was completely clear, allowing a blanket of stars to spread out in all directions, as far as I could see. I leaned against the side of the bar and dialed Neil's cell. It rang once and then Neil answered.

"Hello?"

"Hey, it's Katie."

"Hold on one second."

I waited. There was absolutely no sound coming through my phone. A couple who I'd known since high school walked out of the bar and said goodbye to me. I tried to smile and waved at both of them. I just needed to speak with Neil and to see him for maybe ten or fifteen minutes – a half hour would be great. I just needed to have him beside me, to feel his arms around me.

"Katie?" he finally said. It sounded like he was in a closet, and he could've been. I pictured him squatting down beneath a rod full of dress shirts and pants, standing on a pair of his wife's high heels.

"Yeah, it's me."

"Everything okay? What's wrong?"

"Nothing. Well, it's my sister again. I just need to see you."

"You can't call here at this hour. You shouldn't call me here at all. We talked about this."

I felt like a child who'd been caught watching a rated R movie.

"Sorry, but I need to see you. Like I really need it."

He exhaled loudly. "I'm sorry, but I told you that these next couple of weeks are going to be all about my wife. Her brats are in town for a little while and I have to play the good daddy to them."

"But for like fifteen minutes? Please?"

Now I sounded like that little child too. I hated myself for saying it, and I hated how whiny my voice sounded.

"Katie come on. Is everything else okay?"

"Yeah, why?"

"Just seems like your sister shouldn't upset you so much anymore. At some point you have to get to a place where – I don't know – a place-."

"Where I don't care anymore?" I interrupted.

"No, not care anymore but not care as much, maybe? I mean what do you expect? You can only stick your hand in a fire so much to try and save a necklace you dropped into the flames before you give up."

"Well I guess I'm just stupid."

My voice still sounded too whiny. I really hated that.

"Listen, I have to go," he told me.

"So you can't see me? Like just pick me up at the bar for like fifteen minutes or maybe meet me somewhere? I get out at midnight and we can just listen to music and talk. Just for a few minutes."

I was pretty much begging him. It was demeaning, but I was desperate.

He blew into the phone. "Maybe later this weekend. I'll call you. But not tonight. I mean it's late. I'll call you, okay?"

"Yeah," I said because I had nothing else I could say.

I couldn't keep begging, I couldn't yell at him, and I didn't want to seem mad.

"Are you going to be okay?"

"Yeah, I'll be fine. Go be with your wife and her kids. It's fine."

"Okay. Talk soon."

"Okay. Bye."

What was I supposed to think? How was I supposed to feel? I *needed* him to be with me – not to make love or to even make out – I just needed his company. And yet he brushed me aside like I was an annoying mosquito whining in his ear in the middle of the night.

But I did call awfully late at night and he did tell me he wouldn't be able to see me for the next couple of weeks. I shouldn't have called him. But he didn't have to make me feel like such an incorrigible child.

I walked back into the bar. My shift would be over in about a half hour. Then I'd probably drive over to Sully's Landing and walk out onto the pier. The ocean and the stars would be absolutely gorgeous. It was the perfect night to look across the ocean and think about distant lands where perhaps I could go someday.

I grabbed three empty beer bottles off a table on my way behind the bar. I threw them into the recycling can. Then I walked back toward the sink to grab a rag.

"Hey."

I turned and there was Blake sitting on a bar stool near the other end of the bar. I walked over to him, not realizing I was smiling. "You came back. Everything okay?"

"Kendra is home safe and sound. Steve's pretty pissed at himself."

"For what?"

"For liking her so much and for letting her get so drunk."

"Those are both Kendra's superpowers."

"Superpowers?"

"Yeah, every woman has superpowers," I grinned. "Hers are getting drunk and making guys fall for her really fast. I think it's the whole *beautiful mess* thing she has going for her."

Blake raised his eyebrows while he took a sip from his beer bottle.

"There is a lot to be said about a beautiful mess. So what's your superpower?"

I leaned on the bar and grinned at him. "I'm not sure. Attracting assholes?" I nodded and pushed my hair behind my ears. "Yeah that's probably mine. What's yours?"

"Hmm, my super power? Probably reading people. But I don't think your superpower is working."

"What do you mean?" I asked.

"Because here I sit and I'm proving it wrong."

A thin, warm jolt skidded through my blood. Was he saying what I thought he was saying? I had to play it cool. We would never work.

"Proving me wrong, how?"

"Well you said you attract assholes, and here I sit. And I'm not an asshole."

Then he put the beer to his lips and drank. As he did his dimples appeared, and then he was smiling on each side of the bottle. But his eyes were on me, serious and sincere. In the moment, I knew that no man had ever looked at me like that before. And I suspected nobody ever would again.

"Well, the jury's still out on that one," I said as steadily as I could manage.

Blake laughed and wiped his mouth with the back of his hand. I laughed too.

"So are you okay?" he asked.

"Yeah, I'm fine," I answered without even giving it a thought.

He tipped his head to the side and looked me hard in the eyes.

"You sure?"

I shifted my weight from one foot to the other. I thought to lie to him, like I lie to everyone. I even started to shape the words with my mouth. But I couldn't do it. Something about the way he looked at me, or what I felt when I looked at him, I just couldn't tell him I was okay. So, I shrugged my shoulders.

"It's upsetting to see her like that, you know? And I'm losing hope too. You know?"

"I'm sorry."

"Well thanks," I told him. I smiled as big and wide as I could – it was my *but everything is still absolutely okay so don't worry about me* – smile. I turned to walk back around the bar to wipe down the tables but stopped. "Hey Blake?"

"Yeah?"

"I'm out of here soon. Do you want to stick around until I get out and maybe go somewhere for a little bit?"

I hated myself for asking. The way I felt about him was dangerous. But I couldn't help it. I didn't want to be alone. It wasn't like I was planning on kissing him (and I certainly wasn't planning on screwing him). I just needed some company.

"I can do that. But there's only one problem," he said to me.

Oh crap, here it comes: I don't like you or I'm engaged or I'm studying to be a Priest.

"Yeah, if it's a problem then no worries."

"No, I'll go. But I still don't know anything about you."

"You know my name is Katie and you know what I look like, for most guys that's usually enough."

He laughed and then looked at me with a wide smile.

My God, how had I not noticed how hot he was? Holy crap, how could anyone so beautiful actually exist? He was pretty much off the charts.

"I'm a bartender, twenty-three years old, and I graduated from UNC with a degree in English. Better?"

He grinned. "I would have waited anyway. But thanks. Now I only need to find out about the stuff that really counts."

He offered to give me a ride to the pier but I wanted to drive my own car – it made it all seem less formal and maybe less like a girl going to the ocean at night with a guy who was almost too hot to believe. He followed me as we drove the three miles out to Sully's Landing. It was away from any towns and usually empty. This night wasn't an exception. Blake and I parked on the side of the road and walked up a small hill. When we got to the top, the moon was bright enough so that we could see the water.

"You're not taking me out here to kill me or something, are you?" Blake asked.

"I haven't decided yet."

He followed me as we crossed a small strip of sand and stepped up onto the pier. I was already regretting bringing him with me. What was I thinking? I didn't want to be alone. And despite my uncontrollable attraction toward Blake, he wasn't Neil, and I wanted him to be Neil.

So, what exactly was my plan? Bring this near stranger out to the pier with me to just sit and talk and keep me company? Or did I plan on doing something more with him? Did I need that? A part of me wanted it, but that's not why I brought him out there. I just needed someone to be with me. And he showed up just in time.

"Thanks for coming," I told him. We reached the end of pier and sat down with our legs hanging over the edge, about twenty-five feet above the water. "So what's your story?" I asked.

"My story?"

"Yeah, are you from around here?"

"Nope. I grew-up in a small town in Virginia and then I left home and went to college. I just got done clerking for a State Supreme Court Judge in Virginia. It was a year position that ended in June. Now, I'm here visiting my mom and trying to figure out if I want to work with my brother, Steve, at the small practice he just started up near the Virginia border, or if I want to take a position with a huge law firm in Chicago."

"Choose working with your brother and make a lot of money or choose working for a giant firm in a great city and make a lot of money. Tough choices."

Blake grinned. "Well actually the law firm in Chicago pays more than twice what my brother can pay me, but it is a tough choice. Luckily I have a few weeks to decide."

"A few weeks?"

"Yeah my brother's offer is open and the Chicago firm said I can let them know any time before Labor Day." He grabbed a small stone from beside his leg and threw out into the water. "So what about you? Do you like bartending?"

I shrugged my shoulders. "I like it okay," I said. "It's not something I want to do for the rest of my life but it's a job for now." I looked down between the boards at the waves pouring past.

"So what do you want to do?" Blake asked.

That was the million-dollar question. What the hell did I want to do with my life? What the hell could I do with a degree in English? Go back to school and become a teacher? Write? Edit? None of that appealed to me. I did like helping people. But I couldn't tell him *that*. And according to Chris and mom, there was no money in helping others.

"I want to get in a car and just drive," I finally said.

Blake chuckled. "Don't we all."

"Yeah, I guess. But I really mean it."

"Well, we're still young, you know? Maybe we can help each other decide what the hell we want to do with the rest of our lives."

Maybe it was the tone of his voice. Or maybe the order of his words. But something about what he said made me instantly feel better. I had no idea what the hell I was doing with my life. But maybe that was okay. At least for a little while.

"That's a good thought," I said.

In the distance there was a large ship sliding across the horizon. We didn't speak for a long time. And that was okay. Then Blake reached over and grabbed my hand in his. It made me jump a little – not because it surprised me, and not because I wanted to pull my hand away, but because of how it made me feel. It felt like soft electricity.

"I thought I warned you about holding my hand."

"Yeah. You did. And I warned you too. But feel free to grab my ass, if you're so inclined."

I laughed and slapped him on the wrist.

"Seriously though. Do you want me to let go?"

"No," I whispered.

And then I lay back on the wooden pier and looked up at the stars. Blake did the same. And again, we spent several minutes without talking. We just listened to the ocean waves and stared at the stars above.

"This isn't a date," I whispered. "I mean, I just don't want you to get the wrong idea."

"I know. When I take you for a date, you'll know it."

Not *if* but *when*. I liked that. But I shouldn't.

Because what about Neil?

"So, you must be worried about your sister?"

I licked my lips and considered whether I should just tell him I was a little worried and leave it at that, or if I should share everything. Something about the way he looked and the way he made me feel… it made me want to grab my heart and dump all its contents out onto the pier for him to see.

"I've been worried about my sister for a long time. But with worry comes hope. And I'm starting to lose hope. So, it feels like my worry is turning into fear and grief. If that makes any sense." I turned my head toward him. "Does it?"

"Yeah, it does. Makes perfect sense."

"So what about you?"

"What about me?"

"You're here visiting your mom. Did she just move down here?"

"No. She's lived here for years. My parents divorced when I was six and my dad raised me and my two brothers – you met Steve and then there's our oldest brother Alex. Alex helps my dad run his gym up in Virginia."

"A gym, huh? That must have been cool."

"Taught me how to fight."

"Fight?"

"Yeah, it's a boxing gym. My dad was a Golden Gloves winner back in the early eighties. He used to make my brothers and me box each other and since I was the youngest I constantly got my ass kicked."

"That's horrible."

"Yeah, sometimes my brothers would trick me into fighting them when dad wasn't around and then we'd box without the helmets. Then I'd show up to school with a black eye or a swollen lip. The school got so concerned one time that they called Child Protective. Some lady showed up at the gym when my dad had gone somewhere and Alex told her I wasn't abused; I was just a pussy." He laughed loudly. "I can still see that lady standing there – her eyes the size of Frisbees and her jaw practically on the floor."

I laughed too, but I wasn't sure I should.

"That's horrible!"

"Yeah, but it got straightened out and it all taught me to stand-up for myself. By the time I was fifteen or sixteen my arms were a lot longer than theirs, so I could always keep them away from me with jabs. And I'm still pretty good at throwing them."

I thought about how easily he'd handled Marty. He was very good with jabs. Thank goodness for his brothers.

"Now my dad's gym has turned into more of an MMA gym, but I really haven't done much of that."

"MMA?"

"Mixed Martial Arts? You know those fights in an octagon cage?"

"Yeah, I've seen that a few times. It's pretty brutal."

"It can be. But it's actually pretty safe."

"If you say so."

He looked over at me. "So how about you? Your parents aren't together anymore?"

"My dad left us when were young."

Again, I wanted to say more. But I didn't know if I should. Did I have the right? Did I want to take the risk?

I'd only told a handful of people about my dad and his drinking and how hard those first few years were. I'd never told Neil. But I wanted to tell Blake. I wanted him to know. But what would he think of me? He'd probably stand right up and run off the pier. So, I decided to share something else that even fewer people knew. That information just felt safer to me, at least before I started sharing it.

"I have very choppy memories of him being a cop way back in the day. I remember him coming home and picking me up and twirling me around. I remember it was hard for me to hold my head up as he spun me – it kept wanting to fly back. Then he'd hold me close and I'd rest my head on his chest and it was just the most amazingly powerful feeling of comfort." I shook my head and swallowed hard. "He used to wear a white shirt and a tie every day. I don't know too much about his job but I do know he was some kind of detective. And then one day he started coming home when it was very late or he stopped coming home at all. And within a couple years the marriage was over. He left without even saying goodbye."

I turned my face away from him and wiped away the single drop that slid out of my eye. I was on the verge of tears but I would not cry. I vowed a long time ago that I would never cry for that man again. And I hadn't even come close since high school, until that night lying on that pier under those stars with Blake.

Blake shimmied closer to me so that the side of his body was completely touching mine. The words he spoke next came out slow and cautious.

"Do you know why he left?"

"I know he was an alcoholic," I said before I had the chance to stop myself. "Probably where my sister gets it. I got my dad's eyes and she got his addiction."

"But you didn't get the addiction gene?"

I shook my head. "I don't think so. I mean I guess I need to be careful about it. But I don't like drinking very much. I mean, I drink one or two or sometimes several once in a while, but I don't ever feel like I *need* it, ya know?"

Neither of us said anything for several minutes. We just stayed lying on the wood and looking up at the stars. The feeling of his body against mine made me want to turn on my side and wrap myself around him. But I couldn't do that. I shouldn't even want that. Should I?

"I hope you don't think less of me," I finally said.

"Less of you for what?"

"For coming from such a messed-up family. For my dad being such a loser."

"Not your fault," he whispered. "And I'm pretty sure I could never think less of you."

Something sharp and alive pumped through my blood when he said those words. I loved that feeling, but it also scared me.

"Well, you barely know me so…" And then my voice just trailed off.

"Well hopefully we can change that soon."

He sounded almost too confident and sure. But it wasn't cocky or arrogant in any way. It was just Blake telling me what he was thinking and what he wanted. There was no ego attached to it at all.

I'd never heard someone speak like he spoke or conduct themselves the way he conducted himself. He was sure of himself but it had nothing to do with anyone or anything else. It's tough to put into words even now. And that night I couldn't even begin to try to explain it. I just *felt it*. And it didn't make me feel intimidated or nervous, it made me feel safe.

Of course, the feeling of safety I felt around him was a lot more than just how he talked and carried himself, but that was part of it. So when he told me he wanted to get to know me better, I wasn't unnerved or turned off by it because he didn't mean it to make me nervous or to come onto me. He said it because it was how he felt, and he wanted to let me know. That was all. And I'd soon find out, that was Blake.

I didn't tell him I wanted to get to know him better, even though I did. Instead, I turned the conversation back to where it had come from.

"So what about your mom?"

"What about her? She's a nice lady with a nice life."

I wasn't sure I had a right to ask my next question, but I wanted to know.

"Do you remember her leaving? Did something happen?" I realized how horrible both questions were once the words reached my ears. "I'm sorry," I said. "Don't answer, please. I shouldn't have asked."

"No it's fine. You told me about your dad and I can tell about my mom. It's only fair."

He paused. Somewhere far away a horn blared.

"I don't know why she left," he began. "I mean, I don't know much about addiction and alcoholism and all that – thank goodness – but I do know it's a horrible thing and it destroys relationships and families every day. Just like it destroyed your family. But I can't blame anything like that on my mom leaving. She just left and moved away. She sat me down one day and told me she was leaving and that she was going to start a new life in a new place and that she loved me and would always love me."

He stopped for a while and I waited, picturing a small Blake sitting at a table crying as his mom told him she was leaving him. I didn't know whose story was sadder.

Which is worse: Your dad leaving because he's a drunken idiot? Or your mom leaving just because she wants to? I think I knew the answer but there was no point in recognizing the truth. It was like saying that dying from a head-on car crash is better than dying when you drive off the road and smash into a telephone pole. There is no *better*. Either way, you're still just as dead.

When he didn't speak again I raised my head and looked over at him. He was just staring up at the sky. I put my head on his chest and he put his arm around me and rested his hand on my head. It felt like we'd been like that a thousand times before. It felt like home.

"I don't really like to think about it," he told me "And I don't really like to see my mom either. My brother, Alex, refuses to see her. He's done. But I'm not there and I'm not sure I ever want to get to that place. Anyway. I decided to give it one last go this summer and come down here for a few weeks. It kinda made sense with the family reunion coming up next weekend and everything."

"Did she ever talk to you about it? Tell you why she did it?"

"Not really. Over the years we talked about it a little. But talking to her does no good. She's just not very good at giving me answers, and she never wants to talk about the past. But I already know the answers anyway. As hard as they might be, I know what they are."

"I'm sorry," I told him.

"Well thanks." His voice was suddenly back to being bright and alive. "And I'm sorry about your sister and your dad too. But enough of the depressing shit."

"It's fine," I said.

And it was fine. It felt good to be with someone who was willing to share with me. Neil never would. Neither would any of the older men at college or any of the stupid boys I wasted my time with. Blake wasn't just there to get in my pants and/or to make himself feel better. He was there with me and for me. I just knew it. And until that moment, I didn't know how much I needed that.

"Yeah but I'm supposed to be cheering you up and making you laugh."

"It's fine. But can I ask you something?"

"Absolutely."

"Do you have a girlfriend?"

"Nope. How about you?"

"Nope, no girlfriend."

He chuckled. "Well that answers two questions for me. But do you have a boyfriend?"

I thought about that one for too long. I really wasn't sure what to say. But I looked up out of the corner of my eyes and smirked, playing it off like I was teasing.

"Nope," I finally answered. And I don't even think I was lying.

"Good," he said. "Now I have to be honest, if I stay on this freaking wooden pier much longer my ass and my back are going to hurt so much that I won't be able to walk."

We sat up and my arm hit against my breast in such a way that the bruise flared up and sent pain down into my ribs and up into my neck. I flinched and made the tiniest whimper.

"You okay?"

The pain kept flaring and all I wanted to do was cradle my breast to stop the pain.

"I'm fine," I said.

He cocked his head and smiled at me. "You don't look fine."

I couldn't take it any longer. I reached up and grabbed my breast to steady it. The pain faded away.

"That asshole grabbed my breast during the fight the other night. Now it's all black and blue."

He stood-up and offered me his hand.

"Are you gonna make it, champ?" he asked.

I took his hand and he pulled me up.

"I'll live," I grinned.

"See, I knew going to law school was the wrong choice."

"What?"

"I should have gone to med school and then I could offer to look at your boob, you know to see if it needs any treatment."

I giggled and slapped him on the arm.

"It just needs to be left alone. Now stop talking about it, she's shy and you're going to embarrass her."

But the truth was that I was getting excited and with no bra, I could feel both my nipples beginning to poke through my shirt.

Blake glanced down and then looked me in the eyes.

"They don't look embarrassed to me."

I erupted with laughter and my neck and face instantly grew hot. I turned away from him toward the ocean. My boobs might not be embarrassed but I sure was. I stayed that way for several seconds, fighting the urge to run into his arms and kiss him. When I turned back around he had already started back up the pier toward our cars. I jogged to catch up with him. When I did, he held out his hand to me and I took it. Our fingers linked like a key slipping into a lock.

"Sorry. I probably shouldn't have said that."

"Yeah, not very gentlemanly," I fake scolded him. "And stop looking at my boobs anyway. Don't you know you're supposed to keep your eyes on my face?"

"I'm sorry. I can't help it. You're a beautiful woman Katie. And that includes all of you."

Just when the heat in my face was starting to cool, it flared back up again.

"Is that a line?" I asked him.

"It's only a line if I don't mean it. Or if I'm saying it just to be impress you."

We stopped just before we reached our cars and turned to face each other. I gathered up my hair in my hands and held it on top of my head.

"So was it a line then?"

He shook his head and grinned.

"Nope. Not a line."

"Yeah right."

He shrugged his shoulders. "No, seriously. I said it." He stepped in closer to me. "I meant it." He took another half step toward me and so we were just an inch or so apart. "I stole your momma's credit." He bent his knees and tipped his face down toward me.

"You're a dork," I giggled.

"You're awesome, Katie."

I shook my head. "I think you're full of lines. But you're not so bad yourself, Blake. You're still too tall, but not too bad."

"I'll work on that," he whispered.

I would not raise my face to him. He wanted to kiss me. And I really wanted to kiss him. But I couldn't. We couldn't. So, I took a step back and put some space between us.

"Let me show you. Go out with me tomorrow night," he offered.

I exhaled a burst of air and turned my head to the ocean. Was he really asking me out? I knew the night went well and I believed him when he said he thought I was beautiful (although he was wrong about that), but I didn't really think he wanted to date me. Older guys wanted to date me. Younger guys with sweaty palms wanted to date me. Hell, at the bar I was hit on and asked out by a different looking guy who was a different age every single night – sometimes three of four times in a night. Some were even lawyers. But I never thought a guy like Blake would be interested in dating me.

"Are you asking me out?"

He nodded and smiled. There were those dimples again. Did they only show up when he wanted them to?

"Yeah, I'm asking you out."

My mind was moving so fast that I almost said yes. Then I remembered.

"I have to work tomorrow night. And Saturday night too."

"Maybe Sunday then?"

I shrugged my shoulders. I wanted to see him again before Sunday. (But what about Neil? He wasn't my boyfriend, not exactly at least. But he was something. Probably more than just something. Wasn't he? What would he think of all this?)

"How about breakfast tomorrow morning?" I asked.

"Breakfast sounds good. But it wouldn't really count as a date."

"Right," I agreed much too quickly.

"There's a diner over on Main Street called *Betty's Breakfast and Lunch*. It's pretty good."

"Yeah, I live right around the corner from it. I live above the real estate agency on the corner of Main and Cottage."

"I think I knew where that is," he smiled. "I'll swing by and pick you up at like nine?"

"Nine sounds perfect."

He took a large step forward. He was looking me in the eyes and I knew what was coming next. He was certainly persistent. Did he feel how I felt? Is that why he kept trying. I mean, I wanted to kiss him. I really did. But a part of me didn't want it.

Then he bent down and made his move. I turned my head so he only got my cheek with his lips.

"Sorry," I whispered.

"No, that's fine. Umm, that was probably just a little too fast, right? Sorry, I just thought…" But he didn't finish his sentence.

"You don't need to apologize or explain. My fault. It's fine."

We stood looking at each other and nodding our heads up and down. I already hated myself for not letting him kiss me. How could I be so stupid and scared?

"Well, it's late. You want me to follow you home?"

"No, I'm fine. This is Dulcet, nothing bad ever happens here."

He opened my car door for me and I slid into the driver's seat.

"I'll see you tomorrow morning?"

"Absolutely," he smiled.

Luckily my car started on the first try. I pulled away with Blake watching me. He was standing with one hand in his jean's pocket and the other raised in a wave to me. I should have kissed him. But where would that have led? And I don't mean for just that night; I mean for me in life? I barely knew him but I liked him a lot. And I knew that was a dangerous thing. I just didn't know how dangerous.

Chapter Seven - Then

My dreams that night were filled with Blake. We were at the pier and I was lying in his arms. We talked and we laughed. And then he kissed me and I kissed him back. It felt absolutely perfect. A fire flared hot inside of me. I pulled my clothes off and climbed on top of him. But before we actually started making love, the dream kept ending.

I woke-up a little before eight feeling like everything in the world was perfect. The sun was out, the birds were chirping right outside my window, and I was going to meet Blake for breakfast. And, at least for a little while, that's all that mattered.

I showered, got dressed, pulled my hair back into a pony tail and put on a little make-up. After I brushed my teeth, I put on some lip gloss and then headed for the door.

That's when I saw the sheet of paper sitting on the floor. It had obviously been slid under the door. I bent and picked it up. There were just three small words typed in bold font:

I SEE YOU

I shook as a cold chill washed over my back and splashed into my shoulder blades. But the fear left as quickly as it had come. What the hell was it? Did someone slide it under the wrong door? Probably not. I was the only apartment above the real estate agency. Was someone messing with me? Maybe Kendra stopped by. But that made even less sense. Could it be from Neil? Did he drive by me and Blake last night? I don't remember any traffic but maybe I just didn't notice it. I stared at the paper for several more seconds. Could it be from Blake? That would be creepy.

I pulled my phone out of my pocket: 8:59. So, I folded the paper in half and then I grabbed my keys off the table beside the door and opened my door to leave. I half expected someone to be standing there. But there was no one. So, I locked the door behind me, jogged down the steps, and stepped out into the morning sunlight.

The morning was absolutely gorgeous – sunny and about seventy degrees. The wind was blowing in just the right direction so the scent of the ocean was in the air, mixed with the smell of roses from the bushes that lined the property of a house down the street. It would be a hot one later in the day and probably bring thunderstorms, but right then it was perfect.

Blake was leaning against the front of his Jeep with his arms folded. He was wearing faded jeans and a simple white tee shirt that showed he might be skinny, but his arms and chest were muscular. Holy crap, he was beyond hot. I sort of walked and kinda skipped over to him.

"Morning," he said to me. He looked me up and down. "Don't you look beautiful."

"Well thanks."

"And that's not a line," he added quickly.

I laughed. "Better not be," I said. "You hungry?"

"Yeah. You?"

"Absolutely. Let's go get our grub on."

Blake laughed. "You good with walking?"

"Of course."

We started off toward the diner. He pointed down at the sheet of paper I was carrying. After seeing him I'd forgotten about all about it.

"Whatcha got there?" he asked.

"Oh," I handed him the sheet. "That was slid under my door sometime between me getting home last night and leaving this morning."

I watched him closely to see his reaction. He unfolded the paper and looked at it.

"Someone left this under your door?"

Unless I was crazy, that someone was not him. His reaction made it clear that he was seeing the sheet for the first time.

"Yeah, I have no idea what the hell it is."

"Kinda creepy," he said to me. "You got any psycho exes?"

"Too many to count," I replied, and I was only half joking.

"Maybe it's one of your friends messing with you? Or your sister?"

"Could be."

I took the paper from him and crumbled it into a ball. I threw it in a trash receptacle outside the diner. He held the door for me and followed me down the long row of tables. I chose a table near the back of the diner. I slid into the booth on one side of the table, and he sat across from me.

"So tell me about your choices?" I said to him.

"My choices?"

"Yeah, Chicago or… where was the other place? Your brother's firm?"

"It's in a small town called Chincoteague. It's a beautiful town, but you can't really call my brother's practice a firm."

"Too small?"

"Way too small and too new. It's just him. So, if I go there it will be just the two of us."

"So that would be cool."

"Yes it would."

"And what else: Great town and working with your brother. Anything else attractive about that job?"

He looked up at ceiling and shook his head. "Not really."

The waitress came by and took our orders – I ordered the French toast and Blake got three eggs over medium, bacon, home fries, and toast. I guess he really was hungry. When the waitress left, I asked him what would be good about taking the Chicago position, besides the money. His face lit up and he launched into reason after reason –

explaining how well run the firm was, the types of cases he'd be working on, and things I'd never even think about. He was still going strong when our food arrived.

I knew which choice he was going to make. It was obvious. Didn't he see it? He had to. It was going to be Chicago.

I swallowed down a bite of French toast and washed it down with a sip of coffee.

"So how about cons for Chicago."

"Cons for Chicago, that would be a great band name," he interrupted.

I smiled but stayed on topic. "Any downsides to Chicago?"

He shook his head. "Not really. Other than it's a little farther away from home."

"And farther from me," I added with a grin.

"And of course farther from you," he smirked. "And I'm not huge on cold weather but that's about it."

"So you love the city of Chicago, and this job has more opportunity, more money, more challenging, and about a dozen other awesome lawyer specific things about it, and the other job only has a couple pros, and you still haven't decided which job to take?"

He took a drink of orange juice and wiped his mouth with a paper napkin.

"Right. I still haven't decided."

"I think it's pretty obvious. The Chicago position has everything and your brother's firm – excuse me, I mean practice – has next to nothing."

He shrugged his shoulders. "It's a tough one."

"Why would you even consider going to work with your brother?"

He drank down the last of the coffee in his cup and looked at me with a tiny smile.

"I'm probably going to turn down the Chicago job and go work with Stephen."

That made no sense at all.

"What? Why? The pros and cons are at a ratio of like twenty to one in favor of Chicago. Why would you even hesitate to say no to Stephen?"

"Because that's family. And family is everything."

I loved that answer. And I had no comeback for it.

Could this guy get any better?

I looked at Blake out of the corner of my eyes. "You really are a great guy aren't you?"

"Now that sounds like a line."

We talked and laughed through the rest of breakfast. I had no idea who this guy was or where the hell he'd come from, but I adored him. And I loved how comfortable I felt around him after only knowing him such a short amount of time. He was something special, and he would make some lucky girl a very lucky wife. But I knew it wouldn't be me. He was way too good for me. I wasn't the type of girl that a guy like Blake would ever even fall in love with.

So, why the hell would he waste his time around me? Was it because he was only going to be in Dulcet for a few weeks? Maybe he was okay wasting his time with someone like me while he was waiting for the rest of his life to begin. I didn't know. I still don't know. Maybe I fooled him with my smile and my blonde hair and my big blue eyes. Maybe he didn't realize what kind of girl I *really* was. Maybe he couldn't see what most other guys were able to see – I might be pretty on the outside but underneath the beauty lived an ugly monster. Most other guys did see it and that's why they usually only wanted one thing. Or maybe he did see it and was just waiting until I gave him what he wanted. Maybe. But this didn't feel like that. And, despite having my doubts, I hoped it wouldn't be like that. I *wanted* this to be different.

Blake paid the bill (after I made a lame attempt to try to pay for myself) and we walked back outside. The humidity was already starting to feel oppressive. In another couple hours it was going to be one of those shirt sticking to your back kind of days. Thank goodness for air conditioning.

"So why'd you become a lawyer? You don't seem like the type."

Blake chuckled. "Is that a slam or a compliment?"

"A compliment, I guess?" I teased. "No, it's a compliment."

"Atticus Finch," he said.

"Atticus Finch?"

I looked over at him while we stopped on the corner and waited for a car to pass before we crossed the street.

Blake grabbed me by the wrist. "Whoa, be careful," he said as if I was about to walk in front of the car. "I just saved your life."

"You really are a dork."

"Just a thank you would do. But whatever. And yes Atticus Finch."

His hand slid down from my wrist and grabbed my hand.

"Oh I get it, that's a move. Pretend you're saving me, hold my hand. Very smooth," I said.

"Thank you," he smirked. "And it's still Atticus Finch."

"The name sounds familiar," I said as our fingers locked together.

"He was the lawyer in *To Kill a Mockingbird*. Scout's father."

"Oh. I read that in high school."

"It's my favorite book. Has been since I was little. I must've read it twenty times when I was in middle school. My dad bought me a paperback from a garage sale and I read it so much that it fell apart."

"So you became a lawyer because of a character in a book?"

"I wanted to be a lawyer because of a book. But I became a lawyer because I've always been good at reading people and cracking them open when I want to. Like the other night with that asshole and your sister, I knew if I just stayed calm and confident then he would slither away after getting cracked on the nose a couple times."

"Calm and confident," I repeated. "Seems like you're always calm and confident."

He looked over at me. "Well thank you Katie. That's a nice thing to say. See, you're actually a really nice lady too."

I shook my head. "More compliments. More lines. Blah blah blah. Yuck."

"And the nice moment is gone."

I grinned up at him. "I'm not going to kiss you this morning either."

He acted offended. "You think I want to kiss you? I can't stand the taste of French toast. Talk about yuck," he said trying to mimic my voice on the word *yuck*.

"Well maybe just a small kiss," I said to him.

"Nope, not going to happen," he shook his head.

"Oh we'll see," I said to him.

I was well aware he'd turned things around on me. And the truth was, though I didn't want him to know it, I wanted him to kiss me. I wanted it more than I'd wanted anything in a very long time. I gripped his hand tightly but he tore it away.

"Yeah," he grinned down at me, "I'm thinking we should hold off on the hand holding too. Might lead to something else."

"Fine," I said to him. I wanted it to sound indifferent but I think it came out sounding frustrated. I circled the conversation back. "So what do you mean by reading people and cracking people open?"

A car alarm sounded a couple blocks over and that caused a dog nearby to start barking. But when the alarm stopped, the dog stopped too. Blake and I crossed the last street before my apartment. Just as I was about to step-up onto the curb, he put his hand gently on my lower back. My shirt pulled up ever so slightly in the back and the tips of two of his fingers brushed against my skin. It sent a chill up my spine and I had to fight the urge not to shiver.

"Cracking people open is easy when you can read people," Blake said to me.

He removed his hand and stuffed it into the pocket of his jeans.

"Cracking people open?" I asked.

"Yeah, getting them to say what you want. Getting them to give the testimony you might need, or to agree to some kind of a deal or whatever the case might be. I'm pretty good at knowing what to say and who to say it to. I'm good at reading people. At knowing what they're all about and then using that against them to crack them open. It's a bit of a gift."

He didn't say it like he was bragging. It was true and he was saying it. There was nothing more to it than that.

"So is that like your superpower?"

"Yeah, you could say that. Not as good as being able to attract assholes. But still not bad."

"Not everyone can be as lucky as me."

"One can only hope to be around you long enough to experience such a power."

I couldn't stop smiling. It just felt good to be walking with him, and joking with him, and being with him.

"So you're good at it?" I asked.

"Yeah, I guess you could say that."

"You're like really good?"

"That depends on what your definition of really good might be."

"Now you're sounding like a lawyer."

Blake grinned and nudged me in the side with his hip. "I am a lawyer."

"So crack me open counselor. Tell me all about me."

"I could never do that to you."

"Oh come on super lawyer man, show me what you got."

"I prefer the term superman lawyer."

I pushed on his shoulder but it didn't affect his gait at all.

"Come on," I urged. "Give me your best shot."

He looked down and shook his head. "I have to advise you against that."

I giggled. "Please," I begged. "I think it would do me some good. Tell me all about me. Hell, I don't even know much about myself. You'd be doing me a favor."

"A favor?"

"Yeah."

"Well how about just a sample? How about I just tell you what I read and leave it at that. I'll save the actual cracking you open part."

"Hit me with your best shot."

"Well then, where do I start?" he said. "Let's see you're a woman who doesn't know how great she is."

Oh please don't turn this into another line. Please don't just twist this into another attempt to get into my pants.

But he didn't. What he said was anything but a line.

"There is a fear inside of you that you wish wasn't there, and you're scared of that fear. Because fear has many levels and comes in many shapes and sizes. And sometimes we choose to let people in or to take risks that might make us afraid just so we don't have to face larger fears that already live inside of us. That's something I know very well and I'm pretty sure you do too. You're intelligent and compassionate and quick to help others but you don't always stop to help yourself. On the outside you are this confident, beautiful woman who people watch and admire. But on the inside there is a little girl with big blue eyes who just wishes her father would come back and just give her one more hug. And that in itself isn't a bad thing. It's actually a really good thing – the innocence and the beauty of that little girl. But sometimes you make decisions and allow yourself to be put in situations just because of that little girl. And the grown-up woman inside of you deserves a good life filled with happiness and greatness because you are unique and perfect in so many ways, even your imperfections have beauty because they're a part of you." We arrived in front of the agency and stopped beside his Jeep. "And that's how I read you."

I couldn't speak. I didn't know whether to be angry or flattered, but I was a lot of both. Most of all though, I was just plain upset. I wiped both of my cheeks clear from the tears and tried to hide my face from him. I could feel him watching me and I had no idea what to do or say, so I did what I had to do.

"Well thanks for breakfast," I said, and then I pushed through the door and ran up the steps to my apartment.

He was calling after me but I didn't stop. I jammed my key into the lock, turned the knob, stepped into my apartment, and then I absolutely and completely lost it.

Chapter Eight - Then

What did it really matter? Everything he said about me. It may or may not have been true. I didn't know. So how the hell did he? Still, the part about the little girl inside of me. That hit a nerve that I didn't know was inside of me. And it struck that nerve in a way that I didn't understand.

But after a couple hours I felt like I totally overreacted and made a fool out of myself by running away from Blake like that. But it didn't matter anyway. He'd be going to Chicago soon (I was sure of it) and I'd never see him again. Besides a man like Blake didn't ever truly fall for a woman like me. It just didn't happen. And if I was going to spend much more time with him then I'd just be setting myself up for a fall.

I tried to keep busy the rest of that day before my shift at the bar. I cleaned my apartment, I did all my laundry, and went grocery shopping. Still, I kept asking myself the same question over and over: Why did Blake's words turn me into a puddle?

First of all, to be fair, I pretty much forced him to try to summarize who I was. So it was my fault that he even said anything. He tried to warn me. I guess I just thought he was full of shit. But then he said all of that. And something about it was just too sharp or maybe too heavy to hear. Maybe both. I don't know. But it was when he said the stuff about me being a little child who wanted her father. That's when I lost it. I just couldn't help but cry.

But why? I hated my dad. And I was far from a little girl on the inside, outside, or any side you wanted to look at. Just ask any number of men. Some of the stuff he said might have been sort of accurate, but the stuff about my father, and especially the part about me being like a little girl, was way off. Wasn't it? Yet, somehow it still ripped me open. Though I don't think he meant it to affect me that way.

I made it through the day and worked until two am that night. I kept glancing at the door hoping I'd see Blake walk in. And when the place got really busy, I kept scanning up and down the bar hoping I'd see his smiling face staring at me. But he never came in.

I had no idea how to get in touch with him. I didn't have his number or know where his mom lived. And he didn't have my number either. Why hadn't we exchanged numbers? How stupid. But then again, we probably would've if I didn't go running up the steps like some scared little girl (but no, Blake wasn't right about that part). Maybe he'd show up at some point later in the summer. I hoped so. But that was a foolish hope. He was leaving in a few weeks. And besides, I didn't have a real shot with him anyway.

When I got home that night I felt so lonely. But I didn't even bother to try to call Neil. He hadn't tried to call me either. He was busy with other things. Fine. He couldn't even give me fifteen minutes when I really needed him to. Some guy I barely knew was more than willing to keep me company but Neil wouldn't. (And that other guy made me feel more things in the space of an hour than I'd ever felt with Neil.) So, maybe I needed to rethink everything that was going on with the two of us. We weren't officially dating so it wasn't like I had to break-up with him. Did I? And I wasn't even sure I wanted to break-up with him. I just needed something more. That's all.

The next day Kendra called me and asked me to go to an AA meeting with her. I was thrilled to hear she was going to meetings again. She said there was one at noon in a church basement not far from me. It was an open meeting, which meant both alcoholic and non-alcoholics were welcome. Of course I agreed to go with her.

In the rooms of AA meetings there are so many sad stories, and they're draped in a cloak of hope. I never speak. "Hi my name is Katie," is all I ever say. I never say my name and then admit I'm alcoholic like just about everyone else in the room does. I'm not an alcoholic. Alcohol is not what I've chosen to cope with all the bullshit in the world. It's not what I've chosen to help me manage all the crap that's inside of me.

Kendra usually doesn't speak much more than me at the meetings. That day was no different. She said her name and admitted to being an alcoholic and that was it. Afterward, we decided to walk around the block before going our separate ways.

"So I have a date with Steve tonight," Kendra said with shy smile.

"Really? That's great. He's not mad about the other night?"

"No, not at all. He actually brought me lunch yesterday and asked me to look into going to AA meetings. He said he'd take me to dinner if I went."

"He bribed you?"

Kendra grabbed my arm and held it with both her hands.

"It's not like that," she said. "It was sweet."

"I know. Just remember you have to want to get well for you, not for anyone else."

"Yeah."

I waited to see if she was going to add to her single word response. She didn't so I asked, "Do you want to get better?"

"Yeah. Of course. I've always wanted to get better. Maybe Steve is just what I needed to help me."

"Maybe," I replied.

I'd seen her fall off the wagon too many times, so maybe that's why I didn't like the idea of her dating or going to AA meetings to earn a dinner date. Or maybe it was because I knew a relationship early in sobriety was a recipe for disaster.

"What's wrong?" Kendra asked me.

"Just be careful," I said to her.

"Yeah I know."

"I mean Steve's only going to be here a little while."

"Yeah but he doesn't live too far away," Kendra answered quickly.

"So do you think you're going to keep going to meetings?"

"Every day," she said. "I'm just so sick of the shit. I just have to be done. I have to be."

I put my hand on her hands that were still wrapped around my arm.

"That's good," I told her. "I'm happy for you."

But I wasn't. I wouldn't let myself feel happiness or hope. Because something wasn't right. With Kendra, something was always wrong. And I could feel it radiating off her body: She wanted a drink.

"So how about you and Blake?" Kendra asked.

"There is no me and Blake."

"Steve said he thinks Blake is sweet on you."

I didn't know what to say so I said nothing. Images from the previous day - me running up the stairs to my apartment – played in my mind. I felt bad for leaving him like that. If he was sweet on me before, there was no way he still felt the same way.

"Well I think you two would make a good couple. He's really hot, don't you think?"

"Yeah, he is. But not really my type."

"If he isn't your type then what the hell is?"

Older men who ignore me and refuse to be seen with me unless we're far away from home? Rich men who need a distraction from their boring lives?

"I don't know," I said softly. "But I'll let you know when I figure it out."

∞∞∞∞∞∞

The bar was slow for a Saturday night, even by the latest not-so-busy standards. I had hoped maybe Blake would stop in for a drink. Kendra told me that he and Steven were expected to be back late that night. But he never showed. I'd scared him off, which wasn't a completely bad thing. My feelings for Blake were dangerous in a way I didn't understand. Within another week or so, Neil would be done with his family responsibilities and then I'd be able to see him again and my life would return to normal. Or at least it would return to being abnormally normal.

Linda and Ron both worked late too, so we were able to clean-up quickly. That, coupled with being able to start before two am since all the customers were gone, allowed us to be just about done by quarter after two. I was finishing-up with sweeping the floor, and Ron was gathering the garbage and taking it out back to the dumpsters. Linda took a break from mopping behind the bar to put a song on the juke box. It was a slow country song.

"I love this one," she said to me.

"Yeah, it's an oldie but a goodie," I replied.

"Dance with me?"

"No thanks. I really need to get home."

She pulled the broom out of my hand and leaned it against a table. Then she grabbed my hand and placed it on her hip.

"Come on. We haven't danced in weeks. We used to have so much fun."

We clasped hands and just like that we were dancing.

"If Ron sees us he might pass out from excitement."

"It's been a slow night," Linda grinned. "I barely got any tips. Think if we offer to kiss maybe he'll give us a twenty?"

"I'd do it topless if he'd give us fifty."

We both laughed.

"There's the old Katie," Linda said. "You haven't seemed like yourself lately, everything okay?"

Nothing was okay. My sister was a ticking time bomb, my boyfriend (who wasn't really my boyfriend) was ignoring me to be with his family, and I was falling for some guy I barely knew.

"I'm fine," I lied. "I've just been a little lonely lately and all the crap with my sister. But I'm okay."

"Well, if you need someone to talk to or get drunk with, I'm your girl."

I thought about it. We could go back to my apartment or to her place and get absolutely shit-faced drunk. That actually sounded really good. But that's not what I really needed. What I really needed was a man to make me feel like a woman.

"Thanks," I said to her. I hugged her and she hugged me back. I winced as my sore boob pressed too hard against her arm.

"You okay?" Linda asked.

"I'm fine," I giggled. "I'm just a little sore that's all." I grabbed the broom and walked toward the front of the bar. "Thanks for the dance."

"Any time baby."

I put the broom in the closet that was next to the dartboard. That's when I noticed Buzz sitting in his office, staring out at me. He always went home well before closing, so it was a little shocking to see him still in there. From where he sat he had a clear line to see me and Linda dancing. How long had he been there just staring at us? How long had he been staring at me?

"Hey Buzz," I called to him. He didn't respond. He just kept his eyes fixed on me.

A wave of fear hit me and flowed away as quickly as it had come. I'd known Buzz for years. He was a nice old man. But there was something about the way he was just looking at me. His eyes looked flat, and his jaw was set in way that almost looked like he was about to growl.

"Buzz," I called again. "Hey, Buzz." I moved a few steps closer to him. "Hey, are you okay?"

He blinked and shook his head. "Fine," he muttered. "Just fine."

Then he got up from behind his desk and shut his office door.

"You notice anything weird about Buzz?" I asked Ron on my way out to my car.

Ron had just finished putting the last of the garbage in the dumpster.

"Not really," Ron answered. "Why?"

"Well he's usually not here this late and he was just staring at me kinda weird."

"Yeah I've caught him staring at you a few times."

"Seriously?"

"Yeah but that's not weird. Guys stare at you Katie. Buzz might be old but he's still a guy."

I wasn't exactly sure what he was talking about. I shook my head and shrugged my shoulders. "If you say so. Okay. Have a good one."

"You too."

I unlocked my car and opened the front door. Just as I was about to climb into the driver's seat I saw something stuck under my windshield wiper. I could see it was a sheet of paper and a small part of me hoped it was a note from Blake. I lifted the wiper slightly and pulled the paper out from under it. I sat down in my car and opened it up. Type written in large font and bold print were the words:

I'm watching you and waiting.

My breath caught in my throat and the skin on my shoulders tingled. What the hell? Who would leave such a note and what the hell did it mean? I'd almost forgotten about the other note that was slid under my apartment door. And now a second one?

I sprung up out of my seat and pivoted around in a circle. I couldn't see anyone watching me. But maybe there was someone out there hiding in the darkness? Maybe they were waiting to attack me. I jumped back into my car and locked the door. What if someone was stalking me? What if it was some kind of psychopath or a serial killer?

They never did catch the Zodiak Killer. And there had to be a lot of other serial killers roaming the streets too.

But that was silly. Someone was just trying to play a joke on me. Or maybe this was Neil's attempt at being romantic. Maybe he stopped into the bar just to watch me and I didn't see him? Maybe he's just letting me know that he's waiting, counting down the hours until we can be together again. Yeah, that was probably it.

My car didn't start until the third try and when the engine finally did run, it skipped and jumped and coughed. I put in drive and stepped on the gas. It lurched forward a couple times, stopped, and then finally carried me out of the parking lot toward my apartment. But I only made it three blocks. I was slowing down to stop at a red light and my engine just quit.

"No! Shit! No! Son-of-a-bitch."

I shifted it back into neutral and tried to start it again. It tried to turn over but it wouldn't fire back up. The traffic light turned green as I was just about stopped so I took my foot off the break, coasted through the intersection and pulled off the road. My front tire bumped into the curb and the car stopped. I turned the key and again it tried to turn over, but didn't. I slammed my hand against the steering wheel and yelled out in frustration.

A car passed by going really slowly. A few months ago a mechanic told me my engine was going to need an overhaul. I don't remember what exactly was wrong with it but to make it right it would cost me nearly a thousand bucks. I didn't have a thousand dollars. So what the hell was I going to do? I could hitch rides back and forth to work and maybe look for a second job. Or I could finally stop bartending and go out and try to use my degree to get a fulltime j-o-b. Then there was always the option of asking Chris for the money. But we all knew how hard he made that, and the odds of him saying yes were about as good as winning the lottery.

But I could worry about all that later. Right then I had two options: Walk home to my apartment or call someone. It was too late to call the house and ask my mom to come get me. But I could call the bar and see if maybe Ron or Linda could come get me, or maybe Buzz. But what was going on with Buzz? The way he was staring at me. If I didn't know him so well, I'd say it was almost creepy. Actually it was creepy. No, I couldn't call the bar. I should call Linda on her cell. But then she'll want to drink away the rest of the darkness and I'll end-up watching the night turn to day, drunk off my ass. Actually, that suddenly seemed like a good idea. But before I pulled out my phone, the car that passed me slowly did a U-turn at the next intersection and drove back toward me.

I glanced down at the sheet of paper sitting on the passenger seat: *I'm watching and waiting.*

I grabbed my cell phone and dialed nine-one. I watched the car slowly approaching. When it drew within about fifty feet it veered hard to its left and came straight at me. My eyes blinked and struggled to stay open as the headlights slashed into the car. My chest began to hurt and I had to tell myself to take a breath. The car stopped about two feet from my car and then the entire world stopped. I couldn't move. I simply sat watching and waiting with my finger poised above the final one I'd have to hit to call for help.

I see you and *I'm watching and waiting.*

Chapter Nine - Then

As soon as he closed his car door and started walking toward me, I knew it was him. I could tell by the height and the walk and the place deep inside of me that flared with excitement. Because there was that place deep inside of me that gained a knowledge every time he was near, and when it did it sent a warm pulse through my body. A pulse filled with expectation and hope.

It was Blake.

I opened-up my door and stood up.

"Hey," he called to me.

"Hey," I called back.

He drew closer. "Need some help?"

"What are you stalking me?" I asked with a grin, but I was only half kidding.

Blake laughed. He rubbed his chin.

"Do you wish I was stalking you?"

"I could think of worse things."

"You need a ride or for me to wait with you?"

"You mean you aren't going to ask me to pop the hood and fix my car."

He took a step back and looked my car over.

"I don't know much about cars. But from what I do know, I'm not sure anyone can fix this piece of shit."

"Hey! She can hear you ya know."

"I doubt it. I'm sure her hearing went back in the early nineties while some kid in dread locks was cranking Pearl Jam and drinking a crystal Pepsi."

I couldn't help but laugh. If it weren't so true I might have been insulted, but it was absolutely true. My car was a piece of junk and if it wasn't permanently broken, it was definitely on its last legs.

"Can I get a ride back to my apartment?" I asked.

"Absolutely."

I grabbed my purse and slid my cell phone into my pocket. I locked and closed my door.

"Will it be okay right here?"

"If someone steals it they'd be doing you a favor."

He started walking toward his Jeep and I followed closely behind.

"I meant will it get a ticket or get towed?"

He opened the passenger side door, took my hand, and helped me sit in the seat.

"Again," he said to me, "I think they'd be doing you a favor."

"Hey stop ripping on my ride. Not all of us are lawyers and can afford nice new cars."

But he just laughed and shut my door. I looked around his Jeep. It had leather seats and tons of room. It was nice but not as nice as Neil's Range Rover. In the back seat sat two grocery bags full of food. Blake climbed in and shifted his car into gear.

"All set?"

"Yes."

He drove past my car, turned around, and then headed back toward my apartment.

"I might need some help finding exactly where you live from this side of town. I think I can find it but I'm not one hundred percent."

"Okay," I said. "Just keep going until the next light and then take a right."

I wanted to apologize for how I'd reacted a couple days ago – when I cried and ran away from him. But I didn't know how.

"I swear I hate that car," I said.

"So why don't you get a new one?"

"A new one?" I chuckled. "I'd love to but I don't have the cash money."

"Oh," is all he said in reply, and then there was an awkward silence.

My mind was screaming at me to say something smart or funny or, preferably, something that was both smart and funny.

"So you just coming back from shopping?" I asked just to make myself feel more comfortable. It fit neither category, but at least it was something.

"Me? No, I was just on my way back from running up to Steve's office with him. He had to take care of a couple things so I went up there with him." He glanced into the backseat. "Oh you mean the food? Yeah, I just need to clear my head and cooking helps with that. Plus, all I've been eating is crap for the past couple of days and I could really use a good meal."

"Take this next left up here and then it's just a couple blocks to the right," I directed him. And then I added, "Yeah, it's been a long time since I ate a good home cooked meal."

"Well, are you hungry?"

"A little."

"A little? You just worked your ass off bartending. Tell you what: If it's cool with you I've got the food and you've got the apartment. Is it okay if I come-up and hang for a couple hours?"

I thought for a couple seconds. Something inside of me was whispering for me to tell him no. But something bigger and stronger was screaming hurry-up and say yes already.

"That sounds fun. I'll just need like ten minutes to take a quick shower."

"Excellent," Blake replied. "Just point in the direction of the kitchen and maybe show me where a few things are and I'll get dinner started while you shower."

Then he looked over at me and smiled. His dimples showed-up again and I had to seriously fight the urge to lean over and kiss him.

When I got out of the shower I pulled on a pair of jeans and a plain red tee shirt (being extra careful when I pulled on the shirt since my boob was still sore). I brushed my hair out and pulled it back into a ponytail. I took less than a minute to apply just a little bit of eye makeup. Then I looked at myself in the mirror, took a deep breath, and walked out of the bathroom. The second the door opened I was hit with the aroma of something delicious.

"That smells amazing," I said walking into the kitchen.

"Thanks. It's my grandmother's recipe." He pointed at two beers that sat on the end of the counter. "I like to drink when I cook too. So I have a six pack of beer. You want one?"

"Absolutely."

He grabbed one, twisted off the cap, and handed it to me. Then he twisted off the cap of the other one.

"Cheers," he said holding the bottle toward me.

I clinked my bottle against his.

"What should we drink to?" I asked.

"How about to meeting each other."

I smiled and held up my bottle. "To meeting each other."

And then I drank and watched him watching me drink.

Something was different about him. He wasn't quite as confident, but not in a helpless or shy kind of way. He was more relaxed and seemed softer – but not in a weak way. Maybe it was because it was the first time I'd seen him when we weren't out in public. Or maybe it was because he was doing something he loved. Maybe it was because it was with me, in my apartment, alone. I didn't know. I only knew he'd never been more attractive to me. In fact, I was pretty sure I'd never been more attracted to anyone.

"So listen," I said as I sipped at my beer, "I just wanted to say I'm sorry about what happened outside on the street. You know, after breakfast. Sorry I didn't say goodbye to you."

"It's fine. But you have nothing to be sorry for. I'm the one who should be sorry and I am. I felt horrible. I was trying to show off and said way too much. I didn't mean to crack you open but I did want to impress you and I was showing off. So, I apologize."

"It's fine. Not your fault. But yeah, that is quite impressive how you can do that. You must be one hell of an attorney."

He shrugged his shoulders and frowned. "I'm not so sure about that," he said.

"Well, anyway, I shouldn't have run off like some weak little girl. You just touched a nerve or something. And then everything came bubbling to the surface and I was crying."

"Not a problem."

"I guess it's just that I barely know you and it feels like I've already showed you too many of my wounds. That's wrong. And a little scary."

He shook his head. "It's not wrong. Sometimes you have to show someone your wounds so they can heal. And sometimes that leads to great things happening."

I really liked that: Needing to show my wounds so they would heal. And I liked it that I showed them to him. I'd only just met him, but I felt like I'd known him for my entire life.

I tipped my head back and slugged down a couple huge gulps of beer.

"You care if I put on some music?"

"Not at all. What do you like to listen to?"

"Just about everything." I grabbed my phone and slid it into the docking station. "You know the band honeyhoney?"

He shook his head. "Nope."

"This is them," I said. "They're kind of Americana Folk."

"Americana Folk?"

"Yeah, do you like it?"

"We'll see," he said. "Do you have any salt?"

I walked over and opened the cupboard above the sink. I reached up, pulled down a container of salt, and handed it to him.

"You need some help?" I asked. "I'm really good at stirring, I'm an expert stirrer in fact."

"Certified expert stirrer?"

"Of course."

Blake chuckled and then shook his head. "Nope, I've got this. It's almost done anyway."

"Already?"

"Yep. It's quick, pretty easy, and really good."

I sat down at the small breakfast table, which served as my kitchen table, and watched him move from pot to pan, concentrating hard. Could this man get any hotter? I watched the way the muscles in his arms flexed ever so slightly as he stirred the contents in the pot, and I looked at the shape of chest and how his torso slowly narrowed down to his waist. The answer was: No. This man could not get any hotter. He was the hottest person I'd ever seen and I was sure he was the hottest human being on the planet. It was all I could do to not grab him by the collar of his shirt and kiss him and then do other things that would probably lead to me falling hopelessly in love with him.

"So your grandmother taught you to cook?"

He nodded. "Yes she did. She was a great cook. She owned a restaurant."

"Really?"

He drank down the rest of his beer and set the bottle on the counter.

"Yeah, she started it in the late sixties and by the eighties she was just cooking once in a great while because it was so successful but, yes, she taught me to cook."

"Does she still own the restaurant?"

"Well, she and my grandpa own it, but grandpa owns a bunch of stuff but Grandma ran that all on her own. It was her baby and she did a great job with it."

"Sounds like a great lady."

"She was like a second mom to me, with mom number one being out of the picture so much."

"I'd love to meet her," I said even though I knew it was a little forward of me.

He took another beer out of fridge and twisted off the cap.

"I'd love for you to meet her too. But she passed away almost three years ago." He slugged down a swallow of his beer and wiped his lips with the back of his hand. "You ready for another one?"

"Sure. I'm so sorry to hear that."

"Thank you."

He grabbed another beer and brought it over to me. He twisted off the cap before he set it down in front of me.

"Is your grandpa still with us?"

"He is," Blake said as he walked back to the stove. "He's had better days but he's eighty-four now and fought through two separate bouts of cancer. So, he's doing as well as can be expected. We're almost ready here," he said pointing at the food. "If you want to set the table that would be good."

The food was better than I'd expected – and I expected it to be really good considering how everything about this man seemed to be perfect. We laughed about stupid college stories and silly childhood mistakes we'd made. When he was fifteen, Blake suffered a concussion and a broken arm when he tried to jump into his father's pool from the roof of the garage; I took nineteen stitches to the inside of my thigh when I tried climbing an old silo in short shorts to impress a boy when I was fourteen, and I slipped and slid fifteen feet down the old rusty ladder. Blake got in big trouble for shoplifting a bottle of Geritol when he was five (Why would a five-year-old even think to steal Geritol?) and I stole my mom's car in the middle of the night when I was thirteen and drove around the block. It was the most terrifying and exciting experience of my young life. Mom still didn't know I did it.

After dinner I washed the dishes while he dried. And when everything was cleaned up, it was just after four in the morning and I couldn't stop myself from yawning any longer. So, Blake said he should probably be going and thanked for me for a great time. I thanked him for a delicious meal and wanted to ask him to stay, but I didn't know how.

"So listen," he said to me with one hand on the door knob and the other stuffed into the pocket of his jeans, "I still don't know your phone number, and I'd love to call you and ask you out on a proper date."

"Do you want me to write it down or can you remember it?"

"You better write it down. It's a little late and I'm a lot tired."

I went and pulled out a Sharpie from the drawer in my nightstand. Without saying a word, I grabbed Blake's arm and pulled his hand out of his pocket. Then I flipped his arm over so the inside of his wrist was pointing upward. I wrote my phone number in big loopy numbers from his bicep all the way down to his wrist. And then I drew a heart in the palm of his hand. I looked up at him then and he looked down at me. He moved his other hand from the door to my face and placed his fingers under my chin. Then he tipped my head up and bent to kiss me.

My heart was drumming fast in my chest, blasting the endorphins and dopamine throughout my body. My mouth watered and my fingers itched to touch him. I wanted him so bad. I needed him against me and over me and under me and all around. I wanted to crawl inside him and I needed him inside of me. But just before our lips met, I turned my head and his lips landed gently on my cheek.

I took two steps back and we stood that way - silent and motionless for several seconds.

I wanted him and I needed him. But it was almost too much. He was so hot and smart and sexy. And being with him felt like I'd finally arrived home after being gone for years. He made me feel special and good. And what we had together was special too. But somehow, it just all seemed like too much. Too much of something I couldn't handle or that maybe I didn't deserve.

I needed him. But what it all meant, scared the hell out of me.

I could see the confusion in his eyes and I wondered what he saw while he was looking at me? Was he still reading me like an open children's book? Or was he seeing something else now?

"I'm sorry," I told him shrugging my shoulders. "I just don't know."

I saw the pain in his eyes – genuine hurt.

"It's fine," he whispered. "I umm, I should go," he stammered, "and hey I've got your number." He pointed at his forearm. "So, I'll call you, okay?"

But I knew he wouldn't call me.

He felt it too. He felt the power of us and how right we were for each other.

Did he think I didn't feel it too? Or did he know I felt it but was too messed up to even kiss him? He turned away from me and put his hand on the doorknob.

"Blake, wait," I said to him. "Did you mean what you said about showing wounds? That sometimes it makes everything better?"

"Yeah," he nodded.

I reached down and grabbed the bottom of my shirt and pulled it off. Blake turned back around and looked at me. I dropped the shirt to the floor but Blake didn't notice. His eyes were looking from my face to my chest and then back to my face. My nipples hardened and I almost ran into his arms right then. But instead I unbuttoned my jeans and slid them off. Then I stood tall wearing nothing but my black panties.

"This is the bruised boob that still hurts like hell," I whispered cupping my breast gently in my hand. I turned my right leg outward to show him the scar that ran halfway down my inner thigh. "And this is my scar from when I climbed that old silo." I let go of my breast and brushed my fingers against the scar.

It was a warm southern night in North Carolina and the temperature in my apartment was a comfortable seventy or so, but I suddenly felt cold. I tried to fight the urge to shiver but couldn't stop my hands from shaking.

"So here I am," I whispered. "I'm showing you all my wounds."

My entire body started to tremble.

Blake looked at me with a half-smile curling just the right corner of his mouth. He took one step toward me but stopped. I knew why he was hesitating and I didn't blame him. But I couldn't wait any longer. I launched myself toward him and he caught me in his arms. He lifted me up and spun us around so I was pinned against the wall. His lips were on mine as the passion flowed through our bodies and radiated off our skin. I bit his bottom lip and then licked his upper lip. And then we were kissing and his left hand was cupping my butt and holding me up while his right hand caressed my breast. My hands were inside his shirt, one pressed against his rock hard abs, the other scratching lines into his back.

I wrapped my legs around his waist and squeezed with everything I was feeling at that moment. I grabbed his shirt and pulled it over his head. And then he let go of my breast and clasped both his hands beneath me He carried me that way to the bedroom, the two of us kissing the entire way. And when we got to the bed he laid me down. Then he took off his pants and stood before me naked. I'd imagined how he would look without any clothes, and in my dreams he was incredibly fit and beautiful. But the way he looked then – the sweat glistening on his skin, the ripped muscles, I had never seen anything like it. Not even in magazines.

From my back, I wiggled out of my panties. He knelt down between my legs and traced a crooked - drive-me absolutely crazy - line with his tongue from above my ankle all the way to my cleavage. When he moved to my nipples and began kissing them I was already about to explode. I grabbed each side of his face and pulled him up so we were cheek to cheek.

"Make love to me," I breathed into his ear. "NOW!"

I put my hands flat against his stomach and pushed him over onto his back. I straddled his waist and bent over and kissed him hard on the mouth. When he was finally inside of me, I straightened my back and rode him back and forth, up and down, as he moved underneath me in perfect unison. It was our first time and it felt like the first time, but it also felt like we'd been making love together for years. Just before I climaxed, Blake put one hand gently on my bruised breast and the other inside my hip over the old scar. I screamed out as a runaway freight train of pleasure rolled through me. Blake followed with his own climax soon after. Then I kissed him gently on the neck and laid my head on his chest.

I'm ashamed to admit it, but I'd had sex with so many guys, so many times, I couldn't even remember them all. But I remembered all the good ones, and some of them were very good. Being with Neil was pretty good and bordered on great sometimes (if I had just the right amount of wine in me and he started doing that little trick with his fingers). But what I'd just done with Blake, was not even in the same area code as all the other times. It blew them all out of water.

I was on top of him and his arms were wrapped around me, holding me tightly against him. I felt so safe. And it felt right. Not like, yes we're good together, or we even we fit together like two lost puzzle pieces. No, this was the kind of right where only one right exists in a world of wrongs. It felt that powerful. It felt that good.

"So, is that what you mean by cracking me open counselor?"

Blake chuckled. "Not exactly. That's a little something extra I save for the extra special clients."

I smiled. I closed my eyes and let myself begin to drift away as his left hand played with my hair and his right hand drew light circles on my back. A cool breeze from the open window blew against my bare back and butt. It was so refreshing. And as I was lay there on him, I took in a huge pull of air. Blake's skin smelled amazing. The scent was something I couldn't quite place, something musky mixed with a hint of peppermint. I guessed it was his natural scent mixed with maybe soap or a little cologne that I'd never smelled before. Whatever it was, it was wonderful. Just like everything else about him.

For at least a short time, the world felt right. My life was perfect. A spot inside of me, that I didn't even know was empty, suddenly felt full. And the tiny little child who had always been softly screaming in the back of my mind – for so long that I'd learned to ignore her – became silent. I slipped into an incredibly peaceful and pleasant sleep.

Chapter Ten - Then

It turned out my car needed just under two hundred dollars of work, but the mechanic assured me we were one step closer to retiring the rust bucket for good. But I didn't really care. Once she quit for good, then I'd worry about it. Until then, I was having the time of my life with Blake.

After that night we made love for the first time, the next five or six days were a blur. I worked and spent time with Blake. He spent two more nights at my apartment – one night we spent making love for hours, and the other night we just sat up all night talking about our futures and our pasts. Of course, I left out most of the details and I didn't tell him about any of the older men. Yes, Blake made me feel safe and secure and like we'd known each other forever, but some secrets can never and should never be shared.

But I did tell Blake all about my dad: He'd once been a police officer. And I had memories, though they seemed more like a dream to me after all the years, of my dad pushing me on a swing at the park, of him giving me piggy back rides on walks beside the ocean, and tucking me in at night. I think he'd once been a good man and a good father. But I didn't know for sure. Mom never talked about him and whenever she did it was only to remind us all that dad was an alcoholic who'd lost his job and left his family. I told Blake we didn't know if my dad was even alive or dead. And I told him I didn't care either way.

We talked about Kendra too. She was suddenly doing very well. She was spending a lot of time with Steven, as I was spending a lot of time with Blake. I hoped this was the time she would finally put her life together and move forward away from the drinking. But I would always have my doubts. And though I felt like a traitor for saying so, I told Blake that Steve better be careful.

But Blake assured me that his brother was an adult and knew what he was signing up for. I doubted that. Nobody ever understood what a life with an alcoholic was like – even people who'd lived with alcoholics for years. Hell, I still never knew what the future would bring. But I wasn't going to betray Kendra anymore by trying to make Blake understand, so I didn't say anything else.

It felt awesome to be able to spend time in Dulcet – Blake and I went to dinner, and walked the streets hand-in-hand. We didn't have to hide anything. And the more time we spent together the more I wanted the whole world to know about what we had and what we were doing. I wanted to shout it on every street corner in Dulcet. I wanted it to write it on billboards all around the town. I just wanted – more like *needed* – people to know I had found something extraordinary.

Well, I wanted everyone but Neil to know. There were large chunks of time spent with Blake when I completely forgot about Neil. After going out with Blake on our third date, I knew I had to do something about Neil. He hadn't attempted to contact me and I wasn't going to call or text him. He was busy with his family, and would be busy with them through the weekend. Then his wife's brats (as he called them) would go back with their dad and he'd be available for me to see him.

But I didn't want to see him again. Not anymore.

Because what I had with Blake was so different. It was beautiful and right and thriving in the sunlight. Whereas what I had with Neil was wrong and existed only in the darkness. And it made me feel dirty.

I didn't realize it until I was with Blake, but being with Neil wasn't good for me. Sure, it felt good sometimes – like picking a scab off a wound feels good while I'm picking at it – but in the end it only left me with an open wound. But with Blake it was all different – the hanging out, the texting, the holding hands, the kissing, and having sex. With Blake, all of it just felt right.

To be fair to Neil, what I had with Blake blew everything I'd ever had with anyone out of the water. It was in a different universe. Before Blake I didn't think it was possible to fall so deeply in love with someone so fast. I thought the movies and novels filled with such stories were all just bullshit. And I thought people who claimed to be so in love were just delusional or liars. But now I knew better. True love is real.

Of course there was the problem. Blake wouldn't be in Dulcet forever. He was planning on leaving in a few weeks. If he decided to work with his brother, then we could stay together. After all, I was just bartending and I could pick up and move (if he decided he wanted me to move with him). But if he chose Chicago, that would be a problem. That was too far away and I could never put up with the cold and windy winter days. I loved the ocean and the warm weather too much. I loved the Carolinas. They were my home.

So, I wanted him to choose to work for his brother but I didn't tell him that. It was his decision to make and I wasn't going to allow my own selfish wants to cloud his judgment. It was totally up to him. When he talked about what he was going to do, I could tell he was leaning toward going to Chicago. It had everything going for it. All his brother's practice had to offer was that it was his brother's practice. But I never tried to persuade him one way or the other. I always just mostly listened. Just like when I talked about my future, he usually just listened.

My future. What a joke that is. I had no idea what I was doing with my future. There was nothing I really wanted to do. Nowhere I wanted to go. But I didn't want to keep bartending and living in a shitty apartment in Dulcet either. I'm sure I could get a job with an insurance company or maybe with a large bank or something, but I didn't want to do that either. I hated the thought of slowly growing old while sitting in a cubicle every day tapping away on a keyboard. It just wasn't for me. Helping people would be good. But what kind of job could that possibly be when all I had was an English degree?

"You'll figure it out," Blake said to me.

It was toward the end of the night we stayed up talking. He had his arm around my shoulder and my hand was on his knee.

"I'm not so sure," I replied.

"You will."

He sounded so confident I almost felt better about it.

"First I have to figure it out and then I need to actually get a job. And there aren't many jobs out there anyway. But I'm sure as hell not going to find anything staying here in Dulcet slinging beers."

"So what do you want to do?"

"Get in a car with you and just drive."

"That would be nice, but that's not a job."

"Unfortunately."

"Well, then let's try this: What do you like to do?"

"Be with you."

"Yeah, but that doesn't pay very well."

"Yes it does," I replied quickly. "Just not in money."

"But sex doesn't pay the bills baby."

"Well it could," I said and then paused to smile. "But it's probably best not to go down that road."

Blake laughed under his breath.

"Yeah, probably not the best idea. What else do you like to do? Besides hang out with me and have sex?"

"Have sex with you," I corrected him.

"Hmm, and I thought what we were doing was making love."

I grinned. "No, it's just sex."

I turned my head and kissed him. He kissed me back and then traced a line down my cheek with his finger.

"Well, whatever it is, I'm not so sure you're good enough to make a living with it."

I slapped him on the leg and acted offended. He laughed and pulled me into him. I hugged him back and then put my head on his shoulder.

"Yeah," I said. "I'm a loser who has no idea what the hell I'm doing with my life. I'll probably wind-up homeless."

"That's ridiculous. Seriously, let's try to figure this out. What do you like?"

"Nothing," I said. "Seriously. I did this with my guidance counselor back in high school and she said I should be an entrepreneur."

"Well there you go."

"Yes, I can be my own boss. But still I need to make money."

"Okay, I'll ask again: What do you like? And don't say anything about me."

"I like music. Maybe I can be a rock star?"

"Do you play an instrument."

"I played clarinet in middle school."

"Not many rock stars play the clarinet. Can you sing?"

I shook my head. "Not at all."

"So we should probably cross that off the list. Okay, one down and about ten thousand possibilities to go."

"See? I can't even be serious enough to have an intelligent conversation about it. I don't even want to think seriously about it."

"You'll figure it out," he said. And again he sounded so confident about it.

"How do you know?"

"Because you're too great of a woman and too smart not to figure it out. And the spirit is strong and as long as you're smart and gifted and strong – and you're all three – then everything will be okay."

"If you say so."

"I do say so," he said squeezing me tight. He kissed me on the cheek. "But listen, that family reunion thing I've been talking about with you?"

"Yeah, the one you're dreading?"

"Yes. Go with me."

I'd been waiting for him to ask me to go to it. It was at his mom's house and his whole extended family was going to be there. I was actually surprised that he hadn't already asked me.

"Okay," I answered.

"I guess Steve is bringing Kendra too. So, it should be fun."

"Are your family big drinkers?"

He knew what I was thinking.

"No, not really. But there will be booze and beer there. I guess Steve asked Kendra about it and she said it'll be fine. Why? Do you think it could be problem for her?"

"She's only a few days sober now. But I'll keep an eye on her too. If she says she's fine with it, then it should be okay."

I wasn't sure if he heard the doubt in my voice. I tried to sound sure and unconcerned about it.

"I guess I could tell him to un-invite her."

"No. No. Absolutely not. It will be fine," I said. "It'll be a lot of fun."

And we left it at that.

∞∞∞∞∞∞∞∞∞

The party was at noon and Blake was picking me up a few minutes after twelve. He thought it would be best if we arrived a little late and I had no problem with that. I was both nervous and excited to meet his family. I wondered what his mom might be like and if his stepdad was as big of an asshole as he made him out to be. I was sure he would be. I took my time putting on make-up and putting my hair up. Then I slipped into a sundress that was perfectly between looking casual and being formal.

I had just finished getting ready when my cell phone buzzed with a text message. I figured it was Blake telling me he'd be a few minutes late (he had a habit of almost always being a few minutes late). I picked-up my phone and looked at the message.

Be careful. Or else you will get hurt. Bad.

I dropped the phone back on the table and pulled my hand away like I'd just touched something burning hot. What the hell? First the written notes, which were definitely creepy. But now a text, which was bordering on threatening.

A wave of nausea rolled through my body followed by a chill. I shook all over and then closed my eyes tight, trying to keep myself calm. But I had the sudden feeling that someone was about to grab me from behind so I snapped my eyes back open and spun around.

Nothing. Nobody. Maybe I'd read the text wrong.

I picked the phone back up and there it was. From a number I didn't recognize:

Be careful. Or else you will get hurt. Bad.

Be careful? Be careful of what? They must have the wrong number. I didn't have any enemies. But they also left a note under my door and on my car. Holy shit, they (whoever the hell *they* were) knew where I lived and they knew where I worked. This wasn't good. Holy crap. This wasn't good at all.

Maybe it was someone just playing a joke on me. I ran through all the people in my life and tried to figure out who might think such a thing was funny. I couldn't think of anyone. I had no idea who it could be. Neil maybe? No, he was too sophisticated to play stupid games. Kendra? No, she would never do anything like that. Believe me, she was an alcoholic but she was the last person in the world who would ever try to scare someone like that. Could it be Blake? No, he would never, ever do anything like that. Never. And when he saw the first paper message, he was looking at it for the first time. I was sure of it. It definitely wasn't Blake.

I looked at the message again. Then I carefully typed out:

Sorry. I think you have the wrong number???

I waited. And then after only a few seconds, my phone lit up and vibrated with a reply.

This is Katie, right? Kinda tall... blond hair very pretty... tits could be a little bigger but great ass and legs. Right?

I almost dropped the phone again. For a couple seconds, I considered opening up the kitchen window and throwing the phone into the street. If it would've solved the problem, then that's exactly what I would've done. But of course, my phone wasn't the only connection he had to me (and after that last message I was convinced whoever was doing this was a he). No, this guy – this sick asshole – knew where I lived and worked and he also knew my cell number.

But who the hell was it?

And why?

Fear began to stir in my stomach and slowly it churned out anger. I pictured some small, faceless, hairless, dickless, man sitting in his parent's basement staring at random women's Facebook pages and researching them on the internet to get all their contact information. He was all talk. He got off on making girls scared. If he truly meant me any harm, he would have already attacked me. He wouldn't send me messages and warn me about what he was going to do.

I wasn't going to let him win. I tapped out a quick reply,

That's me. Now who is this?

I waited for a response. My mind was racing trying to think if I'd seen any strange men hanging around the bar or outside my apartment. There were always *strange men* hanging around the bar but I couldn't remember seeing any that looked out of place. Of course, on the busier nights, I could've easily missed some creep who wandered in a for a beer or two. It was impossible to know. But I was pretty sure there were never any weirdos hanging around my apartment.

Maybe this guy would tell me who he was or at least give me a clue. But there was no immediate reply. I waited so long that my chest began to hurt and I suddenly realized I'd been holding my breath since I sent the text. So I sucked in air that felt heavy to my lungs. I watched my phone, biting on the tip of my thumb and waiting for it to light up with a message. Just when I figured he wasn't going to respond, he did.

You will see me very soon.
I'm the one who watches you. A lot!!!

That was a common theme with this asshole, he always liked to point out that he was watching me. He obviously meant it to be threatening and he wanted me to be scared and freaked out. That made my blood boil. It made me so angry that I wanted to reach through my phone and rip this guy's eyelids off. I wanted to beat him to a pulp and then douse the pulp with gasoline and light it on fire.

But... I was also a little creeped out by it. The thought of some heavy-breathing, greasy, psychotic creep watching me. Of course it creeped me out. It was creepy! And of course it scared me. It was scary!

But I would not be pushed around. I would not be reduced to just some frightened little school girl who couldn't stand up for herself. I could not and I would not allow it.

Another text lit up my phone.

**Before long you'll find out who I am
When you least expect it
And if you aren't careful you will feel pain and I will feel happy!**

The anger took over before the fear could calm it down. I typed out a text as fast and my thumbs would move.

**Just let me know when and where and I'll be there.
And then I'll kick the shit out of you!!!
I'm not scared!! Bring it dickhead!!!
Maybe I'll even bring my boyfriend… But just to watch me kick your ass!!!!
Stop texting me or YOU WILL BE SORRY!!!!!!**

The second after I hit *send* I regretted it. Something deep inside was telling me not to make this person – whoever he was – angry. It was telling me not to mess with him. I should go straight to the police and at least make them aware of the situation. I turned my phone over so I couldn't see the screen. I dreaded what his reply might be. But screw it. I wasn't going to be intimated. Chances were pretty high that the creep was just some kind of bully who would never have the balls to confront me face to face. And my text would show him that I wasn't scared. I wasn't intimidated or about to curl into a ball and ask for mercy. And I sure as hell wouldn't let myself be terrorized.

That little voice wouldn't shut-up, so I listened to it.

Go to the police. This is serious. Someone has obviously been stalking you and now he'd taken one more step and threatened to harm you. Go to the police. What's the next step? Kidnaping? Rape? Murder? All three. Don't be stupid. This isn't a game and it's not about somebody trying to make you feel helpless and/or afraid. It's about life and death. Go to the police.

But I couldn't go to the police. What could they possibly do anyway? Probably nothing. But who the hell knew? What was certain is they would ask if I was seeing anyone. And they'd ask if there anyone who might want to harm me. Eventually it would come out that I was seeing Neil. That was not an option. Nobody could know about Neil. So going to the police was out of the question.

But what if Neil's wife had found out about me? Could she be sending the messages? I doubted it. If Neil didn't have time for me while his step kids were visiting, his wife wouldn't take the time to put a message on a car late at night and to slip a note under my door. Would she?

A knock at my door sent me into the air and I banged my hip against the table.

"Who is it?" I called out with a voice about five octaves higher than my normal voice. I could hear my heart beating in my ears.

"Your worst nightmare."

The rushing in my ears grew louder and the room slipped to the side just a little.

"Who?"

"Who do you think?"

I exhaled and my heart began to slow. It was Blake. I walked to the door rubbing my hip.

"Hey," I said as I swung the door open.

"Hey baby," he said as he bent down and kissed me. "You ready?"

"Yeah. Just let me grab my phone."

"You okay?"

"Yeah why?"

"You look a little pale. You sick?"

"No not at all."

I grabbed my phone off the table and glanced at the screen. There was another message.

Which boyfriend?? The tall asshole or the rich old prick?

Nobody knew about me and Neil. Or, hardly anybody anyway. And even fewer people knew about Neil and Blake. Like next to no one knew about them both. How did this creep know? I hated to admit it to myself, but that last line, scared the hell out of me more than all the other notes and texts combined.

"You sure you're okay?" Blake asked again.

I nodded and faked a smile the best I could.

"Yeah," I lied. "Everything's great."

Chapter Eleven - Then

Blake's mom lived in a huge house just outside of the Dulcet town lines. It was in the middle of a relatively new housing development that was full of homes that cost anywhere from a half million dollars up to over a million dollars. As we walked up the cobblestone driveway toward the house, I guessed his house was at least one million dollars. It was a behemoth two story colonial home with stone pillars sitting on both sides of the front door and a porch that wrapped around the side of the home.

"Nice house," I said to Blake as we passed the front door and followed the porch toward the back of the house.

Blake nodded and put his hand on the small of my back. "Yes, it is. My stepfather is quite successful around here."

The thought of the text ran through my mind and I thought to tell Blake then. But I couldn't. There was a chance that it was Neil or maybe his wife doing it. And I had to keep that hidden from Blake. Or it could be some other guy I had been with at some point in my checkered past. But how would just anyone know about both Blake and Neil? I had no idea. But as much as I wanted to tell Blake, I knew I couldn't. At least not yet.

"I have something I want to ask you," Blake said to me.

"Okay."

"I turn twenty-five this Wednesday and I wondered if maybe you wanted to go away with me Tuesday night?"

Of course I wanted to go away with him. But I didn't want to show him how much I wanted to go.

"Where?" I asked.

"Just for the night. But I was thinking we could go to South Carolina. My dad has a friend who owns a house on the ocean, on Long

Bay, but he's never there in the summer. So, he lets us use it. You want to go?"

"Absolutely."

"Yeah?" he said placing his arm around my waist.

"Yeah," I answered.

And all the dread and gloom that was weighing me down from the texts, was suddenly gone. It was only for a night but I was going to get away from everything – the creepy stalker, Kendra's battle with sobriety, my not knowing what the hell I was doing with my life, and everything else. But the best thing was I got to go with Blake. It was going to be awesome.

When we reached the back corner of the house. The full party came into view and I couldn't help but take a step back. There were at least two hundred people there.

"All of these people are your family?" I asked.

Blake chuckled. "Nope, about a quarter of them are family. The rest are friends and associates of my stepdad. Look, there's you sister and my brother."

He pointed at a small table by the pool. Kendra saw us and waved. We waved back and walked over to them.

A tent was set-up between the pool and the patio. Underneath was a bar and several round tables. On the patio was a built in grill and a larger grill that had been brought in just for the day. On the other side of pool, several kids were having a water balloon fight.

"Hey guys," I said to them.

Steve stood and gave me a hug.

"You look beautiful."

I leaned back and looked at him.

"You clean up well yourself. A lot better than your brother here,"

I smiled pointing at Blake with my thumb. Blake shook his brothers hand and patted Kendra on the back.

"You guys been here long?" he asked.

"We've been here about twenty minutes. This place is already packed. Apparently nobody in Dulcet believes in arriving fashionably late."

"Blake does," I replied before the word had left his lips. "How are you Kendra?"

"I'm fine. Just enjoying the sights and sounds of this great party. And trying to stay hidden."

I noticed something in the way she spoke. Her voice was tinged with a slight laziness. There was a strange softness to her words. I looked into her eyes and thought I saw an old familiar enemy in them.

"You okay?"

"What?" She snapped back at me. "I'm fine. Better than fine."

"Okay," I smiled wide trying not to upset her. "I didn't mean-."

But I never finished my sentence. Something cold blasted into the middle of my back. I screamed out in surprise and spun around to find a little boy standing in his swimsuit, laughing hysterically. He'd pegged me with a water balloon.

Blake was on him in two seconds. The poor kid didn't even have time to run. Blake swept him up and threw the boy over his shoulder. The kid was kicking and screaming as Blake ran through the swimming pool gate, picked the boy up over his head, and threw him into the pool. The kid went under and popped his head back up out of the water, half laughing and half screaming.

Before Blake made it back out of the gate, three more kids – 2 boys and a girl – ambushed him. Between the three of them they launched five water balloons and connected with four of the five. The first hit Blake square in the chest and stunned him. The next one hit him in the right shoulder and the next in the left knee. The last one, acting as a perfect exclamation point for the kids' revenge, nailed Blake right in the face. He bent at the waist, covering his face, laughing.

I couldn't allow the punk kids to win. I scanned the lawn and spotted the huge tub of water balloons. I kicked off my shoes and jogged around the pool fence. The kids were too busy celebrating to notice me grabbing four balloons out of the tub. I gripped one in my right hand and cradled the other three in my left arm. Then I jogged around the other side of the pool going straight at the kids.

I got within ten feet of them before they spotted me. The kid who hit Blake in the face was just finishing his last high-five when I chucked the balloon at him. It flipped twice in the air and nailed him smack in the center of his chest. They were all frozen as I launched two more balloons and nailed the girl in the stomach and another boy in the right shoulder. The last kid tried to run away from me. But I sprinted after him and nailed him right in the butt.

"My hero!" Blake called to me. We were both laughing as we high-fived each other. "That was impressive."

"I've got your back," I said to him.

I pushed my shoulders back and tried to look tough. Blake's smile – dimples and all – was as big as I'd ever seen.

"Wow, that was awesome," he laughed.

But his smile quickly fell away and his eyes grew wide. Every kid who was involved in the water balloon fight, had grabbed an armful of balloons and were running at us. There must have been at least fifteen of them.

Blake grabbed my hand and pulled me toward the house. Water balloons flew all around us – over our heads and at our feet – and a couple exploded on our backs. I ran and screeched and kept a hold of Blake's hand. We ran across the patio, nearly knocking into an old man who was enjoying a slice of watermelon, and made it in the door just in time. None of the kids dared to follow us inside. A couple of them shouted at us and called us chickens and cowards, but they all turned and went back to the pool.

We were standing in a large kitchen with several people standing around drinking. The back of me was absolutely soaked.

"Holy shh-moly," I said, aware of my language around the strangers. I knew one of them had to be his mom.

"Wow, they got us but that could've been much worse. We barely escaped with our lives."

Blake and I both laughed.

"Yes, those punks are ruthless. Kids these days," I said looking down at my drenched dress.

And then we laughed some more.

"Still partaking in water balloon fights? Honestly, Blake Alexander, will you ever grow up?"

An attractive older woman, who had the same eyes as Blake, walked over to us.

"I'll get you both some towels. But first I'll introduce myself."

"This is my mom, Angela," Blake interrupted. "Mom, this is my girlfriend, Katie."

"Nice to meet you Katie," she said.

We shook hands and smiled big at each other. But just before she let go of my hand, she looked me up and down and I could've sworn I saw disgust on her face.

"Nice to meet you too. I've heard a lot about you."

"Not all bad, I hope?"

I looked at her for a hint that she was kidding, but she seemed as serious as cancer.

"Umm no," I shook my head, "it was all very good actually."

"Well, to be honest, I haven't heard anything about you. I just know he's been spending a lot of time with some girl. I assume you're the girl." She smiled when she said that and then looked at Blake and winked.

That was the first time I'd ever seen Blake blush. He looked down at his shuffling feet. The always confident, always in control Blake suddenly looked like a little boy.

"Of course it's her," he said to his mom. Then he looked at me and rolled his eyes. "Of course, it's you."

"I hope so."

I pulled my lips down at the corners and shrugged my shoulders. I knew it was me, but it was kinda fun to make Blake think I didn't know for sure.

"You two wait here. I'm going to grab some towels for you both. Blake, introduce your friend to your aunts and stepdad."

Blake pointed at the three ladies who were standing around a large kitchen island with glasses of wine.

"That's my Aunt Marcia, my Aunt Emily, and my Aunt Pati. Aunts this is Katie."

They all smiled and waved and said it was nice to meet me and I said it was nice to meet them. One of them, I have no idea whether she was Aunt Marcia, Emily or Pati, told me she'd hug me but she didn't want to get wet, and everyone laughed.

"And that's my stepdad Neil sitting way over there in the corner drinking his beer."

Holy freaking shit. Son of a bitch.

I couldn't believe it. Neil – *the Neil!* – *my Neil (no, not exactly my Neil)* – stood and walked over to us. He didn't let on that he knew me. He extended his hand to me.

"Nice to meet you Katie," he said to me.

I shook his hand and said nothing.

He slammed back a big gulp of his beer and grinned at me.

"Don't I know you from somewhere?" Neil asked.

He had a total shit-eating grin on his lips and a glint in his eyes. What was he about to say or do? I looked at him and then looked at Blake. Blake squinted and raised his eyebrows in wonder as he must have recognized the desperation in my eyes.

This was very bad. And was about to get much worse.

Chapter Twelve - Now

A woman who looks to be about my age walks in carrying a camera. She takes pictures of my arms and my neck. She asks in a hushed voice if I have any bruises that are hidden underneath my clothes. I shake my head no. She asks if I'm sure and I tell her I am. And then she leaves.

"So before that party you had no idea that Neil was Blake's stepfather?" the detective asks me.

I shake my head. "Of course not."

"And Blake had no idea you were seeing Neil?"

I shrug my shoulders and shake my head again. I look down at the table, embarrassed.

"He had no idea."

"And this is the party where your sister died?"

I nod slowly.

"And you had no idea that was about to happen?"

I draw in a deep breath and fight back the tears. I try to swallow but my throat is too swollen.

"May I get some more coffee and maybe a bottle of water or something?"

The detective frowns. He writes something in his notebook and then drops his pen onto the table. He rubs his eyes with the heels of his hands and spends several seconds staring at the ceiling.

"Of course," he tells me. "I'm ready for a break myself. You want a sandwich or something?"

I shake my head and whisper, "no."

What I really want is to get out of here. I need to put this all behind me. But that might be impossible.

The detective stands and stretches his arms high over his head. Then he puts his hands on the bottom of his back and bends backward at the waist. He starts to leave but stops halfway out the door.

"Just to clarify before taking a break: The whole mess with your sister and everything, was that right after the water balloon fight and finding out about Neil and Blake, or did it happen a while after?"

I try to swallow again but can't.

"It was right after," I croak. "I found out, then Neil threatened me, and then I heard screaming and Blake came running and told me about Kendra."

"Neil threatened you then?"

I nod and look at the detective for a while, feeling my eyes well up. He looks at me for several seconds. I look back at him. I'm trying not to see Kendra's lifeless hand bouncing up and down; I'm trying not to think of everything that led to all that blood on my apartment floor. Finally, the detective nods his head and leaves.

I put my head in my hands. I can't hold on any longer. I hear the door shut and I know I'm alone. Now the tears come fast and hard, and I let myself get washed away.

END PART ONE

Part Two

Chapter Thirteen - Just Before Now

I walked out of Wright Regional, the small airport that feels more like a bus station, and I climbed into my car. It started on the first try (thank God for small miracles). I cranked up the AC and the radio, threw it into *Drive* and away I went.

But I didn't make it far.

I was singing along with the radio and tapping out the beat on the steering wheel trying to get lost in the music, trying not to think of anything that happened during the summer, trying hard not to think of the mess of the past few days and especially the last several hours. There was smoke surrounding my memory of the last couple of hours. I couldn't quite see through it. But that was fine with me. And to be honest, I couldn't think clearly enough to even try to see through the haze, to remember everything.

But I was mostly succeeding in just losing myself in the music (I guess). That's why it was a little surprising when a tear slid out of my eye and down my cheek. The cool air pumping out of the vents dried it before it made it all the way down my face. But I could still feel the line it traced down my cheek – just like I can still feel all the lines he traced on my skin and I can still feel him beside me… and over me… and all around me.

Stop that. You're going to make yourself a mess. Stop it now!

And I did stop. Because out of nowhere a police cruiser raced up onto my bumper. I glanced down at my speedometer: I was only going forty-four in a forty-five (I'm pretty sure). I glanced in the rearview mirror at the police officer speaking into his radio. And then his lights flashed on and his siren whooped twice at me.

I flipped on my right turn signal and pulled into the parking lot of Mason's Market, which is right next to *Take a Shot*, the bar where I worked. For more than a couple seconds I actually considered bolting from the car and running into the bar. Not to get away or try to hide, but just so I could be in a familiar place and maybe feel a little comfort for just a couple minutes. But of course I can't do that. And the bar's closed any way. Closed for good. And yes, it is at least partially my fault.

I rolled down my window and looked up at him. He had his left hand on his hip and his right gripping the handle of his gun. (*Do they stand like that for every stop or am I in some special class that forces him to be ready to draw his gun at any given second?*)

"Go ahead and turn your car off for me."

His voice was incredibly deep, like unnaturally so. And not in a good way but more of a freakish carnival barker kinda way. It's been that way ever since the seventh grade.

"Really? Do I have to turn it off?" I asked because I know it might not start again.

"Turn it off."

And I did. The engine kept running even after I turned the key, but very soon it started to choke, then sputtered, and stopped.

"May I see your license, registration, and proof of insurance please?"

"Seriously Rick? You know who I am."

"Well I thought I did. And it's Officer Daniels."

The way he said it made my stomach turn over and my palms start to sweat. Maybe things were as bad as I feared. But they can't put me in jail for that, can they? It was too much to think about all at once so I threw-up a wall in my brain.

Just take it a minute at a time – a second at a time if you have to. It will be okay. It'll be fine.

I grabbed my wallet from the passenger seat beside me and flipped it open. I handed my license to Rick (Officer Daniels) and then leaned over to grab my registration out of the glove compartment.

"Was I speeding?" I asked, holding out hope that maybe this is just a routine traffic stop.

"No. And it's okay Katie, I don't need anything else. Why don't you go ahead and step out of the car for me?"

I sat up and looked up out of the window at him.

"Right now?"

"Please."

He opened the door for me and I pulled myself out of the car. I had an overwhelming feeling that I was forgetting something. But before I made it all the way out, he stopped me.

"Grab your keys and your wallet, Katie."

"Okay." I got out of the car with my keys in my right hand and my wallet in my left. "And it's Ms. Sanders," I said with the brightest smile I could manage.

We walked to the back of my car. His hand was still on his gun and with his other hand he grabbed his radio. He spoke too low and fast for me to hear everything. But I caught a couple numbers and my name. He paused for a few seconds and responded with "ten-four."

Then he looked at me and frowned. "You know what this is about, right Katie... ugh Ms. Sanders."

"I think so."

"And you know we need to talk to you down at the station?"

"Nope," I said.

I was struggling to keep my nerves from making me lose it, and I was fighting to keep myself from saying something fresh. It wasn't an easy fight.

"Well, we need to talk to you. But there's no reason to make a big scene or anything. Mind just getting in the backseat of my cruiser and I'll give you ride?"

"Do I have a choice?"

"Not really."

"Can I drive myself?"

"Your car will be fine where it is, just make sure you lock it up."

"Okay," I said.

I was losing the battle to keep my nerves in check.

I'd never been in the back of a police car before. I hope I never have to be there again. I wasn't in handcuffs, so it could have been worse. But it was bad enough. There was a stench of antiseptic overlying the smell of something else vial. I think it was the smell of urine, feces, and vomit all rolled into one.

We took a left then a right. Then the station came into view, two blocks up on the right. I looked all around at the trees and a couple holding hands walking on the sidewalk. I noted the darkness of treetops and the sky behind them.

How long would it be until I see all of that again? Later today? Maybe tomorrow? Weeks or months from now?

My mouth went dry and I wiped my hands against my pant legs. I was being ridiculous, of course. They wouldn't officially arrest me. And they couldn't charge me with any type of felony. Could they?

He pulled into the police station parking lot and drove around to the back. For a second I was sure I was going to add to that underlying stench of vomit, but I managed to swallow it down. I stared down at my hands, which were shaking as I tried to link my fingers together so that maybe I could get some comfort from holding my own hand. I tried to make my mind go blank but it was racing away to wherever it wanted to go.

Thankfully, Ricky got out of the car and opened the back door. He reached out his hand and helped me out of the car. Another officer, a woman I'd never seen before, was holding the back door open.

Ricky led me to the end of a hall, into a room with just a table and four chairs in it.

"You can have a seat. I'll let the detective know you're here. This shouldn't take too long."

"Thanks."

He turned and looked at me. "Are you okay?"

Of course not. I'm about as far from freaking okay as I've ever been.

"I'm fine," I answered softly.

"Can I get you anything?"

"No, I'm okay for now."

He left me alone and I couldn't stand it. Two images kept racing through my mind: Blake's beautiful smiling face and blood running across my floor.

Hold on. Just hold on.

And then, mercifully, the door swung open and an older man with no hair on his head and a white goatee walked in.

"Ms. Sanders, I'm Detective Alexander."

Chapter Fourteen - Now

And here I am, all alone again. Except I'm not trying to hold it together anymore. I just absolutely lost it for a few minutes. And now I feel a little better. At least I can swallow again and my headache has almost disappeared. And slowly the fog is lifting from my mind. And the pieces are starting to snap together. I'm starting to remember.

I'm sure I look like absolute crap, but I don't care. I don't have anyone here that I want to impress. Truth is, there may not be anyone in the entire world left for me to impress. But the world is a big place so maybe I'm just being overly dramatic. I don't know. I only know that it shouldn't be taking the Detective this long to come back with a coffee and a water. They are probably watching me right now – gauging how I act when I'm alone.

They just got quite the show seeing me wailing like a two-year-old baby.

Finally, the door opens and the Detective walks back in holding a cup carrier in his left hand. He sets it down and pulls out a cup of coffee and a bottle of water. I grab the bottle, twist off the cap, and take a big swig. It feels wonderful, like it's been days since I had a drink.

"Coffee black is still okay, right?"

"Yes."

"Are you okay or do you need a longer break?"

He must see how hard I've been crying. I bet my face is streaked and red and my eyes are probably all blood shot. But I don't want to wait any longer.

"No," I tell him. "Let's get this over with."

Chapter Fifteen - Then

Neil kept looking at me with that big beaming smile, but it wasn't his real smile.

"Seriously, haven't we met somewhere before?" he asked.

I opened my mouth to speak but nothing came out.

Hurry up and say something or Blake will see you struggling and know something's going on.

Talk!

"She bartends at that bar you own," Blake answered.

The warm relief swept over me.

"Yes, Buzz's bar. You're the owner right?"

Neil tipped his head to the side and kept right on with that fake grin. It resembled a painted-on clown's mouth.

"Maybe that's it," he said. "But somehow it seems like I know you better from somewhere."

I shook my head and shrugged my shoulders.

"I don't think so."

Then I shoot him a millisecond long glare.

"Well, I'm soaked. I'm going to run upstairs and change," Blake said.

"Didn't your mom tell us to wait right here?"

I don't want him leaving me,

Blake rolled his eyes. "Yeah, she did. Are you okay or do you want me to try to find something else for you to wear? I'm not sure what my mom has."

"No, that's fine. I'm not that wet. I'm just dripping all over the floor."

Blake grinned. "I can stay in these clothes."

I looked at Blake and then at Neil. I've never suffered from panic attacks in my life, but I swear, standing between the two of them, I nearly had one then.

"No, go get changed."

"Okay," Blake said. "And then I'll run you home really quick to get changed too."

"Okay, yeah," I nodded.

That sounded like a great idea. Then once I got back home I'd do everything in my power to not have to go back to that reunion.

Blake kissed me on the cheek and tugged on my dress. "I'll be right back."

"Okay."

And then it was me and Neil standing there, in Neil's kitchen, in Blake's mom's kitchen, staring at each other. Angela hustled back into the room carrying a stack of towels. She handed me two and I wrapped one around my waist and used the other to dry my shoulders and arms.

"Where's Blake?" she asked.

"He went upstairs to change."

"I swear, that boy never listens to anything I say. Some things never change I guess."

"Hey," Neil said shaking his finger at me, "Katie right?"

"Right."

"Are you going to see Buzz in the next couple of days?"

"Yeah."

"Good, I have something in my office for him. It's just some paperwork but I have to explain something to you so you can explain it to him. Do you mind taking it to him for me?"

I started to object but Neil didn't even wait for an answer.

"It will just take a couple minutes," he called over his shoulder. "Come back to my office and I'll show you."

I had no choice but to follow him. It would look suspicious if I refused.

So, I smiled at Blake's aunts and his mom, and I followed Neil down a long hallway to his office. I walked in and he slid the glass doors shut behind us. Of course there was a huge desk and a leather couch in the room. And a little corner bar with bottles of expensive liquor filling the three shelves. The office smelled like Neil, and when I caught a big whiff, a memory of Neil - naked and sweaty, lying on top of me - pushed into my mind. For a brief second I actually felt his skin on mine.

I moved the towel up and down against the back of my hair and waited for him to speak. Neither of us said anything for a while. We just stood face to face looking at each other. I felt like a child who was about to be lectured.

"Were you going to tell me about Blake?"

"Probably not," I answered honestly. "But I haven't seen you since I met him."

"Did you think I'd be angry?"

"Are you?"

I reached around and rubbed the towel against the back of my shoulders.

"Here let me help you with that." Neil took the towel and turned me around. He drew thick lines on my back with the towel, starting at my shoulders. "I'm not angry. It's fine. I mean, I am married after all. And I don't expect you not to see other people." The towel made it down to my lower back and then went back and forth across my butt. "You're a beautiful girl, of course you're going to see other men – men closer to your age."

He dropped the towel at my feet and grabbed a handful of my right butt cheek. Then he kissed the back of my neck.

"Don't do that," I told him, turning around and putting my hand against his chest. "Your wife is twenty feet away."

"And your boyfriend's upstairs. So what?"

He leaned in to kiss me but I stopped him.

"No."

"Okay." He bent down and picked up the towel. He handed it to me. "This Tuesday night, we'll meet in Wilmington. I already reserved our regular room."

"I can't. I already have plans."

"Well cancel them."

I glared at him and started rubbing the towel against the back of my head again.

"No. I can't cancel them. I'm going away with Blake."

"Really? Don't you think that's a little fast?"

"You took me to a hotel room in Wilmington and screwed me when we barely knew each other."

"I seem to remember you walking out of your room completely naked."

"I had underwear on."

He shrugged his shoulders.

"Practically naked. You're still the one who started it. You came onto me."

He had a point. but that didn't give him the right to question my relationship with Blake.

"Well, anyway, Blake and I know each other pretty well. And I'm going away with him."

"That's fine. I get it. It's weird to see both of us at once and I'm not going to make you choose." He pushed a lock of my hair behind my ear. "Blake will only be around for a couple more weeks. I can wait for you."

I shook my head. "No, I'm done seeing you Neil. I'm sorry but I really like Blake and I don't want to mess this up."

"What?"

His eyes turned hard.

"I'm sorry. But I really care about Blake and I don't know how long he'll be here or if he's going to go to Chicago or to work with Steve, but I want to give us a chance. I don't want to be the one to mess it up. So, I can't see you anymore."

Somewhere far away there was a scream followed by shouting. A door slammed and that was followed by more shouting. Neil ignored it all.

"You aren't ending this. I say when this ends," he said jabbing his index finger against his chest. "I say when it ends."

"Excuse me? I can say it too. And we're over. The end."

"And what if I tell Blake about us?"

A yellowish-green sickness popped in my stomach. The fact that he would even threaten such a thing. Would he be that stupid? He had as much to lose as I did. Didn't he?

"Then it's your choice to ruin your marriage and whatever relationship you might have with Blake and his brothers," I replied. "And if you want to ruin that then-."

"You'll be ruining it," he interrupted me. "And besides, what kind of relationship do I have anyway? Honestly, I can't stand any of those little brats and if I never see them again it won't matter to me at all. It would actually improve my life."

"But if you tell Blake or anyone else, then your wife will find out. I'll spread it all over town. I'll ruin you."

"You can't ruin me," he said with far too much arrogance. "Look. You want to end this and threaten to tell others then I'll tell everyone how you seduced me and I just couldn't resist you."

"You're an asshole."

"No, I'm just in love with you."

That stopped everything. I looked at him trying to figure out if he was bullshitting me. In the distance, from the back of the house, there was more shouting, followed by a door slamming.

"You don't love me," I said softly.

"I think I do. And I'm not going to let you go. What we have is something special and I want it – no, I need it – to continue. And if you decide to throw that all away, then I will make you pay for it. I'll make you pay in ways you can't even imagine."

"Are you threatening me?"

"I'm warning you. I'm simply telling you what will happen."

I thought of the notes and the threatening texts.

"Did you know about Blake and me before this? Have you been-."

But before I could finish the question, the office doors flew open. I spun around and there was Blake, his shoulders heaving up and down.

"Katie! It's Kendra. There's something wrong."

"What do you mean?" I asked.

"Come now!"

From the look on his face and the sound of his voice, I knew something very bad was happening. I followed him out of Neil's office and ran through the house toward the back. I remember hearing someone crying as we went through the kitchen and I remember the scent of onions and steak as we crossed the patio, but I don't remember seeing anything until I saw Kendra.

The table Kendra had been sitting at was toppled over. And Kendra was lying on the ground, beside that table. A woman was kneeling beside her head and a man was on one knee leaning over her. He was pushing on her chest. Then he stopped and the woman breathed into Kendra's mouth. And then the man started back with the chest compressions.

CPR.

My God, Kendra!

I tried to get to her. I wanted to grab her on each side of her face and yell at her to open her eyes. I wanted to shake her until she snapped out of whatever was happening to her.

These people did not know her. They were complete strangers. They didn't know the first or the last thing about Kendra. But I did. I was always there for her. And I wasn't about to let her down when she needed me most. I had to get to her and help her.

But someone grabbed me before I could. Strong arms were wrapped around me and my face was pressed against a chest. A scent of musk mixed with cinnamon and a distant hint of chlorine surrounded me and I knew who was holding me. Despite it all, the paranoia subsided and my mind and muscles relaxed. I felt safe. I felt like everything was okay, at least for a few seconds. At least while I stood there being held by Blake.

"It's okay, it'll be okay," he whispered into my ear. Far away there were sirens wailing. "They're both doctors. They'll help her. Don't worry, it'll be okay."

She was being helped by two doctors. So, I didn't need to help her. She was getting all the help she needed. I could just stay in Blake's arms and close my eyes, and wait for everything to be okay. The sirens grew louder and then stopped. Then I heard a different set of voices and I knew the rescue and ambulance had arrived.

I pushed myself out of Blake's arms and turned to see them still performing CPR on Kendra.

"What the hell is happening?" I asked to nobody in particular.

"I don't know," Steve answered from beside us. I hadn't noticed him standing there. "She grew quiet for a couple minutes and wouldn't speak to me and then her eyes did something weird and she fell out of her chair and started having a seizure or something."

"That doesn't make sense," I told him.

He just shook his head. He looked like he was about to be sick.

"I know," he whispered.

"Did she take anything?" one of the paramedics called out.

Nobody answered.

"Did she take anything?" he repeated. "Any drugs, medications, anything?"

All eyes were on me. I shook my head and shrugged my shoulders. Then I looked at Steve.

"Do you know? Did she?"

"No," he replied. He sounded offended, but maybe it was just fear. "I think she may have been drinking. I'm not sure."

She had been drinking. Of course she had. I heard it in her voice and saw it in her eyes when Blake and I first arrived at the reunion. But I'd never seen her drink to this point. I'd never seen her have a seizure and stop breathing.

My God, she isn't breathing.

She is dead.

They loaded her onto a stretcher and they kept pressing on her chest and squeezing a bag that was connected to a mask over her mouth. I could only see a sliver of her cheek. It was so white that it was almost no color at all. And one of her hands was bouncing off the side of the stretcher as they wheeled her across the lawn. Her fingers were crooked and locked into a bent position. And I remember thinking: *Oh God, don't let that be the last image I always remember. Please don't let that be it.*

The world slowed down as she disappeared around the corner. Then the sky tipped forward in front of me and stopped for a few seconds. I wasn't standing anymore. But I wasn't falling either. I was suspended somewhere in between. And then everything swirled and sped forward at a hundred miles an hour. The sky toppled down behind me as my head grew too heavy and rolled back causing me to fall back with it.

Blake caught me in his arms and held me to his chest.

"You okay?" he whispered into my ear.

"I don't know," I gasped.

And just like that I was in his arms. He was carrying me like a baby with one arm under my knees and the other arm under my back, cradling my head in the crook of his elbow.

"I've got you," he said. "I'll drive you to the hospital."

I closed my eyes, wrapped my arms around his neck, and rested my head on his shoulder. The world was spinning out of control and crashing down all around me, but Blake was my pillar and my protection. When we got to his Jeep he set me on my feet and kept one arm wrapped tightly around me.

"Hey, hey," a voice yelled from behind us. "I grabbed your keys and I'm coming with you all." It was Steve.

"We might need those," Blake replied.

He helped me into the front seat while Steve got in the back. Then Blake ran around and climbed into the driver's seat. I tried to open my eyes but everything was too bright. So, I closed them again.

"Did she take any drugs?" I asked Steve.

"I don't know."

We pulled out of the driveway and sped off toward the hospital.

Please live. Please live. Please Kendra. Please live.

"How much did she have to drink?"

"I don't know. I'm sorry Katie. I didn't know she was drinking at all. She didn't seem right when I picked her up at the park this morning."

"You picked her up at the park? That's weird."

I felt like I was looking over myself talking to him. I wanted to be angry with him, but couldn't find the energy to muster that much emotion. So I just kept being a viewer.

"Yeah she called me and asked me to pick her up there," Steve told me. "She said she'd gone out for a walk."

"Oh shit. I have to call my mom."

And that snapped me out of whatever funk I was allowing myself to exist in. I opened my eyes and blinked away the brightness. I pulled my cell phone out of my dress pocket and made the hardest call of my life. I called and told my mom her oldest daughter had stopped breathing and was being rushed to the hospital.

I didn't say she was dead though. I almost did. But I didn't.

Chapter Sixteen - Then

Blake dropped me off in the semi-circle just outside the Emergency Room. I stepped out of his Jeep and ran toward the doors. I nearly slammed into them. I had to slow down and turn sideways to fit through as they slowly slid open. I ran over to the guard's desk and was rather shocked to see him drinking a cup of coffee and reading the newspaper, as if nothing out of the ordinary was happening.

"Excuse me," I said as calmly as possible.

"May I help you, ma'am?" he asked with a slow southern drawl.

He was looking at me with a half-smile, like I might be crazy. And I'm sure I looked pretty ridiculous with my soaked clothes that were just starting to dry and my face all red from crying.

"My sister was just brought in by ambulance. Can you tell me where she is?"

"Right through that door," he said (painfully slow) pointing to a door behind me

"Thank you," I said.

I hurried to the door. I pushed on it but it wouldn't budge. I pushed harder but still nothing. I turned back around and looked at the guard.

"Sorry, you can't go in there."

"What?"

I was about to go over to him and grab him by the soiled collar on his shirt. I had to see Kendra. I had to be with her.

"Only auth-er-ized per-son-nel are allowed in there," he explained.

"Excuse me?" I snapped at him. "I have to see my sister."

I took three steps toward him. The decision had been made. I was going to grab him, and shake him, until he either let me through the door or until his head fell off his shoulders. But before I got to him, the door opened. I spun around and nearly knocked into an EMT who was walking with his head down.

"Hey," I said to him. "Were you in the ambulance with my sister?"

He nodded. "I think so. She the one who overdosed at the party?"

"Overdosed?" I was stunned. My sister was an alcoholic but not a druggie. At least not that I knew of. "I mean yeah, the girl from the party. How is she?"

He put his hands on his hips and rubbed his chin. He was trying to gauge if I was able to be trusted. He must have saw what he wanted.

"I'm really not allowed to say. But we were able to revive her on the way to the hospital. I'm not a doctor and I can't make any guarantees but her chances of being okay are one hundred percent better now than they were fifteen minutes ago."

"She's breathing?" I grabbed him by the shoulders and couldn't help but start to smile.

He smiled back and nodded.

"Yes, she breathing."

And then I was hugging him tight. He didn't hug me back but I didn't care.

"Thank you," I said to him. "Thank you so much."

"You're welcome. Like I said, she still has a long way to go, but she has a decent chance."

She did have a decent chance. Better than decent, actually. Kendra was a lot of things and a fighter was one of them. She would figure out a way to pull through. Sure, she couldn't figure out how to save herself from her addiction, but she always somehow found a way to stay alive.

By the time my mom and Chris arrived at the hospital – maybe twenty minutes after I called them – the doctor came out to tell us Kendra had regained consciousness. It was too early to tell exactly what had happened but they drew blood that would be tested to see what was in her system. She was responding well to the treatment. They didn't think there was any brain damage, but again it was a little too soon to tell. They were definitely going to keep her overnight but they didn't think they'd have to transfer her to a larger hospital in Wilmington, and it was possible she could go home tomorrow.

When the doctor, left my mom and I hugged each other for a long time. Blake and Steven stood off to one side and Chris stood on the other. I took a step back and pointed over at Blake.

"Mom, this is Blake and Blake this is my mom."

"Nice to meet you," Blake said to her. "I wish it were under better circumstances."

"Nice to meet you too," my mom said.

She rubbed her hands on the front of her shirt, and gave me a curious look, but she didn't ask why I was wet.

"Do you know Steve?" I asked.

"Yes," my mom nodded. "He's been over to the house a couple times the last few days."

"Blake that's Chris, my stepdad."

Blake and my stepdad shook hands and smiled and nodded at each other. I sucked in a deep breath and raked my fingers through the hair on top of my head.

"So you think she's going to be okay."

My mom bit on her bottom lip and shrugged her shoulders.

"Did the doctor say they suspect she overdosed? Since when does Kendra do drugs?"

The question almost sounded like an accusation directed toward me.

I put my hands out at my sides and shrugged. "I have no idea. I thought alcohol was her drug of choice."

"Steven, do you know anything about this?"

Now the question sounded like an accusation directed at him. Mom looked Blake up and down. Apparently, she was thinking about accusing him too.

"I don't," Steve said with a soft voice. "I know she has a drinking problem but I've never seen her take any drugs. She's never even talked about doing drugs."

"And you're clean?" my mom asked.

Steve's entire face wrinkled, as if he'd just smelled something rancid.

"Of course," he said.

"And what about you two?" Mom fired at me and Blake.

"What?" I replied sharply.

"Yes ma'am," Blake said softly. "I do not do drugs."

"Mom, come on," I begged. "Don't try to shift the blame for this."

My mom looked closely at Steven and then fixed her stare on Blake.

"I don't know what to think," she said.

"I think she needs help," I said.

I looked at Chris with my eyes narrowed. Yes, I was blaming him for not agreeing to pay for Kendra to go somewhere and get the help she needed.

Chris just looked at me and said nothing. He knew better than to open his mouth.

We waited for more than two hours before a nurse finally came out and told me and mom that we could see her, but just for a couple minutes. The nurse said Kendra was very tired and wasn't in much shape to visit. Maybe later tonight, she said, once Kendra was settled in a room upstairs. Or maybe tomorrow we'd be able to visit longer and possibly even take her home.

The nurse took us through the door (after punching in a code) and led us down a hallway. There was the dual stench of shit and disinfectant. There was either beeping or groaning (or both) coming out of every room that we passed. But when we got to Kendra's room everything seemed too quiet. She was lying in bed with an IV running out of each arm and an oxygen line hooked into her nose. Her eyes were closed and mom and I looked at each other wondering if we should disturb her.

"Ken?" mom said softly. "Mom and Katie are here."

She opened her eyes and looked at mom. Then she ever so slowly shifted her gaze over to me. A fraction of a smile curled the left corner of her mouth.

It felt so incredibly wonderful for her to look at me. She was alive! She really was.

"Hey there," I said to her fighting back the tears.

"So sorry," she whispered with a voice that made my throat hurt. "I didn't," she said but her voice trailed off. She closed her eyes and was silent.

Again, mom and I looked at each other and weren't sure if we should disturb her.

"Kendra?" Mom said. "Katie and I are going to let you sleep, okay?"

She opened her eyes for all of two seconds and then closed them again. She nodded her head three times and then was still again. Her face looked horrible. It wasn't as white as it had been earlier but it was still pretty much devoid of all color, except for a few bright red splotches on her cheeks and forehead. I bent down and kissed her on the top of her head. Mom kissed her on the cheek and then pointed toward the door.

We walked back out to Blake, Chris, and Steve. They were all sitting in a row, staring down at the floor, not saying anything.

"She's okay," my mom said to them. Chris stood and put his arms around her. "She's okay, but pretty tired. Probably has a sedative or something."

"That's awesome," Chris said. "Best news I've heard in a long time."

Sure, it's the best news you've heard in a long time. You know what would be even better news? If you coughed up just a few thousand of the hundreds of thousands of dollars you have and sent her to a place she could get some help. That would be the best news of all!

But I didn't say anything. I just sat next to Blake and grabbed his hand.

"I really am sorry," Steven said.

"I know. But it's not your fault."

We all hung around the ER waiting room until Kendra was assigned a room. That took close to three more hours. Once we knew her room number, mom gave her cell number to the nurse's station and made them promise to call if anything new happened. Then she left with Chris.

Steve stuck around for about another half hour and then Blake gave him the keys to his Jeep and he left. I wasn't about to leave Kendra. It just didn't seem right. But I didn't want Blake to stay there too. Well, actually I did *want* him there but I didn't want him to have to do it. If that makes any sense. But he told me he'd stay and be there with me at least until I was ready to go or until they kicked us out.

Blake and I wound up killing over five hours in the hospital. We watched some television in the ER waiting room. We spent way too much time staring at our smart phones. We ate dinner in the cafeteria, which wasn't as bad as I'd feared. It wasn't exactly restaurant quality stuff but it was much better than prison food. Then we sat outside for a while and waited for the street lights to kick on. All the while, Blake was right beside me. Holding my hand when I needed it held. And just sitting in silence when I needed the quiet. Somehow, someway, when it came to me, he just knew the right thing to do.

"Sorry I ruined your family reunion," I told him.

We were sitting on the curb on the street side of the hospital, staring up at the dark globes on the street lights.

"Believe me, you didn't ruin anything. I didn't want to be there anyway. It's not even my reunion. It's my mom's and Neil's party. Not mine."

No, it wasn't his party. It was Neil's. The man I was having an affair with. Correction: The man I *had an affair with.* Blake's stepfather. I hadn't even had the time to fully process that.

What the hell was I going to do? And did Neil threaten me? He told me if I tried to end it then he would make me pay. Those were his exact words: *If you try to end it then I will make you pay*. That was probably just the jealousy talking. He was hurt and angry to be losing me. And he was losing me to Blake. I'm sure that made everything one thousand times worse.

But he did threaten me.

And what about the creepy notes and texts?

"You okay?" Blake said.

I had to tell him. I had to come clean. About everything – the notes and of course about my history with his stepdad.

"Not exactly," I replied.

And then there was a tiny click and the street lights started to illuminate.

"There they go," Blake whispered.

"Yeah, we better go back inside and check on Kendra."

"Okay."

"You can go, you know. Call Steve or whatever to come and get you."

"Do you want me to go?"

"No."

"And I don't want to go. So, I'm staying."

We walked through the doors back inside the hospital and headed toward the elevators.

"Thank you," I said wrapping my hand around his wrist.

"You're welcome. But no need to thank me. Is your mom planning on coming back?"

"I don't know. My mom gets pretty sick of all Kendra's drama and stuff. Sometimes she literally can't take anymore and just withdraws."

"But you don't ever get sick of it?"

The elevator door slid open and we walked in. Blake hit the number *five* and the door slid closed.

"I'm always sick of it."

"But you stay beside her anyway?"

"It's not about me. And she needs someone."

I knew how that sounded. It made me seem selfless and caring. But it also made me sound sad and pathetic and weak.

Blake nodded once. "You're an amazing woman, Katie," he said to me.

"No, I'm not. My weaknesses are just really strong. And so are Kendra's."

So are my parents' weaknesses. Obviously their weaknesses are superhero strong.

Blake didn't say anything. He just turned to me and wrapped his arms around me. He held me that way until the elevator dinged and let us off on the fifth floor. We walked hand in hand to the small waiting area at the end of the hall. It only had four plastic chairs with a small coffee table in the middle, covered in old, ripped magazines. I pulled out my phone and checked my text messages. There was nothing new. Thank goodness for small miracles.

"Excuse me, are you Kendra Sanders sister?"

I stood up, trying not to get too worried.

"Yes."

"She's asking for you. You're Katie?"

I nodded. "She's awake?"

"Yes, she is. You can go in and see her whenever you want. But I wouldn't wait too long. She's due for her next dose of medicine in about forty-five minutes and she will be sleepy after that."

"Okay thank you."

The nurse walked away and I turned to Blake.

"Do you want to come in with me?"

"No, absolutely not. You go see your sister alone."

"Are you sure?"

"Of course. Don't worry about me." He leaned over and grabbed a magazine from the table. "I'll be fine and waiting patiently. I've been meaning to catch-up on this issue of *Guns and Bows.*" He looked closely at the cover. "Apparently it's already been over three years since it came out. So, I'm way overdue. Now go see your sister and tell her I said *hey*."

"Okay."

I put my hand flat against his cheek and bent down and kissed him. He kissed me back. And before I went I looked deep into his eyes. He really did care about me. A lot. And while Kendra was still struggling to overcome her demons and to live a happy life, with Blake all my demons had run away and I was beyond happy.

Well, all the demons in my head are gone anyway. But there may be a very real demon stalking you.

He's not stalking me. Stop being dramatic. But someone is trying to scare me.

And there's Neil who might ruin everything. Did he really tell me he loves me? And did he threaten me? Yes and yes.

Kendra was sitting up in her bed with a cup of ice in her hands, resting in her lap. When I walked in she smiled at me and then looked down at the cup.

"Hey there," I said to her.

I hugged her tight and she hugged me back.

"I'm so sorry."

"Stop," I told her. "No apologies. I'm just glad you're okay."

I sat in a chair in the corner of the room, only about three feet from her bed.

"The doctors said I was officially dead for a few minutes." Her voice was low and flat when she said the words. "That's pretty messed up."

"Yeah it is. How are you feeling now?"

"Like I got hit by a dump truck."

"Do you remember anything from when you were gone?"

She shook her head. Then she grabbed a piece of ice from the cup and popped it in her mouth.

"I was just gone." She crunched up the ice with her teeth and swallowed. "I don't remember anything. It must have been horrible for you at the party. And for everyone else there. Does Steve hate me?"

"No. Absolutely not. He was here for a while. He was really worried about you."

She didn't say anything for a long while. She just stared at her cup of ice. I tried to focus on something else in the room so that I didn't make her feel nervous. This was the time when there were no more worries and no judging. Of course, she'd never been this sick and in the hospital because of her drinking, but we'd been in that spot dozens of times before. It was the sweet spot after Kendra had fallen hard and worried me sick, but now was okay and safe. No decisions had to be made right away and it was not the time for lectures or for worrying about the future. It was a time to rest – to be thankful – and to just love and embrace the moment.

"How are things with you and Blake?"

"Good," I said. "Really good."

"You guys make a good couple."

"Thanks."

"Do you think me and Steve make a good couple?"

"Of course."

"Me too."

And then she was quiet again.

"I'm sure Steve isn't mad. I think you guys will be okay," I told her.

And I really believed it. I could tell Steve was really sweet on her.

"He's not really my type," she whispered.

She rubbed an ice cube against her lips and then slid it into her mouth.

What is your type: Scumbags? Drug addicts? Abusers? Alcoholics? All of the above?

But I didn't say that. "I think you guys make a cute couple," I said instead.

"Yeah, he's a super good guy. And super cute too. What a great looking family."

"Yeah, they really are," I agreed.

His mom was beautiful and his stepdad was gorgeous. But an asshole.

"But I was stupid to believe I could be with Steve. He's way too good for me."

I pushed myself off the plastic chair and sat down on the edge of her bed.

"Don't say that. You deserve the best."

She shook her head. Then she held up her cup of ice to me.

"You want some?"

"No thanks," I grinned.

She shrugged her shoulders and popped another cube in her mouth.

"Can I ask you a favor?"

"Of course."

"Will you talk to mom and Chris for me? Will you ask Chris if he'll help me? There's a great rehab center in Malibu and I think it's prefect for me. I really need to go there."

"I'll ask him. I'll go talk to him and mom first thing tomorrow morning. But you know how he is. I don't think it will do any good."

"But maybe this time it will."

"Maybe. I just don't want you to get your hopes up. You know, I don't want you to bank on this and then have him say no and it causes you to…"

"Causes me to drink again?"

"Yes. Or whatever."

"What do you mean whatever?"

I grabbed one of her hands and held it in my lap. It was cold and clammy. That could have been from the cup of ice, or maybe not. But I wrapped both my hands around her hand and warmed it.

"I just mean whatever caused you to wind-up here."

"I don't do drugs," Kendra said. "I never have and I never will. Who needs drugs when alcohol does the trick? Takes all my cares away and screws up my life. Why would I need to do drugs?"

"I don't know," I answered honestly.

"I don't do drugs," she said softly. "But you need to help me. You need to use all your charm and that pretty girl bullshit stuff you do to make guys like you and do stuff for you."

"Pretty girl bullshit?"

We both laughed.

"You know what I mean," Kendra said. "Maybe you don't even realize you're doing it. But please use it on Chris."

"That never works with Chris. The whole point of it, the whole reason it works, is completely off the table with Chris." I wasn't sure if she knew what I was talking about. Or if she even cared. She was beginning to get upset. "But I promise I'll try," I added.

She squeezed my hand so hard it hurt. She tipped her head down and looked up into my eyes.

"I have to get out of here," she whispered. "I'm not safe."

"You mean the hospital?"

"Not just the hospital. Dulcet. North Carolina. The east coast. I have to get away. Please, Katie, I can't stay here or I'll wind-up dead. I will."

Her hand was still gripping my hand too tight, and now it was shaking too. All of her was trembling. I'd never seen her like that. Never. I'd seen her in all kinds of crazy states: Too drunk to talk; so sick she couldn't move; hung-over with puke dried in her hair; passed out in her own vomit and feces. These were all moments that never should be lived. And they should never be viewed, either. But I'd never seen Kendra like she was in that hospital bed.

"I'll try." That was the best I could do.

"I'm sorry, Katie. I'm sorry to put you through so much shit all the time. And I'm sorry I'm asking you to do this too. But I have no choice. Chris hates me."

"No he doesn't," I interrupted her.

"Yes he does," she replied. "I can see it in his eyes He can't stand me being there or taking so much of Mom's time and attention. He can't stand me. But it's okay, I can't stand me either. But maybe you can use that. Maybe you can make him see that if he sends me across the country then I'll be out of his house and out of Mom's hair. It's a ninety-day program and they could put me in a type of halfway house after the ninety days for another six months. They'll even help me find a job and get back on my feet. It will be a new start in a new place."

"You've really looked into this, huh?"

"I have. I just need to get away. I have to get out of here. And you can come visit me. We can hang out in Cali by the Pacific Ocean."

"That does sound great," I said.

"What is it they say about the Pacific?"

"That is has no memory?"

"Yeah. I like that. Don't you?"

I did like the sound of it, ever since I first heard it said in a movie many years ago. I remember sitting on a couch as a sophomore in high school, holding the hand of a boy who was a freshman in college, and thinking maybe that's where my dad went. Maybe he went west to the Pacific to find a new life. Because wouldn't he have to have forgotten all about his past in order to be able to leave his wife and two little girls? If he had any memory of us, he would have to come back. Wouldn't he?

I believed it then, but I didn't believe it anymore. Back then I was just a young girl being silly. I was a little girl trying to stop the sadness. As I grew older, I'd found other ways to cope.

"I do like it," I said to Kendra. And I left it at that.

"Maybe you can come out once I'm all set-up and cleaned-up and we can live together. We can both start over."

"Maybe," I answered.

And I hoped she didn't hear the hesitation in my voice.

Over the years, Kendra and I talked hundreds of times about getting out and starting over. We always had a nagging feeling in our souls that we needed to go somewhere else and start over doing anything else. The grass had to be greener. And there had to be a better life than the ones we were both living. I supposed that feeling was a gift left behind by dear old Dad.

But, for the first time in my life, I didn't feel the need to run. I didn't want to start over or forget my past or anything else. I was finally happy. I wasn't content with my life, but I felt good and my life finally felt right. It almost felt like I had stepped into the light and left Kendra behind in the darkness. And I felt guilty for that. But I couldn't help it. I was finally happy and excited about today and tomorrow. That was a gift given to me by Blake.

"I just feel like this is my last shot. And I need to go as soon as possible. Maybe tomorrow or the next day."

"I don't know, Ken. Like I said, I'll talk to Mom and Chris. I'll see what they say. But either way, I'll make sure you're okay. Okay?"

"Okay."

She finished her cup of ice and tossed it toward the trash can across the room. It barely made it past the bed. I picked it up and threw it out for her.

"Blake says *hey,* by the way."

"Tell him I said *hi*. Is he here?"

"Yeah he's out in the waiting room."

"Oh, I feel bad. He's out there by himself?"

"Yeah, it's fine. He has his favorite magazine to read."

My joke amused me but Kendra had no idea what I was talking about. She gave me a strange look and then patted the bed next to her.

"Will you lie down with me for a couple minutes. Then I'll let you get back to Blake."

"Of course."

I got on the bed beside her and we wrapped our arms around each other. We hadn't lain like that in years. When we were children, there were some nights we fell asleep like that. But once she'd grown older, Kendra didn't like so much touching. But maybe she'd matured enough now so that she was fine with it. Or maybe, she was once again that little girl who often asked me to cuddle with her.

"Love you, sis," I whispered and kissed her head just above her ear.

"Love you too."

"Don't ever scare us like that again. Okay?"

"Okay. Katie?"

"Yeah?"

"I'm still scared. I mean really freaking scared."

"It's okay," I whispered. "Everything is okay. Please believe that. It's all okay."

And I tried to believe it too.

But things were not okay. Kendra was on the verge or possibly, in the middle of some type of breakdown. I could feel it coming off her skin and I could see it in her eyes. On top of that, I was falling in love with Blake while his stepdad claimed he was in love with me.

How could I possibly tell Blake about me and Neil? I mean, obviously I was free to date whomever I chose. Neil and I were never an exclusive thing. And, technically, Blake and I still weren't an exclusive item either. So, all of that was fine. But it was his stepdad. And, it meant I was the girl who his stepdad was cheating on his mom with.

So, the whole history of having sex with his stepdad was creepy. But me being the mistress who wronged his mom was unforgivable.

And then there were the notes and texts.

Obviously Neil was the primary suspect for that. But I didn't think he was capable of such things. He was above all that. Right? Well, I believed he was until the little scene in his office. He was always a bit of a pompous prick and always acted like he was a little better than me. But that was pretty standard with older guys who I spent time with. On the outside, they always acted a little above me, not fatherly (obviously), but sort of like they were more of an adult than me. Although I could sense that deep down it was actually the opposite. But with Neil, I honestly thought he was better and he knew it. That was different than just acting better. Neil had accomplished so much and had his life all together. Or so I thought. Sending crazy notes and texts seemed so far beneath him. But now, I wasn't so sure that was true. Jealousy and love make villains out of heroes and turns angel to devils.

So, maybe it was Neil doing it. In all honesty, I hoped it was. At least then I could be sure I wasn't in any real danger. Deep down Neil was not truly capable of hurting me. Not physically anyway. And I believed he was too smart to actually hurt me in other way too. He wouldn't tell Blake about our affair or anyone else, because he knew it would destroy his marriage and his life too.

But what if the threats weren't from Neil?

What if it was some psycho?

No. It couldn't be.

Could it?

"Tell me it's okay again," Kendra whispered.

Her body was shaking against mine and her breathing was chopped and heavy.

"It's okay," I said softly. "Everything is okay. Everything is fine."

Chapter Seventeen - Then

It was amazing how early Chris woke-up and started his day. He's one of those people who only needs like five hours of sleep a night. I can remember during my college years, coming in sometimes from a fun night out and finding Chris already awake sitting in the kitchen, tapping away on his laptop or just sipping coffee and looking out the window. It felt so weird. Like we lived in separate worlds, which we kinda did.

But, that's the same feeling I got that morning when I went over early to talk to him about Kendra. I wanted to see him alone – before Mom got up. It was Blake's idea. He thought that maybe if I went to Chris, without the protection of my mom, then maybe I'd have better success. It would show Chris that I was an adult and deserved to be heard like one. It would take away the blanket of comfort that we both used when in the company of my mom. And it would also potentially strip away any type of behavior that Chris might exhibit around my mom.

I was nervous about it all. I could count on my hands the number of times that Chris and I had been alone in the same room over the last five years. And when we were alone, the conversations were always sparse.

Of course, I was also nervous because I wanted to succeed for Kendra. There was something urgent about her words and actions the night before. I don't know.

There was just something different about her. She was scared. She was desperate. If I failed, I honestly didn't know what the hell would happen next.

I let myself in at just before six a.m. and found Chris reading a paperback book at the kitchen table. A full coffee cup was to his right and two cell phones sat on his left. He jumped when he looked up and saw me.

"Hey Katie," he said. "You scared the hell out of me."

"Hey. Sorry."

"How's Kendra?" He looked concerned. "Everything okay?"

"Yeah. Yeah, she's fine. Well, as well as can be expected anyway. I was able to visit her for a little while last night."

"Good. Your mother talked to her on the phone last night."

"Oh. How was she then? Did Kendra say anything?"

Chris shook his head. "No, your mom said she was very quiet. But I guess your mom is going to go up there later today." He put the book face down on the table and sipped his coffee. "Do you want a cup of coffee or a glass of juice?"

"I'd love some coffee."

"Well help yourself."

"Thanks."

I pulled a red mug out of cupboard and poured coffee into it.

"Your mother doesn't usually get up before seven and with all the stress she needs her sleep. So, you might be waiting awhile."

"Actually I came to talk to you."

He looked slightly alarmed but I figured it was just for show. He was a smart man and he could put two and two together. The minute he saw me walk into the kitchen, he had to know why I'd come.

"So what's going on?"

"I just wanted to talk to you about Kendra." I sat in a chair across from him. "I wanted to ask you a huge favor."

Chris frowned. He took off his glasses and rubbed his eyes.

"We should probably wait until your mom gets up."

"Kendra is really messed up right now. I mean, like more messed up than usual. There is something different about her. And she really thinks if she can go to a rehab facility in Malibu then it will give her a new life. A new start."

"And you want to ask me again if I'll pay for it?"

He stressed the word *again* like I'd asked him a million times or something.

I sipped my coffee and nodded. "Yes. I have no idea how much it costs but I'm sure it's expensive. But I really think-."

"It's over eighty thousand dollars a month," Chris interrupted me.

That stopped me. Eighty thousand dollars? Seriously? I knew it was expensive but that was like ten times what I figured. Did Kendra know it was that much?

Did it really matter?

"Wow, that is a lot."

"Yes it is."

"So you looked into it?"

That had to be a good thing - the fact that he took the time to research the cost.

"I always do my homework. If I'm going to say no to something, it's usually even more important that I do my homework. I can't shell out eighty thousand dollars or a lot more for rehab that probably won't even work."

"But maybe it will work this time."

"Has anything ever worked with Kendra?"

"I think it's different this time," I told him. "I think she's hit rock bottom."

"You know I hope she gets better. I hope so for your sake and for your mother's sake. Hell, I love both you and Kendra like you're my own, so I *want* her to get better too. But sending her across the country and shelling out that kind of money is insane."

"Why?"

It was just a one-word question but it threw Chris off. His eyes snapped wide and he looked at me for several seconds before answering. During the silence I raised my mug and was able to steady it just enough to take a small sip.

"Why?" he repeated.

"Yes. Why?"

"Because it won't work. And I'm not paying for it. And if you want to talk about it any further then we better wait for your mom to get up."

For a second I was going to accept his answer. I'd asked and he'd answered. And then I asked him why and he answered me again. I did all that I should have to do. He wasn't going to pay for her to go to Malibu. We all knew it. So, I should just finish my coffee and leave.

But I was sick of it all. I was sick of being so weak and small. I was tired of feeling like the good little girl who just wants to be accepted by everyone who matters.

I can't explain exactly what happened or how it happened, but something inside me shifted. Suddenly I wanted to be someone just a little different. I wanted to be strong and confident and an adult.

The truth was this: The Malibu rehab facility was very expensive but Chris had the money for it. He was wealthy. He was very rich – by most people's standards. It wasn't that he couldn't shell out eighty thousand or even a quarter of a million dollars to help Kendra, it was that he wouldn't.

"I'd rather we finish the conversation ourselves," I said. "Just the two of us."

Again he looked shocked. He smiled and put his glasses back on.

"Okay, then the conversation is done. I'm sorry Katie but I can't pay that kind of money."

"But I think it will help this time. I think this is it."

"I hope she has hit rock bottom, but she needs to get well herself. Unless she does it herself, it will never work. Believe me, all the money and the tears and the worry, won't help her. The only one who can really help Kendra is Kendra. She has to want to get better."

"And I think she does this time. This is different. Please Chris. I've never begged you for anything. I'm begging you now. Please."

"Katie I'm sorry."

"I'm sorry Chris. I don't want to put you in this spot. But damnit, here we are – both of us are in this spot. I'm afraid for Kendra. And it's not the same fear that's been inside of me for years. This is different. I really think it's Malibu or that's it. She's going to die."

"But you don't know that, Katie." He grabbed my hand and held it in his. "Kendra has made this mess and she needs to get herself out of it. She's the only one who can help herself."

I pulled my hand from his and wrapped both my hands around my mug.

"And I think she's ready to be helped."

"Good. I hope she is."

"But you won't help her?"

"I'll be there to support your mom and her and you too, if you need it. But paying for her to go to rehab is out of the question. I appreciate you coming here so early and speaking to me one on one. But Katie, I can't help her. None of us can. And throwing a ton of money at the problem won't do any good."

"But you don't know that. Please Chris. Please." My voice was too high and whiny and I hated that. But I couldn't help it. I was failing Kendra. "I'll pay you back. I know it will take years but believe me, I'll do it."

Chris grabbed his book. "I won't continue repeating myself over and over. This is starting to feel a little too much like you're twelve and begging for the latest doll. You're sounding a little too much like a spoiled brat." Then he flipped the book over and started reading it.

The words spoiled, brat, and twelve lit an anger inside my chest. But I tried to keep it down.

"I never played with dolls."

"That's not the point, but your response proves my point."

It was obvious he was growing angry too.

But I wasn't going anywhere. I wouldn't back down. The Katie everyone knew would apologize and go crawling away. But I was pretty much sick of that Katie. That Katie had a sister who had died yesterday for a few minutes and was battling addiction; that Katie was being harassed (and possibly stalked) by some unknown man; that Katie had no idea what she was doing with her life and didn't feel worthy to be with a man like Blake.

That Katie was gone.

"I'm sorry," I said softly. "But I haven't ever asked you for anything. I have my own apartment and my own shitty car and I rise and fall on my own. But I am asking you this one time. Please. Please. Help Kendra. It's a matter of life and death. I can feel it."

He set his book back down and took off his glasses again. He sipped his coffee and stared at the ceiling for what seemed like forever.

"I'm sorry, but the answer is still no. And if you want to talk about it anymore then you need to go to your mom and talk to her. I won't talk about it anymore. Now if you want to sit here and have a conversation like an adult then I'd love your company. Otherwise, you can leave and come back in a couple hours to see your mom."

Are you really threatening to kick me out? Seriously? You're nothing but an old, rich prick, just like so many other rich pricks I've known.

"And that proves my point," I said to him.

He exhaled loudly and rubbed his eyes.

"Okay, against my better judgment, I'll bite: What is your point?"

"That you're not actually a part of this family. You've never bothered to get to know me or Kendra."

"Now that's completely unfair."

"Is it? Have you ever done anything for us that you weren't *required* to do?" And I threw-up air quotes when I said *required*.

"This conversation is over. You have no right to come into my home and speak to me this way. Call your mom later or stop back on by when she's up. And I'll forget all about this."

He put his hand on the table and used it to push himself into a standing position. I grabbed his wrist and looked up into his eyes.

"I thought this was *my home* too," I said, spitting the last three words at him. "And that's the problem, isn't it, Chris? You've never considered me or Kendra a part of your family. Or, to be more accurate, you've never considered yourself a part of our family and you don't know my family. You were more than happy to take the best years of my mother's life and to have her there on the cold and lonely nights. And you think just because you put a roof over our heads and clothes on our backs and then paid for college then that's all you have to do. You can wipe your hands of any further familial responsibility. And that's fine. Just don't expect me to ever think of you as my father ever again."

"I was more of a father to you than your own father."

"Bullshit." I snapped at him.

But I knew he was right. He had been more of a father to me than my own dad. That was knowledge so cold that it hurt to hang onto it, but it was true. But being better than the worst should never be confused for sufficiency. He could have done more for us, and he could have been more to us too.

"You don't know the first thing about my father. So how dare you compare yourself to him?"

"I know he left your mom and two little girls when they needed him most. So forgive me, but it's pretty easy to be sure I'm a better father than that. And your daddy still hasn't come back and I'm still here helping to clean up his family's messes."

And he said the last three words like they were the worst curse words ever uttered.

His hand stayed on his cheek and my entire life slowed to a stop. At first, I didn't even realize I'd done it. I just stood facing him, my mouth wide open, and tears stinging my eyes. His eyes were popping out of his head with shock and horror.

Neither of us could believe what had just happened.

I'd slapped him across the face. I'd struck my own stepdad.

I half expected him to hit me back. A part of me wanted – almost needed – him to slap me back. But he didn't. He just sat back down in the chair and stared at the table.

"I'm so sorry," I said. I reached for him, to maybe touch his reddened cheek or to hold onto his arm. But I didn't know where to place my hand. It was still tingling from striking him. So, I tugged on my ear lobe a couple times and then put the hand safely beside my cup of coffee.

"Okay," he said softly. "Okay."

"I'm a horrible person. A horrible daughter," I added hoping it would help at least begin to fill-in the gap I'd just blown between us.

He said nothing. He just kept looking at the table. And I couldn't stand to be beside him any longer. I might not ever be able to stand to be in the same room with him again. Not only had I not convinced him to pay for Kendra to go to Malibu, I'd ruined what relationship Chris and I had together.

"I'm… going to go."

I wanted to say more. I had to. But I couldn't find the right words. I couldn't even think the right thoughts. So, I had to get out of there. Fast. But before I got to the door, Chris stopped me.

"For your information, I knew your father. He was a good friend of mine."

"What?" I turned back to him.

"Your dad. He and I were good friends."

I returned to the table and sat on the edge of the chair. I couldn't quite believe what I was hearing. Never, had he or my mom ever mentioned such a thing.

"I've never heard that. You and Mom never said anything. You knew of my dad or you were friends with him? Like before he left?"

"Before he was married to your mom. Before he even knew her."

"What? But you never said anything."

He sipped at his coffee. The red spot I'd left on his cheek was already starting to morph into just a pink hand print. Chris looked at me and sighed. Then he swallowed down the last of his coffee and went to the counter for more.

"Your mom never wanted me to talk about my friendship with your father. In fact, she never wanted me to talk about your father at all."

He poured a new cup of coffee and returned to the table.

I didn't know what to say. He knew my father? He was friends with him? And my mom didn't want him to talk about it? My mom never wanted any of us to talk about my dad. It was always: Move straight forward and never look back. Don't look back at the bad times or the good times. Don't talk about dad at all and maybe we can pretend he was never here at all.

"How well did you know him?" I asked.

Chris tipped his head back and forth. Then he nodded. "I knew him pretty well. After we both finished college we were pretty good friends. We both worked at the same insurance company before your dad went to the police academy. We used to hang out quite a bit. And we raised a little hell together too."

"So you liked my dad?"

"Of course. Your dad was a good guy. Liked to drink from time to time and raise a little hell, but he was a lot of fun and a good person. He was a hell of a cop, too. Went from patrol to detective in less than five years. Of course, it wasn't long after he made detective that he married your mom and then you came along not too long after that."

"Wait," I said, "You knew my parents when they got married and when they had me? You knew me as a baby?"

"I did."

At least a thousand questions bubbled in my mind. But I had to pop most of them.

"Did you like my mom back then? Did you two ever date or-."

I stopped myself from asking the question. Did he and my mom have an affair? Oh God, is that why Dad started drinking? Is that what really broke-up their marriage?

I tried to think back when I was a little girl. Was Chris always in the picture? I couldn't remember. But I didn't think so. And I knew that we'd suffered through at least a couple years of pretty severe poverty. Chris couldn't have been around then. Could he?

"I always thought your mom was beautiful and attractive in more ways than just physically. I mean, she is a good looking woman. A great woman inside and out. And back then she liked to raise a little hell too. She was a lot of fun. But no, we never got together until years after she and your dad split up."

I tried to picture my mom inside a bar having a lot of fun. But I couldn't. And I tried to envision her raising hell in half a dozen different ways, but I couldn't do that either. The mom I always knew was somber and straight-laced. Had my dad's alcoholism and the marriage splitting apart changed her that much? How tragic.

"So if my dad was such a great guy, what the hell happened to him?"

"You should probably ask your mom that question."

"I have," I said. "Or at least I've asked versions of that question hundreds of times over the years. And she'll never talk about Dad at all. So now I'm asking you. Please Chris, what the hell happened with my dad?"

He sipped his coffee and stared at me for nearly a minute. The ticking of the clock above the stove was the only sound in the room. I knew he was struggling with honoring his word to my mom or helping to relieve my pain. There was no excuse for my mom forcing Chris to keep quiet about his friendship with my dad and what had happened to make my dad go off the deep end. And it was equally wrong that she never told us anything about my father. That decision by my mother was almost as bad as what my father had done to me and Kendra. But until that moment, sitting across from Chris while my mother slept peacefully upstairs, I didn't realize just how much my mother's forced gag order had messed us all up.

"Why does any alcoholic ever go from just being a drinker to running off the rails?" Chris began. "Sometimes it's something traumatic that happens in their life – the loss of a loved one, an accident, something like that. Other times maybe it's something as simple as the marriage hits a bump in the road or money gets a little tight. I can't say for sure why your dad went off the rails and threw everything away. Honestly, we lost touch right after your mom and dad met and then reconnected maybe a month before their marriage. Then we lost touch again about a year after you were born and didn't reconnect until after your dad started drinking heavily. I just happened to run into your mom at the grocery store and I could tell there was something wrong and she told me about what was going on with your dad.

"So, I agreed to talk to him and try to figure out what was going on. Long story short, I talked to him and that did no good. So, I tried to help him by being there for him and I even took him to rehab twice. But both times he left early, and the second time he left and went away for good. But before that, I tried everything I could to make him sober up.

"I remember going to your house and seeing your mom and you two little girls. It was so sad. My heart broke for the three of you. And I thought: Your dad is a good man. He was a great cop and an even better person. He just needs a little help and then he will go back to his family and raise his girls in a loving home. Because that's what good people do, right? Good people who are parents always put their kids first. Their love for their children is more powerful than anything else. Right? So, I knew if he just got some help from me, your dad would straighten himself out for your mom and his sweet little girls. But no matter how much I tried and how much money I spent, it did no good. None."

"Money you spent on him? Did you help pay for rehab?"

"By the time he went to rehab the first time, your dad had already been fired so he had no insurance. And your mom wasn't working. So I paid for both rehabs. And back then I didn't have a lot of money so I actually took out a loan to help pay for the second one. But I figured it was a charitable thing, a noble thing, to help you guys out. And when that didn't work, I was a mess. A mess with a five-thousand-dollar loan at a ridiculously high interest rate. And sure, the money mattered to me – money has always mattered to me – but just the fact that your dad chose to leave the three of you and didn't accept my help at all, it just rocked my world. I'm not sure why. Maybe deep down I loved your mom even back then. Maybe I cared too much about your dad. Or maybe I just had a naïve belief that the world was a generally decent place to live. I don't know. But when your father left everything behind and just pretty much vanished into the wind, I was a mess. So, I picked up and moved north to Boston for a couple years. And that's when my career really took off in banking. I was eventually offered a VP job back here at home. I accepted and eventually reconnected with your mom and the rest is history, as they say."

I sat for a while looking at the floor between my feet. I saw everything that he said playing out before my eyes. Everything except the part where my dad left rehab and vanished. All I could see of that scene was my dad walking off into complete darkness.

"Have you ever heard from my dad again?"

Chris shook his head. "I haven't. Sorry, but I never heard from him again. He left me a message saying he was leaving rehab and he was sorry but he was going to start over. That was the last time I heard from him."

"And did he even bother to call my mom and tell her?"

"No," Chris said softly. "He told me to do it for him." He ran his hand through his hair and rubbed his eyes. Then he put his glasses on and downed more coffee. "It wasn't easy for me. And when I told your mom, that was my main concern. Me. And that's why I went to Boston. I couldn't take the defeat of not being able to save your dad and I couldn't take the pain of seeing you and Kendra and your mom suffer. So, I left. I ran away."

"Did you help get my mom the job at the bank?"

He nodded his head just once. "But she worked her way up fair and square. That was all her. I just gave her a shot. It was the least I could do."

Chris had told me more in fifteen minutes than he'd told me in almost fifteen years. I was looking at him with new eyes. He'd always been my stepfather and I'd always seen him as such. He did the things that good stepdads do. And he was good to all of us. But I resented him anyway. Or maybe I resented him because he was good to all of us. He did what my own dad refused to do. Rather than be thankful for that, a part of me hated him for it. That hatred was so woven into all the other crap that was living inside of me, I didn't realize it was there. Not until that morning. Not until I let it go.

And just like that, in the span of about one quarter of an hour, I went from disliking Chris more than I ever had, to loving him like a father.

He wasn't just some interloper who came into my little family, he'd always been there, trying to help my family. He was a good man – a very good man. And he deserved my respect and my love. Though it hurt to admit it, he was more of a father to me than my own dad. And it was time that I accepted that.

"I see a lot of your dad in Kendra. And I know that's not fair. But I do."

"But she's not my father."

"I know. I know." He picked up his cup of coffee and held it to his mouth. "But I know alcoholism too. And I just didn't want to throw good money after bad. I vowed to myself, a long time ago, that I would never shell out money to try to help someone with an addiction. And I truly believe that it won't do any good. I mean, I tried everything I could think of to help your dad. And it did no good."

"But Kendra isn't my dad," I said again.

"I know."

"She's your daughter. And I'm sitting here as your other daughter begging you, please just help her. Please just do this. Maybe it will restore your faith in the world."

"Or maybe it will make me feel like an idiot. Fool me once shame on you, fool me twice and I deserve everything I get."

He took a drink and set the cup of coffee back on the table.

"Kendra has never fooled you when you sent her to rehab. And besides, isn't it better to be fooled then to be the one who goes to his daughter's funeral and thinks to himself: *Maybe I should have done more for her? Maybe it would have worked.* I'm not that old and I'm pretty stupid, but I know that regret for not doing something is far worse than regret for doing something."

"Fine. You're right. If it works, I would give a million dollars to turnaround Kendra's life. Hell, I'd give a million dollars just to make your mom stop worrying."

"You'll really do it? You'll pay for her to go to rehab in Malibu?"

I wasn't so sure I'd heard him right.

"Yes," he nodded. "I'll do it."

The balloon of sweet, warm relief burst in my chest and flooded my entire body. Somehow, someway, I'd convinced him. I did it! Now Kendra had a chance.

"Can I hug you?" I asked him.

"I guess so," he replied with an embarrassed grin.

"Just don't tell your mom about this," he whispered as we embraced.

"Okay."

That hug felt different than it ever had. It made me feel like a little girl being held by her daddy. And maybe it was the relief of getting him to agree to pay for rehab, or maybe it was that feeling I had in his arms, but I was suddenly fighting back tears.

"I'll tell her when she wakes-up that I decided to pay for it. And I'll make some calls and hopefully they'll have a bed for her and we can get her there within a few days."

"Okay," I whispered again. "Okay. And thank you."

"Okay," he said softly. "It's okay."

Chapter Eighteen - Then

On the trip down to South Carolina, I finally discovered Blake's one fault. Everyone has at least one, even those who might seem perfect. It might be their feet or a terrible taste in movies, but every single person has at least one fault. For Blake, his fault was a unique ability to always sing off pitch and slightly behind the lyrics of a song. He was able to sing for just about the entire trip because I was quiet. But I didn't mind his singing. It was horrible but cute. I knew someday, it might annoy the hell out of me. I could only hope we'd make it far enough to see such a day.

I was thinking of the shift that had occurred within me over the last couple of weeks. The way I saw the men who affected my life - and men in general - had changed.

It all began with meeting Blake. He showed me how a true man acts and how a true man loves. I never knew someone's touch could be both gentle and firm at the same time. I didn't know it was possible to make love and have crazy-good sex at the same time. But Blake showed me that it was not only possible but it was easy when it involves two people who fit together so well.

Of course the way I saw Chris had changed too. And so had my view of my dad. He was a real person. He wasn't just a dream or a nightmare. He wasn't just a hazy memory of warmth with a deep voice. He was more than an asshole who left his family. He was so much more than that. I felt like a fool for not realizing it before. I mean, obviously my dad was a human being with real emotions. He had faults and talents and a million different thoughts and feelings. There was depth to him. I mean, that's obvious. And I have no idea why, but I never realized any of it until I spoke to Chris.

And there was Neil. Why did I get involved with him? Why did I sleep with him? I'd give just about anything to take it all back.

Did I really want to be that woman who cares nothing about other people's commitment? I was the *other woman*. And I did it willingly and, for the most part, happily. I tricked myself by thinking I was doing the wife a favor. If it wasn't me, it would be some other bimbo who might get all crazy about everything and demand to be the only one. Or she might go all psycho and wreck the marriage once he broke-up with her. I wouldn't do any of that. I knew what Neil and I were doing. It was an affair. And affairs are fun but they never last. And I suppose it was that fact that allowed me to get involved. What did it really matter? It was *only* an affair between two consenting adults. We were the only two involved and nobody would get hurt. What was the harm?

He was married. He'd committed himself to another person – Blake's mom! And whether she ever found out or not, we were hurting her and her marriage.

Driving down the coast with Blake, there was just one question weighing on my mind heavier than everything else: Do I tell him about Neil?

I still doubted Neil would actually carry through with his threat to tell Blake about the affair. But what did he mean by: *I'll make you pay in ways you can't even imagine*? Other than telling Blake, what else could Neil do to me? He did own the bar and he could get me fired from there. But I could easily find a bartending job elsewhere. So, that wasn't a big deal. And other than that, he had no other options.

He was probably just bluffing. Just trying to scare me.

About two hours into the trip my phone buzzed with a text. I grabbed it out of the cup holder in the door and looked at it, making sure I kept the screen tipped away from Blake.

I can still see you.

I'm always watching. Always.

Shit. Oh no. Somehow I'd hoped the texts would simply stop. I was certainly ready to be done with them. I just wanted to move on and not have to worry about a potential stalker. I just wanted it to end. But now another text.

And I before I left, there was yet another note slid under my door too. It simply read:

Soon. Very soon. I will get you.

Was it Neil doing this? Who else could it be?

But it seemed completely out of his character. Why would a man like Neil resort to such ridiculous tactics? If it were a stranger, then it was extremely creepy and scary. But if it were Neil, then it was just childish and stupid.

"Everything okay?" Blake asked me, taking a break from his off key singing.

I looked at him and almost told him everything in one long sentence. I had to tell him. It didn't matter if Neil really would or not. If we were going to be together, I had to let him know. But not right then.

"Yeah, everything's fine," I replied.

He tipped his head and furrowed his brow. "You sure?"

"Of course. Everything is fine."

He accepted my answer and went back to his singing. I stared out the window and wished for the strength to tell him everything. And I hoped that my past sins wouldn't ruin our perfection.

Before long, we turned off Route Seventeen and after a few quick turns, we arrived at his friend's house.

It was a small bungalow located right on the beach, about fifty yards from the ocean. There were much larger houses on each side but neither house was very close to the bungalow. By the size of the bungalow, I assumed it must be the neighbors who owned a lot of property on both sides. But the house was cute and nice. It was the perfect place to spend a night away with Blake.

Inside there was a large kitchen and living room. There was a small half bathroom off the kitchen and a full bathroom between the two bedrooms, which were located in the back of the house. The bedroom Blake and I would share had a large sliding glass door that overlooked the ocean. We dropped our bags and made the bed together. Then we went to the glass door and looked out.

"Not a bad view, huh?" Blake said.

"Not bad at all."

We spent a couple hours walking the beach. We talked about everything and just about anything. The conversation moved so fast and was so easy that I never even thought to come clean about Neil. Besides, tomorrow was Blake's birthday. I should probably at least wait until we got back and his twenty-fifth birthday was over. Right?

After dinner we went into town. There was a half farmer's market - half party going on in the park. The band was just okay – they played mostly country and classic rock – but Blake and I had a ball anyway. We drank a couple beers and ate freshly made strawberry pie.

I've never been the type of girl who got all sappy about relationships. I know, that was partially because I'd mostly been only in unhealthy relationships. I can admit that. But there were a couple guys along the way who were close to my age and had a lot in common with me. I liked them too. But I never wanted to spend every minute of the day with them. And it scared the hell out of me to think that maybe someday this would be the only man I'd ever be intimate with. That idea in general freaked me out.

But with Blake, all of that was gone. I was that sappy, head-over-heels hopeless romantic puddle. I was that girl that the old Katie would rip-on with her friends. And I didn't even care. Not one bit.

I knew he wouldn't, but if Blake had gotten down on one knee that day and asked me to marry him, I would have said yes. I would've jumped up and down and screamed to everyone within a half-mile radius that I was the luckiest girl in the world.

I grew-up believing that true love didn't really exist. And I knew, that I would never find anything even close to being *in love*. Yet, there I was, walking hand in hand with Blake. And we were in love. At least I was in love with him. Madly and hopelessly. Though I didn't want to admit it – especially to Blake, but even to myself – it was an absolute fact.

Lying in bed with Blake, later that night, I studied every inch of him as he slept. The air conditioning in the bungalow was working but not very well. So, we had no covers or clothes on – we were both in our underwear. I wanted to freeze that moment in time and live within it for eternity. How had I managed to attract such a perfect man? He was smart, funny, considerate, and caring. And he was the most beautiful man I'd ever seen. I mean, ridiculously gorgeous.

My eyes started at his feet and slowly worked their way up to his head, studying every inch closely. He had a small scar just above his left knee. He had a tiny birth mark, roughly in the shape of Texas, just below his ribs. He had tan lines that made it obvious he wore a tee shirt when he was in the sun some of the time, and just shorts sometimes too.

I don't know how long I watched him, but it was a while. I imagined what he could have done to get that scar. And my mind played imaginary movies of a child Blake playing kickball and a teenager Blake hanging out with friends. I even imagined an older Blake, with grey hair on his head and wrinkles covering his face, and me sitting beside him on a park bench. I wished I had always known him. I'd wasted so much of my life without him in it. And I also wanted to be there with him for the rest of my life. Yeah, I knew that thought might be slightly ridiculous and a little dangerous too. But it's what I wanted. It was nearly what I needed.

Just before midnight I rolled off the bed and went to my suitcase and pawed through the bottom of my clothes until I found the bag with Blake's present in it. Then I went back to the bed and stared at my phone until the time turned to midnight.

"Hey, happy birthday."

Blake's eyes snapped open and he looked wildly at me for about a second before reality was able to take hold in his mind. Then he smiled.

"Happy birthday old man. Twenty-five years old."

I kissed him.

"Thank you."

"Here I got you something," I said placing the gift on his chest. "It's not too great so don't get your hopes up."

Blake laughed. He pulled himself into a sitting position and leaned against the headboard of the bed.

"You didn't have to get me anything."

"Of course I did. I'm your girlfriend."

"You're my girlfriend?" he asked.

"Aren't I?"

"Are you?"

"I thought so," I said slowly.

I looked at him closely, desperate to find a hint that he was teasing me. And then I saw his dimples appear and he grinned.

"Of course you are. I hope anyway."

I started to laugh but his kiss stopped me.

I am your girlfriend and anything else you want me to be. Just say we'll be together forever.

"Come on, open your present."

He unwrapped it and looked at the book. It was *To Kill a Mockingbird*. The book that had first inspired him to become an attorney.

"Thank you," he said opening the front cover. "Katie, is this a first edition?"

"Yes it is."

"Wow. Thank you so much. I love it. I really do. But I'm sure it was too much. Like way too much."

"Shush," I told him. "And later I have a card for you and I want to take you out to dinner when we get back home."

"Okay, but I'm paying for dinner."

"Umm no you're not. It's your birthday. It's on me. Anywhere you want to go."

"Anywhere?"

"Absolutely."

"Because there's a great Italian place in New York that I would love."

"Then New York it is." I grinned.

He kissed me on the lips, soft and slow. Then he put the book on the nightstand, and laid back on the bed. I slid myself against him and put my head on his shoulder. I drew circles on his chest with my middle finger and he played with my hair.

"I wonder how Kendra is doing," I said. "It's three hours earlier in California but she should be all settled in by now."

It turned out that the rehab facility in Malibu did have an open bed but they couldn't guarantee it would stay open. So, right after Kendra was released from the hospital, she got on a plane with Mom and Chris and flew right out. Before she left, I went over and said goodbye to her. She seemed so hopeful and relieved.

Mostly relieved.

We hugged and she thanked me over and over for all my help. She promised she'd make it up to me. And I told her it was okay and that's what sisters are for. And she told me when she got out of the rehab facility and got settled, she hoped I'd go out and see her and maybe even move out there. I just smiled and said okay. Living in California could be awesome. But, until I fully gave me and Blake a chance, I would never move out there. I knew she'd understand that. But there was no point in discussing it then.

"You're an amazing sister to her," Blake told me.

I wasn't so sure about that. I tried to be a good sister, I knew that. But when it came to helping Kendra, usually I was too weak. But this time, I'd actually pushed myself to go further and I convinced Chris to help her. That was impressive. So maybe I really was a good sister. Maybe.

"Did you talk to Steve about any of this that's going on?"

"I guess they agreed to give each other some space and let her focus on her recovery. Did Kendra say anything about him?"

"She likes him. But pretty much the same. She needs some time and space. And I think she's planning on staying out there in California. So, probably not going to work out."

"Yeah. Probably not. But Steve likes her a lot."

"Yeah," I agreed. "Kendra likes him too."

With everything that was happening – Kendra's drinking, the affair with Neil, and the creepy messages – there was still one more thing I was worried about. It managed to overshadow all my worries. What would happen with me and Blake?

I shouldn't care about it. I was head over heels over him, and he obviously was into me too. That should be enough. I mean, I was never one to worry about the future with men. I was happy to just be with them. If they showed up tomorrow then that was fine, if not then that was okay too. But lying there with Blake, I was suddenly scared that maybe he wouldn't show-up tomorrow. And maybe it was his plan to just leave me behind.

But I wasn't that girl. I wasn't going to ask him about us and our future. I would not do it.

"So what is this?" I asked. I couldn't stop myself.

"What?" Blake replied.

"What is it we're doing? I mean, I don't need you to commit to me for the long haul, and I know we're *dating*," I said throwing up the air quotes, "but is this just a summer fling or is it something more?"

"A summer fling?" he asked as if the thought had never even crossed his mind.

"Yeah. I'm sorry. I've just never felt this way. Never. About anyone before. I like it. But it also scares the hell out of me."

He inhaled and exhaled, causing my head to rise and fall with his chest.

"Do you know how perfect you are to me?"

"No," I answered honestly.

"Absolutely perfect. Everything about you. There isn't one thing I'd change."

His words made me want to climb inside of him and live there forever. But they also made me want to run and hide.

"I'm not perfect," I whispered to him.

"Maybe you're not perfect but you're perfect to me."

"My boobs could be bigger. Don't you think?"

It was mostly a joke to deflect him from complimenting me anymore. But a fraction of it was truth – a truth that had been placed inside me by Neil.

"What? Your boobs are perfect. Just like everything about you is perfect. I mean, they aren't porn star huge, but most guys can't stand that anyway. At least, I know I don't. They feel perfect, look perfect, they are perfect." He smiled at me, his glorious dimples appearing. "It's a tragedy that you can't see yourself the way I see you – the way you really are. You're freaking perfect. So accept it and move on."

"Oh," is all I said. Because there was nothing to add. He always had a way to say the right things to me.

"But listen," he continued, "I don't know where this is going. I just know that you make me a mess. And that is me being one hundred percent honest."

"A mess? Well, that's insulting."

He slid up from under me and sat looking down at my face.

"No," he whispered. "No, it's not insulting. Listen, I don't know what the hell is going on between us. But I do know that I always have everything neat and tidy in my life. I've always known exactly what I was doing with my life and I always had a plan. And getting involved in a relationship had never been a priority of mine. Never. And that's because I knew I wanted to excel in college and then in law school and then get my career off the ground before I even thought about having a woman in my life."

"I'm not the first woman whose ever been in your life," I said.

I didn't completely understand what he was trying to tell me. There was no way a guy who looked like Blake had never had a girlfriend before.

"No, you're not the first woman in my life," he said. "I've always dated off and on and I've been in a couple committed relationships. And I've liked other women. But with you it's different. Honestly? This scares the hell out of me too."

I looked up at him and he continued just to stare down at me. Neither of us spoke for a while.

"I don't know," he finally continued. "Maybe my mom messed me up. But I've never believed much in relationships. I always thought they were for someone else. And then I met you. And, just like that, my feelings and my thinking changed."

"And I make you a mess?" I asked.

A gust of wind shook the bungalow and rattled the windows. Blake looked out the glass door toward the ocean and shook his head slowly.

"Yeah, you make me a mess," he said with a grin. "You do. And I'm the guy that always has his shit together. But you make me a mess." He looked at me and kept on grinning. "And I like it. I like it a lot."

"And you make me feel like everything makes sense," I said softly. "You make my life not a mess."

The smile on his face dissolved and he put his hand flat against my cheek.

"I don't mean it in a bad way. Do you understand what I'm trying to say?"

I didn't. I wasn't sure what he meant. I made him a mess? He seemed to think that was a good thing. But I knew it wasn't. Was it?

"I don't really know what you mean," I told him. "But it's okay. It's okay."

"I'm just trying to be honest. That's all," he said softly. He shook his head. "It's not a bad thing. It feels too good to be bad, you know? But I'm just being honest with you. Because, to me, honesty in a relationship is the most important piece of a relationship. And while I'm being honest, I have something else I need to tell you."

Here it comes. He knows about me and Neil. Oh God. Should I deny it? Blame it all on Neil? Try to play the helpless, innocent young woman who was taken advantage of? No, I was far from an innocent young woman, and I was as much to blame as Neil. Probably even more to blame. No, I'll be honest about it. I have to be.

But it can't be that. He doesn't know. He wouldn't be here with me if he knew.

Is he seeing someone else? Is he engaged? Is it something else?

"I'm suddenly pretty rich, Katie."

"What?"

Now I was really confused. Why was he acting so weird? And what the hell was he really trying to tell me?

"I just want you to know because I don't want you to hear about it from Neil or my mom or whatever. And the exact number isn't really important. But it's a big deal. So I want you to know.

"My grandfather was a very wealthy man. And he set-up trust funds for me and my brothers that we gain access to when we're twenty-five. So, all that money just became available to me like fifteen minutes ago."

"So what kind of rich are we talking?" I grinned.

"It's really not that important."

"Are we talking like Bill Gates kind of rich?"

"Not quite."

"Like retired school teacher kind of rich?"

"Maybe slightly better than that," he said.

"Like buy an airplane kind of rich?"

"Like how big of an airplane?"

"Seriously?" I asked with wide eyes.

"Maybe," he smirked.

I decided to stop teasing him. "So, wait a second," I said. I sat up in the bed and sat cross legged with my knees touching his legs. "You're telling me you're an attorney, you're hotter than hell, you're smart, and you're rich?"

He nodded his head and frowned. "Well, the first and the last statements are facts. The others not so much. But I don't want you to be freaked out about it or to think I'm bragging or anything. I just wanted you to know. I'm just being honest. That's all. Okay?"

It was more than okay. And yet, it wasn't okay at all.

He felt the need to be honest with me. He cared about me that much. And he valued what we had together. And, to be honest with myself, the fact that he was rich made me want him even more. I know that's shallow. But it's the truth. And though I may hide secrets and occasionally tell lies to others, I can't keep secrets from myself or tell lies to myself. Not anymore.

And that's why Blake being so honest with me was pretty far from okay. I had a secret I was keeping from him. And that made everything I did less than honest. The kisses, the touching, and the sex. The laughs, the late night talks, and every moment we shared. It was all just a little dishonest. That knowledge made me sick to my stomach.

But it wasn't okay for a much larger reason: I wasn't worthy of this man.

What the hell was he doing with me? Couldn't he see how messy my life was? Couldn't he tell how undeserving I was?

But he did know me. In fact, after meeting him, he brought me to tears because he was able to tell me more about myself than I was willing to even acknowledge in the hidden confines of my own mind.

Blake knew me. So, maybe, just maybe, he wasn't completely wrong. Maybe, I was worthy. At least a little bit.

Or maybe I was the one who was completely wrong.

What if I was worthy of Blake? What if I was better than I gave myself credit for being? Maybe I wasn't so bad that I couldn't have a good guy in my life. Maybe I was good enough to have a good job. And maybe I wasn't so bad that I couldn't live a good life.

That thought both excited and terrified me.

In the distance thunder roared and I turned in time to see lightning knifing down above the ocean, several miles away.

"Enough about me. What about you? What do you want to do with your life? What are your dreams? Assuming you don't want to sling drinks for the rest of your life."

"Dreams? I can't afford dreams."

"Nonsense," he said brushing a lock of hair behind my ear.

"Dreams are only for the rich and the sleeping. So, Mr. Rich Man you can dream all you want, but I'll just keep busting my ass mostly for dollar tips."

He chuckled. "Bullshit. Everyone has dreams. And see, I knew I would regret telling you about my money."

I laughed and pinched his arm playfully. "Maybe I don't."

He drew his face within an inch of mine and looked at me seriously.

"I know you do," he said softly.

I bit on the tip of my thumb and looked out the glass door. Again, thunder rumbled in the distance. Blake was staring at me, waiting for an answer.

"I don't know. I've always wanted to help children."

"Like be a teacher?"

"No. Not teach. I could never do that. But just help kids who need help. You know?"

"Like a counselor."

I thought about that. Yes, exactly like a counselor. Maybe the inner city somewhere? I didn't know. I just wanted to help kids who'd experienced loss so that their entire lives wouldn't be messed-up.

"Yeah, like a counselor," I whispered.

Outside, far off above the ocean, two bolts of lightning snaked across the sky. I jumped off the bed and grabbed a tee shirt from Blake's suitcase.

"Mind if I borrow this?" I asked.

"Of course not. Why?"

I went to the door and slid it open.

"Because I want to go out and watch the storm move over the ocean."

And then out I went.

The air was electric. It was both cool and warm at the same time. I ran down the beach toward the water as three more bolts of lightning lit up the distant sky. It felt great to be outside breathing the fresh air, with the wind blowing through Blake's tee shirt, cooling my skin.

"Hey!" Blake called behind me.

But I kept running until I was about twenty feet from the water. The sand beneath my feet went cold as a wave sent the water creeping toward me until it washed over my toes before receding.

"Haven't you ever heard you're not supposed to be near the ocean during a storm?" Blake called from behind me.

I turned and faced Blake. He was wearing only a pair of denim jeans. Lightning cracked, much closer this time, and caused me to jump. I started to laugh but I only got as far as my lips pulling back to reveal my teeth. A huge roar rolled right up my back.

I was blasted forward, my beginning laugh turned to a shocked scream for help.

My head snapped back and my knees buckled. Then I was on my stomach skidding forward a few feet before sliding back for what felt like forever. If I wasn't so shocked, it might have been fun. But it all happened too fast for me to feel anything other than surprise and fear.

The water was gone and I was lying on the cold sand. Blake's shirt was soaked and sticking to me like skin. In the distance I heard him yelling for me. He sounded alarmed, but I was okay. I just needed a few seconds to regain all my senses.

Everything was okay.

I got onto all fours and started to smile.

Yes Blake, I had heard the ocean shore was a dangerous place to be during a storm. But I love storms and I wanted to be a part of it. Sometimes I'm a stupid girl. And sometimes I purposely do stupid things to ruin perfect moments.

I began to lift my head to tell him I was okay, but my ears were overloaded with sound and then the crash of cold water hit me again. I only had time to try to move forward. And then I was whipped toward Blake's voice. I tried to scream but the water rushed into my mouth and down my throat. I tried to cough but only choked. I was moving backward, under the water now, surrounded by darkness and the sound of a roaring engine.

My instincts kicked in and I let the water take me where it wanted me to go. When the movement stopped all around me, I sprang into action.

I kicked downward with my feet, hit sand, and pushed off with all my might. I wasn't too far from shore. But another wave or two and I'd be pulled out to sea. And then, despite the fact that I knew how to swim, I would drown.

I had to keep the panic far down inside of me. My life depended on it.

I swam upward and reached the surface of the water. I coughed and gagged and spit. Another wave hit me in the face but it barely moved me. I popped back to the surface and tried to yell out. I only coughed some more. Lightning flashed above me and took a picture of everything around me. There was nothing but water. And then a huge boom shook my bones.

Oh crap. Swim Katie. Swim for shore!

I tried to breathe again and this time air went into my lungs. I coughed a half cough but was able to exhale. And then I heard the familiar rumble baring down on me. I had just enough time to close my mouth and try to hold my breath. But it wasn't enough.

The wave hit with all its force and tossed me like a helpless piece of driftwood. The water pulled me under and sent me tumbling and twisting, head over heels and side to side. I was thrown one way and then back another way. And when the pull lessened, I kicked my legs and flapped my arms, trying to crawl to the surface of the water. But another huge wave rolled over and all around me. And I was sent spiraling backward and downward.

I just let the force take me. I was no match.

My lungs screamed at my mouth to pull in another breath of air, but my mouth screamed at my brain that there was no point. Try to pull in air and quickly die from drowning. Stay closed, and at least we'd have a several more seconds before passing out. Either way, the result was the same. But when times are desperate, living even a minute as opposed to living thirty seconds is a huge deal. In fact, it's doubling your life expectancy.

I knew that was it. I was so tired. Another flash of lightning popped - far overhead. The surface was maybe twenty or thirty feet above me. And it didn't matter anyway. I was done. I was at the mercy of the ocean and the storm. And though I didn't know much, I knew enough to know mother nature and water, shows no mercy. It is unforgiving and relentless. And I was going to die.

They say that right before you die, your life flashes before your eyes. But that's not true. At least it wasn't for me. There were no flashes back in time to my father holding me, or him leaving my mother, or Kendra and me lying in my mom's bed all night, cuddling with her, trying to get her to stop crying. There was no vision of my first kiss or the first time I ever drank a beer or even to the best day of my life. Though, to be fair, I had no idea what the best day of my life was. It was either the day I met Blake, or the day I convinced Chris to pay for rehab for Kendra, or ironically enough, the last day of my life. But none of it came to my mind as I was under the water, still alive in what was about to become my grave.

Instead, I viewed my life with perfect clarity. And that clarity was not twisted around any distorted views of life or of myself. It was truth. Because, at the intersection of where life meets death, truth is all that's left.

There is very little pure love in this world. A parents' and child's love is usually pure. And sometimes we are lucky enough to find pure love with another person in this life. But most times we just fake it. My love for my mother and my father was always pure. And it was the unreciprocated love for my father, that shaped far too much of who I'd become. And it was the love I had for Blake that was about to mold who I was about to become in the future. Yes, I loved Blake. But I did not have a future. So what did any of it matter?

All I could smell was iodine. Darkness surrounded me. So, I closed my eyes and let myself drift in the cold ocean water. This was my end. And it was as it should be. One stupid mistake – going too close to the water because I felt restless and needed to run – would be the last mistake I'd make. But it was just one blunder in a life filled with them.

Dying because of a seemingly inconsequential mistake, was absolutely appropriate.

It was the end.

The cold ocean water began to feel warm to my skin. And there was humming far away. My lungs were desperate and shrieking for air, but everything else inside of me was relaxed and prepared.

And there was nothing but me, and the ocean, and my love for Blake.

Chapter Nineteen - Then

All I saw was Blake's face, right in front of me, revealing his glorious dimples while he smiled.

And then everything turned to chaos again. I moved through the water with a hook stuck in the crook under my shoulder, hoisting me upward. Just before I burst above the water, back into the night air, I realized it wasn't a hook at all. It was a hand.

My face exploded up out of the water. My mouth opened and sucked in ocean spray and oxygen. Precious oxygen. It was then that I started kicking my feet again and treading water. Lightning lit up the world for three divided split seconds, like a reel of film at the end of a movie.

Then it boomed.

"Swim!" a voice screamed from beside me.

It was Blake. He wrapped his arm around my chest and started pulling me in a direction that I had to assume was the shore. So I kicked my legs and pumped with my arms, as hard and fast as my body would allow. When another huge wave hit us, Blake stopped swimming and wrapped his arms and legs around me. So, I did the same. I wrapped my arms and legs around him. The two of us became one.

The wave hit us both and sent us spiraling forward. And I had just enough time to think: *This is better. Connected to Blake. This is a better way to die.*

Because I still didn't believe I stood a chance.

And then the wave crashed past us and bounced back from the shore. And Blake let go of me and started swimming again. So, I did the same. I swam with everything I ever was and everything I hoped to be. I was so tired but I knew this was my last chance – it was our last chance – to survive.

Again, a wave roared up behind us and Blake grabbed me, so I grabbed him back and held tight. We exploded forward with the wave and when the wave was past us, I kicked to swim upward, and I hit the ocean floor. Blake grabbed me and threw me forward. His height allowed him to stand once again. And with the extra few feet I gained from his toss, I could stand too. But I only had time to take two steps before the water pulled me back out toward the ocean.

I lost my footing and went sliding backward. I felt Blake's hand scrap against my hip and then tug at the bottom of the tee shirt I was wearing. But he couldn't get a grip.

Oh no…no… no!

If I got swept back out I would never stand a chance. I was too tired and as the storm moved directly overhead, the force of the water would only grow stronger. If I kept sliding that would be it for me.

If I believed I was going to die before, now I knew it.

Except, my hair was nearly yanked out of the top of my head and my entire body jerked and wiggled like a snake. Blake had caught a fistful of my hair and was holding tight.

We both slid slowly toward the ocean but Blake was offering enough resistance to keep us close to shore. I flailed out with my arms and managed to grab a hold of the waist of Blake's jeans. And then my feet were in the sand and I was part running and part swimming through the water just as another wave smacked into our backs.

I left my feet and shot forward toward the shore. And then I landed on all fours. Blake was a few feet behind me and he pushed on my butt, urging me forward. Although I didn't have any energy to do anything but lie down and sleep, I crawled forward.

Again, the water slid back out and started taking me with it.

"Dig in!" Blake yelled. "Hands and feet!"

So I pushed my hands and feet into the sand. But it wasn't enough. I started to skip backward and then I lost my grip. The water flipped me over onto my back and, just like that, I was gliding back out again. Blake hooked me under my left arm and dove on top of me. Lightning flashed again and that's when I saw the look of desperation on his face. His jaw was clenched and his lips were drawn back, baring his teeth. His eyes were wider than eyes should be able to open. He was looking at me, and I was looking back at him, as slowly we both slid back out away from shore.

Then I felt his hands on my hips. He flipped me over and suddenly I was going forward again, the tops of my feet scraped against the sand. And Blake slid off of me and away.

I kicked and flailed, and then ran and propelled myself forward. Another wave hit me and again I flew forward. But this time I landed in water that was only knee-deep. I jammed my hands as far into the sand as they would go and dug in with my toes. As the water pushed back at me my feet went deeper into the mushy sand and I stayed planted.

Once the water washed back out, I bear-crawled forward until the sand started to warm beneath my hands and feet. Another wave hit against the back of my legs and I lost my balance and tipped over onto my side. I glided forward a few feet but dug in again and stopped myself. The water pushed against me and tried one last time to pull me back out. But there wasn't enough of it to grab me. And once it washed away and left me in only a couple inches of water, I stood and ran. My legs wobbled the entire way, but they didn't give out on me.

The sand turned warmer where it hadn't been touched by the ocean water, but I kept moving forward another twenty steps or so. I didn't want to be anywhere near the water. And once I was far enough away, I collapsed.

I coughed for several seconds and spit into the sand beside me. My chest was too heavy and burned like hell. I sucked in a deep breath and then coughed some more. Two more deep breaths and the coughing stopped and the burning cooled. Slowly, the heaviness lightened too.

As I lay there, the skies opened up and rain pelted my body. I didn't care. I couldn't get any wetter and I was alive. Alive! Somehow, someway, I'd survived.

Blake.

I scrambled up to my knees and looked all around. Lightning flashed and I could see the bungalow about one hundred feet off to my right and higher on the beach. I didn't see Blake.

"Blake!" I screamed. "Blake!"

He'd been there right behind me. He was just with me! He'd saved me. Surely he didn't get sucked back into the ocean. He was too strong… too smart… and too full of life for that to happen.

The wind gusted and the rain fell even harder. I scanned the beach. I saw nothing and nobody.

"Blake!" I yelled until my throat ached. "Blake!"

Desperation gripped me hard and I stood-up and started walking back toward the water. I had to go back in after him. I barely had enough strength to walk, but I couldn't leave him out there all alone. I couldn't let him die.

Both my thighs twitched and my knees buckled. My legs turned to spaghetti and I was on my ass sitting in the sand. I had no strength left. And I couldn't even save myself. It would be stupid to go in after him. I'd only die myself. But I had to try. I had to. Life before Blake was nothing but a mess. And life without him, knowing I had a hand in his death, would be even worse. I had to go back in the water and at least do something. If dying was all I could manage, then that was okay. It was better than living by doing absolutely nothing.

I managed to get back on my knees and then put one foot down into the sand. Lightning flashed directly over my head and the boom that followed made my right ear ring. I pushed myself into a standing position and then slowly staggered back toward the water.

The sand began to turn cooler beneath my feet. A few more steps and I'd be far enough for a large wave to topple me over and drag me out toward Blake. Toward my death, Toward our fate.

There was movement to my left. I sensed it more than saw it. I turned that way as the water washed over my feet up past my ankles. A lightning bolt popped behind me. And there he was less than fifty feet away, walking toward me up higher on the beach.

Every muscle in both of my legs threatened to give out on me. But I ignored them. I ran away from the water and then straight toward Blake. My legs buckled a couple times, but I managed to stay on my feet. I managed to keep moving forward. And when I got close enough to see the outline of his body, he took off toward me. Our bodies clapped together and we both fell into the sand. And though mere seconds earlier, there was no energy left in my body and no will left in my mind, I was suddenly alive and felt as strong as a million horses.

We hugged each other tightly and uttered phrases with the words "alive" and "love" in them. And when his mouth met mine, I tasted salt and I kissed him harder and deeper than anyone had ever been kissed. I felt everything inside of me. And I mean everything.

My scalp popped from my hair being pulled, my lungs burned from lack of oxygen, and my skin felt the water pushing me around. But I felt even more than the physical stuff that I'd just experienced. There was the loss of my father along with the loss of my innocence. There was the regret of being with Neil and the other older men too. There was regret for being with just about all of them. I was better than that. And there was shame for living the life that I lived. But there was also the pride of finding Blake and not messing it up. That was brightest of everything that was inside of me. And there was no doubting that love was all a part of it. I loved Blake – madly, deeply, and completely.

It was my very life that the ocean had just about pulled out of me. Death was about to rip away my everything and take it for good. But I cheated death at the last second. Nothing left me. But it was still on the surface. It hadn't yet seeped back inside of me. And now it was setting me on fire.

Blake peeled off the tee shirt I was wearing and then my panties. We managed to tug his soaked jeans off of him. Then as the rain pounded down on us and the thunder and lightning were everywhere, Blake climbed on top of me.

We were still alive. We survived. And that knowledge pushed us to a place I never knew existed. It was a place filled with the love we felt for each other, and made of everything that we were: both together and as individuals.

He kissed me and touched me and moved above me as I writhed under him. I dug my nails into his back and bit on my lower lip until I tasted blood. He was all around me and inside me, and I was all around and inside of him too. And while we made love, we were no longer on that beach. We were in a place that knows nothing but pure love and passion. His lips were on my breast and my tongue was on his neck, but forever was what we were tasting. And eternity was in our mouths.

We were not dead. We were alive. More alive than ever.

And everything Blake ever was or would be, exploded out of him and into me. And then all that I was and ever would be burst into flames and consumed us both. We burned together. And we screamed in pure pleasure as the rain poured down on our naked skin, and the lightning crashed overhead, and the ocean roared everywhere.

∞∞∞∞∞∞∞∞

We slept until almost noon. And then we loaded up the car and headed back toward Dulcet. I slept most of the way, dreaming of the ocean and sailing to distant lands with Blake. We got home just after three in the afternoon. Blake walked me up to my apartment and we stood kissing outside my door.

Blake tipped his head back and smiled at me. "Are you okay?" he asked me.

I nodded. "I've never been more okay."

"Okay," he said softly.

"Okay," I replied.

He let go of me and stood at the top of the stairs.

"See you in a couple hours?"

There was a birthday dinner for him at his mom's house. Of course I didn't want to be around Neil, but what choice did I have?

"Sure you don't want to come in?" I asked. "We could just get takeout and spend the rest of the day naked."

He smiled. "That sounds great. But we have to go to dinner. You know, my mom is cooking this big meal, and she never cooks. Which means two things: We have to go and the food is going to be horrible."

I shook my head and grinned. "Sounds absolutely perfect."

Blake started down the stairs as I slipped my key into the deadbolt. He stopped and turned back to me.

"Hey baby?" he said.

"Yeah?"

"Last night on the beach. Did you say you loved me?"

My cheeks grew warm and my stomach flipped. Did I tell him that? I mean, I absolutely did love him. But I didn't want him to think I was silly.

"I don't know," I said. "Did I say that?"

Blake nodded once. "I think you did."

"And I think you did too," I replied.

"That's because I do."

"You do?"

"Yeah, I love you Katie. I do."

I stood there frozen. I felt my eyes growing teary.

"And I love you," I said slowly.

He walked back up the steps and stood inches from me.

"I mean it. I've never told a girl I loved her because I never have before. But I love you."

And then he bent down and kissed me. I whispered "I love you" over and over again as he kissed my neck.

"And if you keep doing that I'm going to pull you inside and not let you ever go home."

He stopped and kissed me once more on the forehead.

"Okay, sure you don't want me to pick you up later?"

"No, I have to go pick-up my check anyway. I told Buzz I'd be in this evening for it."

"I can take you there after dinner," Blake offered.

"No, really it's fine. I'll be at your moms at about six."

"Okay."

He walked down the steps and was just about out the door.

"Hey Blake," I called to him. "Are we talking like buy your own private island kind of rich?"

He smiled up at me and shook his head. Then he went outside and disappeared from sight. I unlocked my door and stepped inside. On the floor was a sheet of paper folded in two. I bent down and picked it up.

I missed you. But soon you will see me.
Soon….

Somehow, for some reason, it barely affected me. Maybe I was just getting used to it or maybe I had changed in a way so that stupid middle school notes couldn't creep me out anymore.

I crumpled it up and threw it in the kitchen garbage. It was getting old. And I didn't have the time or the energy to worry about what kind of nut job was sending me the notes. I knew I'd probably have to face up to it, one way or the other, eventually. But that was not the time. I had to shower and get ready for Blake's birthday dinner.

Just before I got undressed, my cell phone buzzed with a text. It was from that blocked number again.

Welcome home.

Don't forget about me.
Don't you dare.
I'm still here.

Son-of-a-bitch.

∞∞∞∞∞∞

I showed up at Blake's house (his mom's house, which was also Neil's house) at a little after six, carrying a bottle of wine. His mom, Angela, met me at the door and let me in. She led me down the hall, past Neil's office, and back into the kitchen.

"Blake's running a little late," she explained. "He just ran up to take a shower. He should be down in a few minutes. Neil guilted him into cleaning the pool and it took a little longer than I think he thought it would."

"Oh," I smiled. "No problem."

I looked around. There was no sign of Neil. Not yet.

"And I don't know if Blake told you, but Stephen decided to go home today. So, it's just going to be the four of us for dinner."

The four of us: You, me, Neil, and Blake. Sounds lovely.

"Stephen went home? Is he okay?"

"Oh yes, he's fine. He wanted to get back to his practice."

"Oh okay."

"He was a little upset about your sister but he'll be fine."

"I'm really sorry about that."

"It's not your fault. Really. It's not anyone's fault. I feel bad for your sister and for your family. Addiction can destroy families. I hear it's one of the biggest destroyers of marriage too. Well, that an infidelity."

I didn't know what to say. She may have looked at me for a couple seconds too long when she said the word *infidelity*. I wasn't sure. Maybe it was just my guilty conscience imagining it.

"But anyway," she continued, "today is day of celebration. My baby is twenty-five." She held the bottle of wine I'd brought and studied the label. "Oh this is my favorite."

"I know. Blake told me."

"Well, do you want a glass? Or don't you drink?"

"I do, sometimes. But no thank you. I'm fine."

"Yes you are," Neil said walking into the room.

"What?" his wife asked laughing nervously.

"From what Blake tells me, she is very fine."

He walked around the island and kissed his wife on the mouth and then patted her butt. He looked at me the entire time.

"Don't embarrass the girl."

"Oh I wouldn't think of it," Neil replied. "How are you Katie?"

"I'm fine," I said before I could catch myself. "How are you?"

Neil raised his eyebrows up and down at me. "I'm fine as well." He grabbed the wine bottle from his wife and took a bottle opener out a drawer in the island. "Do you want a glass Katie?"

"No thank you."

"What? I thought you loved wine?"

"And how would you know that?" his wife asked with her hand on her hip.

Neil shrugged his shoulders and smirked. Angela smirked back.

I prayed she only thought he was teasing me.

"Oh that reminds me." Neil popped the cork and poured three glasses of wine despite what I'd said. "That report I have for Buzz is still in my office. The one I started to explain to you the other day, I still have that. Here, I'll show you in my office."

I didn't want to go with him. Of course I didn't. But what choice did I have? If I objected, it would look worse than him inviting me into his office. He carried two glasses of wine and handed one to me.

"It'll just take a couple minutes," he said.

"Don't you bore her by showing her any of your art either? Or anything else you value so much. Not in this house. You hear me Neil?" His wife called to him as we walked down the hall.

"Oh, maybe just a little," he called back over his shoulder.

And then we both walked into his office and he closed the door.

My mind was racing. I tried to slow it down to form a single thought but I was too slow. Within the privacy of his own office, Neil moved close to me and leaned into kiss me. I turned my face so his lips landed on my cheek.

"I've missed you," he whispered.

I shook my head and stepped away from him. "I'm sorry."

He took a sip of his wine. "Tell me you haven't missed me?"

"I haven't missed you."

My voice was as flat and cold as a sheet of ice.

Neil chuckled. "Well, I don't believe you. And I don't think you're thinking clearly."

"I've never been thinking more clearly in my life. I'm sorry Neil. This is over. We're over. I love Blake."

While I spoke, his eyes went from amused to shocked to angry. With a shaking hand he raised his wine glass to his mouth and gulped it down. His eyes softened and his smile returned.

"I don't believe you."

He moved toward me. I backed-up until I was against the wall. He pressed his entire body against mine. I could smell the wine on his breath and his after shave on his face.

"I've really missed you. And I reserved the Honey Moon Suite at the hotel in Wilmington for this weekend."

"And what are you going to do?" I whispered. "Screw me right here while the man I really love – your stepson – is upstairs and while the woman you supposedly love – your wife – is in the kitchen making our dinner?"

"No. But a passionate kiss would be nice."

"Kiss me if you want. But I'm not kissing you back."

And so he did.

He bent his face toward me and pressed his lips against mine. His tongue came out and licked at my lips, tried to invade my mouth, but I clenched my teeth tight. After trying for so long that it almost turned comical, he finally stopped and walked over to his desk.

"That's how it's always been for you, hasn't it?" I said wiping his saliva off my mouth and chin. "That right there sums it up perfectly."

He heard me, but he didn't acknowledge my words. He grabbed a manila envelope and shoved a small stack of blank paper into it. He handed me the envelope.

"I warned you. But because I really do love you – in some strange way – I will give you three days to change your mind."

He started for the door but I didn't move. I wasn't scared of him anymore. And I wasn't intimidated either.

"And then what?" I asked.

"What?"

"Then what will you do? Tell your wife about us? Tell Blake? Does it make you feel like a big man to threaten me? You want to ruin my life by ruining your own life? Do you think that makes you a man? You have far more to lose in all of this then I do."

Of course I didn't believe that. Losing Blake would be the greatest loss ever. Neil's stupid reputation and his fake marriage were nothing compared to the love Blake and I shared.

"This has nothing to do with me being a man or not being a man. And it has nothing to do with my reputation either." Now his voice was as flat and hard as steel. "You have no idea how much I can mess up your life. And believe me, I'm smart enough not to do anything that will mess-up my own life."

"Yeah I'm sure your wife would be thrilled to learn you've been screwing her son's girlfriend."

"Maybe she already knows. Maybe."

I studied his face for a hint as to whether he was bluffing. But if he had a tell, it wasn't obvious.

"Bullshit," I said.

He shrugged his shoulders and turned back to leave.

"One more question?" I said.

"What?" he asked sharply.

"Is that you sending and leaving messages for me?"

"What?"

He looked like he had no idea what I was talking about.

"Messages for me. You know, like threatening messages?"

His eyes narrowed and he pressed lips together into two thin pink lines.

"Someone's been sending you threatening messages?"

"Is it you?"

"Did you try to trace the number?"

"Neil," I said sharply. "Is it you?"

"Do I look like the kind of person who would send you stupid messages? Do I seem that petty and childish?"

He wasn't answering my question and I was getting sick of asking. All I needed was a simple yes or no.

I shook my head. "I have no idea who you are. So just answer the question. Is it you?"

"Of course not," he replied.

And then he opened the door and was gone.

I followed him down the hall to the kitchen. This night wasn't going to be easy. It made me sick thinking about sitting at the same table as Neil and pretending to like him. I hated what I had done with him and I hated what he was doing to me. I just wanted to run out of the house and never look back. But I wouldn't do that to Blake, especially not on his birthday.

Blake was sitting on a stool at the kitchen island with a bottle of beer in his hand. He turned and smiled at me. That smile. It lifted my entire mood. It made me want to fly. Even then.

"Hey baby," he said to me.

I put my arms around him and leaned my head against his chest. The beating of his heart stopped my own heart from racing so fast.

"You okay?" he asked me.

"Yeah, I'm fine. Happy birthday again."

"Thank you. But you seem upset. Did something happen with you and Neil."

And that sent my heart racing again.

Did something happen with me and Neil? Oh, you have no idea all that's happened between Neil and me. And I hope you don't ever find out.

"No, he just had to give me some papers for Buzz," I said holding up the envelope.

And then I took a long drink of my wine.

I barely spoke during dinner. I politely answered all the questions about my childhood and where I went to college and what I wanted to do with my life. I never liked talking about my childhood, and I didn't even know what I wanted to do with my life. So, even if I'd been feeling less nervous, my answers probably wouldn't have been much more than a sentence or two anyway.

Thankfully Neil behaved himself. He seemed interested as I explained my brief history, though he already knew all about it. And he didn't even take any jabs at me or throw any strange looks my way. He acted like I was nothing more to him than some random girl his stepson had brought home. Maybe he thought that would hurt my feelings. But he was wrong.

After dinner, we ate birthday cake and shortly after that, at a little before eight-thirty, I excused myself to go pick-up my check at the bar and drop off the fake paperwork to Buzz. Neil and his wife both hugged me and thanked me for coming over. I thanked them for having me and for the delicious food. Neil told me he'd see me soon. And I didn't say anything back.

"You okay?" Blake asked me.

We were standing next to my car at the end of his driveway.

"Yeah. I'm just a little tired. And I'm still a little shaken up about last night."

"Almost dying?"

I laughed, because hearing him say it so plainly seemed strange. I mean, some people tell stories about *almost dying* and they didn't actually come anywhere near to being killed. But I was right there. I was closer to death than I was to life. And then Blake saved me.

I hoped he'd always save me. And I hoped somehow, someway, he would figure out a way to save us. Because eventually he would find out about Neil.

Three days. That's what Neil had said to me. He'd give me three days until he did whatever he was going to do to ruin me or whatever. And I knew I should just tell Blake the truth. That would make it a little better. But I didn't think it would make it enough better to actually save anything. So, I had to just keep my mouth shut, deal with the huge secret that was stuck through our love, and hope Neil was just bluffing.

"Yeah, that just has me a little shaken still."

"Seems like we're too young to be dealing with all this scary, heavy crap," Blake said.

He wrapped his arms around me and hugged me tight.

"All this heavy crap?" I asked, my voice muffled by his chest and arm.

"Yeah, with Kendra and everything. I mean she died and then we almost died. We're too young to be dealing with all this shit."

"Yeah, we are," I said.

I stepped away from him and opened my car door.

"Are you sure there's nothing else?"

"What else could there be?" I asked.

But my words sounded way too clumsy as they dropped out of my mouth.

"You okay with me telling you I love you?"

"Of course. I love you too."

"Because I've never told anyone that before. And I don't know what happens next."

He leveled his eyes on me. He looked too serious. It scared me, but I'm not sure if it was in a good way or not.

"And I've always known what happens next," he continued. "I've always had a plan and I stick to it. Everything has always been nice and orderly with me. But with you, I don't have a plan. I feel like things are a little messy inside of me. But in a good way, you know? Like in a very good way. I hope that makes sense to you."

I tipped my head to the side and couldn't help but grin. He was off balance, a little left of center. And it was me – or our love – that was doing it to him. Maybe it shouldn't have, but that made me happy. But he – and our love – was doing the exact opposite for me. Finally, things in my life were making sense.

"I kinda understand," I said to him.

"Yes, just kinda, right?" he said. "Because it doesn't make any sense. And I'm not usually like this. Never. It's new to me." He shook his head back and forth and half laughed, half coughed. "But despite my mind being a little freaked out by it all, my heart has never felt so full and happy. And that's because of you. It's all because of you."

He cleared his throat and smiled nervously. "I've never met anyone like you Katie. I didn't even know anyone like you existed. Or a love like this existed. I've never been the sappy type. So, this isn't easy for me. But I don't care. And I know it doesn't make sense. And I know it's messy. But I just don't care, because I love you. I mean like freaking head over heels love you."

I wanted to kiss him and hold him and never let go. I wanted to cry. I wanted to scream. But most of all, I just wanted to love him and have him love me back forever.

"I know, it's crazy. But I never thought a guy like you would ever fall for a girl like me. And I never knew I could love someone so much either. And it scares the hell out of me. But I don't care either."

"Would you ever consider moving to Chicago?" he asked so fast that the sentence sounded like one word.

And that was the problem that I didn't even want to think about. I knew that wasn't our biggest problem. But for Blake, it was. Because he had no idea about the issues I was dealing with. But it didn't make it any less of a problem for us. Very soon, Blake was going to have to choose where he wanted to go. And that decision could make or break us as much as any decision.

"I don't want you choosing anything because of me," I said slowly and softly.

"What do you mean?"

"Choose for you, not me. Okay?"

"But would you move to Chicago? I mean, I'm not saying that's my choice, and if it is my choice, I'm not asking you to commit to moving there. Obviously. But I am asking: Would you ever consider moving there? Or are you dead-set against ever moving that far north?"

I looked at the darkening sky through the corners of my eyes. I couldn't exactly picture myself in Chicago among the tall buildings, with the wind whipping against me. I tried several times and I was able to picture the buildings and the people walking the streets, but I could never bring myself to picture me amongst them.

But I could always picture myself with Blake, no matter where it was.

"I can picture myself with you," I said, still looking at the sky.

"And that includes Chicago?" he asked with a smile.

"That includes anywhere."

He kissed me and held the door while I slid into the driver's side. He shut the door and I unrolled my window.

"So is it Chicago then?"

"Maybe. I don't know yet."

"Okay," I said.

I slid the key into the ignition and turned it. The engine rolled over, hiccupped a couple times and then was quiet. I looked at Blake with a big, fake smile. How embarrassing. I turned the key again and this time it just sort of burped and then nothing.

"Hey Katie?" Blake said to me.

"Yeah?"

"Anything wrong with you and Neil?"

"What?" My heart thumped hard in my chest. "What do you mean?"

"I don't know. I'm not really a big fan of his and it seems like he has a bit of creepy interest in you. I don't know. Like I've caught him looking at your ass a couple times and I know you went into his office with him tonight and at the party that day. Is there anything I should know about?"

I opened my mouth but nothing came out. I wanted to tell him the truth but I couldn't. I wanted to tell him to get into my car and we could just drive forever and never stop.

"No," I shook my head. "Of course not. He just had some paperwork to give me for Buzz, that's all."

"Okay."

"And I just feel a little weird around him because he owns the bar and all. It makes it kinda weird."

"Okay."

I turned the key again and, mercifully, the engine turned over, coughed, and then roared to life. Blake stuck his head through the window and kissed me.

"I love you," he said.

"I love you too," I said back.

"You sure you're okay?"

"How about you get in the car and we drive west until we hit the Pacific Ocean?"

Blake cocked his head to the side. "That sounds great."

"Then let's do it. Let's just get in the car and drive."

He stood and wrapped his hand against the top of the car.

"Someday baby. Someday."

I backed out into the street while Blake watched me.

"Happy birthday again. I'll see you tomorrow."

And then I headed toward the bar.

∞∞∞∞∞∞∞∞

"Hey, where is everyone?"

Buzz was sitting alone at the bar. There were no customers or bartenders. He turned his head slowly toward me.

"Hey Katie, what brings you here on this fine night?"

"I'm here to grab my check. You okay? Where's Linda? I thought she was working tonight."

"I sent her home. Didn't you notice the closed sign out by the road?"

I hadn't. I wasn't the most observant person in the world, especially when I had a million things on my mind.

"Why are you closed? Everything okay?"

"It's okay," he said. "This way we'll be able to talk alone for a couple minutes."

"What's wrong?"

He patted the stool next to him. "Have a seat," he offered. "Are you thirsty? You want a drink?"

I sat next to him. "No, I'm good."

"Suit yourself," he said raising his glass of bourbon toward me and then taking a long slurp from it.

"Are you okay?" Something wasn't right with him.

"I'm just ducky," he said. "How are you?"

"I'm fine. Just need to grab my check and then I'm going to head home and call it an early night. Things have been a little crazy lately."

"I bet. Not hanging out with that boy tonight?"

"You mean Blake?"

I didn't know he even knew about Blake.

"Of course. He's Neil's boy, isn't he?"

"His stepson."

Something definitely wasn't right. Buzz drank down the last swallow of his bourbon and slid off the bar stool.

"Right his stepson. Tall guy, right?"

"Yeah."

He walked around to the other side of the bar and poured himself another glass of bourbon. Then he started back around the bar again.

Something about the way he walked and talked. Something about the way he was looking at me. It made me feel like I should get up and run out of there. And it wasn't because he was drunk either (and I knew he was drunk). I'd seen Buzz drunk too many times to count. He was usually a lovable, jovial drunk. But that night, something was strange.

And then I remembered the other day when I caught him staring at me. The little blond hairs on my arms started to rise.

"I think you should stop seeing that guy. He's no good for you." As he sat back on the stool his drink sloshed over onto his hand that was holding the glass.

"How do you even know about Blake?"

"Oh I just know," he said licking the bourbon from his fingers. "I see things. I watch a lot. Even when you don't know it."

A cold chill slid down my spine. And I was suddenly aware how alone we were.

"I just need to grab my check. Is... Is that okay? I'm in a hurry. B-Blake's actually waiting for me out in the car."

"Oh he's out in the car?" Buzz asked.

"Yeah, I...I really need to be going," I said and I started to slide off the stool.

Buzz grabbed my wrist tightly. I could feel his saliva on my skin.

"Just sit with me for a minute, okay?"

I sat back down. I'd known this man for years, but suddenly he was a stranger – a creepy stranger.

"Buzz," I said softly. "You're hurting my wrist."

He looked down at his hand and released his grip. He left behind four red and slimy stripes on my skin.

"May I have my check please? Or should I just come back and grab it tomorrow?"

At that point I was fighting the urge to run out of there without saying another word. But there was still a tiny slice of me thinking that maybe I was just being silly, maybe I was reading him all wrong. Maybe all the stress was just getting to me and I was overreacting.

"Can you promise you'll stop seeing Blake? I mean seriously, you're too beautiful for him anyway. You're way too good for him."

"I can't make any promises." I was choosing my words as carefully as I could without making them sound too unnatural and all chopped up. "Blake and I are just kids. R-Really. Just having fun. It's not that serious," I lied.

Buzz frowned and then took another drink.

"So you won't stop seeing him?"

To tell too big of a lie seemed disloyal to Blake. And despite my fear, I wouldn't do that. I was already being disloyal enough by not telling Blake about Neil.

"No," I said.

"Then that won't be good. Bad things might happen."

"Are… Are you threatening me?" Despite my best efforts, my voice started to quiver. "I really j-just want my check. But I can get it some other t-time."

I jumped off the chair and started for the door. I expected Buzz to spring at me and try to run me down before I made it out the door.

He had to be the one leaving me the notes and sending me the messages.

But why? Why did it start so suddenly? I had no idea. And it didn't really matter. All that was important was getting the hell out of there.

"I'm sorry," Buzz called out. "I'm not threatening you. Come on Katie. Let's get your check."

He waved his hand for me to follow him as he made his way back toward his office.

"I'll just wait here, okay?"

He nodded his head once. "Okay."

I leaned against the wall just to the right of the door. If I needed to, I could easily run out the door. But then what? Would he chase me down in the parking lot and pull me back inside? At this time of night traffic out on the road wouldn't be heavy but there should be some traffic and somebody would have to see something. Plus, Buzz was getting to be an old man, if he wasn't already. I could outrun him and if he somehow caught me, I'd stand a decent chance of fighting him off.

But he was bigger than me and could be armed with a knife or even a gun. He could stop me from leaving the bar if he really wanted to. So, should I just run or wait? I really needed the money from my check and there was still that tiny possibility that I was just overreacting.

I just needed to grab my check and get the hell out of there.

"Here you go," he called to me as he walked out of his office. "You'll notice that it's a couple days short because I changed the pay period. I hope that's okay."

"It's fine."

He drew within fifteen feet of me. His right hand was holding my check but his left was behind his back.

"So I would think Blake will be leaving soon and then that will be it for the two of you. Right?"

"Yeah. We'll see."

What the hell was behind his back? He drew within ten feet. It could be anything. A gun? A knife? A cloth with something on it that would make me pass out?

"Well, just think about it. Ah shit, maybe I should just tell you. Maybe I should just come clean."

He was less than five feet from me. There was a glaze of sweat on his face and his hand shook as he handed me my check. I took it and smiled.

"Come clean about what?"

I put my hand against the door and pushed it open a couple inches. My muscles were tensed and ready to spring into action.

Then Buzz started to bring his left hand around. It swung in a wide circle and came up and rubbed his chin. It was empty.

"Never mind. You'll find out soon enough. I won't ruin your night now. Have a good night Katie."

He turned away from me and I watched him until he was back at the bar. Then I pushed my way out the door, jogged to my car, jumped in, and locked the doors.

Chapter Twenty - Now

"And you never suspected Buzz of sending any of the messages before that night?" the detective asks me.

"No," I shake my head. "Why would I?"

I look inside my empty coffee cup. I shrug my shoulders, start to say more but I don't.

Looking back, I can think of several times when I caught him looking at me, especially that one day when he was sitting in his office. But it was never something that alarmed me. Some men stared at women, or at least stared at me. It didn't mean anything more to me. Not before that day when I was sure he was considering attacking me right there and then.

"He never showed any other signs of stalking you or anything?"

"Not at all. Of course not."

"And you didn't think to run out of there when he went back in the office?"

"I thought about it."

"But you didn't run out? Were you not really that scared?"

"I really needed my check. I had about three dollars in my wallet."

He nods and then both of our heads turn toward a knock at the door.

"Yeah," the detective calls out.

The door opens a couple feet and a woman's head appears.

"Can I have a word?" she asks.

The detective nods.

"You want anything else?"

"I really have to use the ladies room."

"Okay? Just give me a minute."

He leaves the room and shuts the door. I'm alone again. I just want to get the rest of the story over with. I want to be done with it all. I'm so exhausted. But if and when I'm able to walk out of this police station and back into the real world, then I'll have to face the reality of my new world: I have no job, no concrete plans for a future, and no love.

It's the no love part that I can't think about. I just can't.

But I need to get out of my own head and move forward. I have no other choice.

The detective walks back and calls over his shoulder.

"Tell him we'll only be about another fifteen minutes or so. Then he can see her."

There's a muffled voice at the end of the hall, I can't make out the words. And then the detective calls back, "Yep, that's fine."

Then he looks at me and tips his head toward the other end of the hall.

"You need the restroom?"

"Please."

"This way," he says holding the door open for me.

I walk past him into the hall. The air's much cooler out here and I have to fold my arms over my chest to keep myself from shivering. The detective walks me down the hall, past an office with a television blaring, to a door with golden letters stuck to it that spell *Lad-es*. It's missing the "i" but when I walk into the bathroom, I realize the missing letter is the least of my worries. It looks like the toilet and sink haven't been cleaned in about fifteen years.

So, I carefully do my business while sitting on about a half inch of toilet paper. I wash my hands, being cautious where I touch the faucet and the soap dispenser, and then I walk back out. As I walk back past the office, I hear the television talking about a potential homicide. Despite every ounce of me not wanting to, I stop and watch for a second.

We are getting word now that one deceased male was found in the apartment above this real estate agency you see behind me. You can see the yellow police tape surrounding the building. There are both Dulcet Police and North Carolina State Police on scene.

Here is what we know so far:

Just a couple hours ago, police responded to the scene of what they are calling a domestic disturbance. When they arrived on scene they found two males inside. Both names are being withheld at this time. But what we do know is one of those males was found deceased and it is believed it was the result of some type of altercation.

Police are being very tight-lipped regarding exactly what happened but a source has told us that it is believed that one other person fled the scene and was believed to have tried to fly out of Wright Regional shortly after the incident. Police were able to apprehend that individual and two people are currently in custody. No one else is believed to be involved and police have stressed that the public is in absolutely no danger.

My mind slips and I remember. I see the blood on the floor. I see the body. I see the familiar eyes right before me.

Yes, he is dead.

And yes, Blake is still gone.

The world swirls around me. I reach out and grab the door jam and try to stay upright. The detective's hand on my back helps a lot. I draw in a deep breath and hold it in my lungs. Then I exhale through circled lips.

Just move forward. Don't think about it. Don't think about it. Do... not... lose it!

"You okay?" the detective asks.

His voice is a hundred miles away.

I nod my head and look up at him. He tips back and forth in my vision for a few seconds, but eventually comes to center and stays there. He keeps one hand on my back and grabs my arm with his other hand. We walk back to the interrogation room and he helps me sit down.

"You need a couple minutes?"

"I remember a little more about what happened."

"Do you remember everything?"

"I think maybe," I say.

He sits down across from me and picks up his pen.

"Then we better continue, as long as you're up for it?"

I nod my head and look him in the eyes, but all I'm seeing is Blake's smiling face.

Chapter Twenty-One - Then

For the next two days, Blake and I were inseparable. I began to believe that Neil was bluffing. He wouldn't say anything and he'd let me and Blake alone. And I believed that somehow Blake and I would make it work. I mean, like make it work forever. Maybe Blake would choose to work with his brother and we do the long distance thing for a while, or maybe he'd choose to go to Chicago and I'd go with him. Who knew? But I believed Neil would leave it up to us.

I was wrong.

It turned out my paycheck from the bar was actually 18 hours short. When you live mostly off tips, it doesn't matter that much. But still, almost a hundred dollars short is still a hundred dollars I didn't have. But I wasn't about to go confront Buzz about it. I wasn't sure if I'd ever step foot back in the bar again. I didn't care to see Buzz ever again and I figured I could avoid him.

Again, I was wrong.

I called into work the day after the craziness with Buzz. He wasn't there and Linda said she'd give him the message that I wasn't feeling well. The next day, I called in again and Buzz answered.

"Are you really sick or are you hanging out with Blake?"

"Buzz," I breathed heavily into the phone. "Does it really matter?"

"Actually it does, Katie. It matters more than you understand. Now listen, I know I was drunk the other day but-."

"Buzz," I interrupted him. "Buzz. It's okay. Let's just agree to forget about the other night and move on."

I almost quit right then and there but I couldn't make myself say it. Somehow, for some odd reason, I still liked Buzz and I still felt an allegiance to him, or at least to my job.

"Well I'm sorry Katie," he said.

"It's okay. It just has to stop," I told him.

We both knew what I was talking about without me even saying it.

"And it will," Buzz said.

It will? Did he mean for it to sound like it wouldn't actually stop until sometime in the future? I wasn't sure. Buzz didn't always have the tightest grasp on the English language, or how to express himself properly.

"It's done, Buzz. Like now. Okay?"

"Katie I don't think you understand," he said. "There is more going on here. More than I can say right now. But I need you to do this for me. Please. Just say you'll be done with Blake. Like right now."

I didn't understand. I'd worked for him at the bar for years, and never had he once shown any interest in me beyond being my boss and a sometimes almost uncle-like advisor/protector for me. I even suspected that he knew about me and Neil. But he never mentioned it. And he never showed that he cared. Not one bit.

Now, out of the complete and total ocean blue, he suddenly turns into a stalker? And not a very good one at that. First, he lets me know I have a stalker by leaving me notes and then sending me texts, and now he's just completely giving himself away and trying to control my life. Didn't he know stalkers were supposed to attack their prey? They weren't just supposed to annoy them.

"Buzz," I said through gritted teeth. "You don't control me. I already have a father and he's an asshole. I don't need another one."

Of course I knew he didn't see me as his daughter. I didn't want to think *how* he felt about me. Or *what* he felt about me either. But I was hoping that maybe I could cast things in more of a father/daughter light.

"But Katie. What if I told you your job depended on it?"

"I'd say tough shit."

And that was the end of our conversation. I hung-up on him, went out and climbed in Blake's Jeep, and off we went to grab some dinner and see a movie. After the movie Blake dropped me off and went back to his house to grab some clothes. He said he'd be right back. And then more than two hours passed. But I'd learned that Blake's mom (and sometimes Neil too) often slowed him down. So I wasn't concerned at all. But I was a little annoyed.

Blake was going to stay all night at my apartment. I was so excited. The thought of him sleeping beside me, the two of us curled around each other, still caused my breath to catch in my throat and my stomach to flip and twist. This was the night when we would take things to a new level. Or so I hoped.

But level was that exactly?

We met – check. We playfully flirted – check. We kissed and fell hard for each other – check and check. We made love – big check. And we fell in love with each other – a titanic check.

So, what level was next? Moving away together? Is that what I was hoping for? Honestly, at least a small part of me did hope for that. And I didn't care if it was Virginia or Chicago. (Okay, I cared a little. I wanted to stay near the ocean.) But maybe I was moving too fast. I probably was. But as long as Blake was right along beside me, I didn't care.

I examined myself in the mirror once more. I dabbed on a little more perfume and walked back out to the living room. Finally, I heard a knock at the door.

"Hey!" I swung the door open, smiling wide.

"Hey."

He walked past me several steps into the apartment. The first thing I noticed was that he didn't have a bag slung over his shoulder. Maybe he left it in the car. When he turned around, his face was longer than usual and his eyes were watery, like he'd just stopped crying or was about to start. He looked at me, from my feet to the top of my head and said nothing.

"So before I forget, I have to ask: Are we talking like vacation for a year kind of rich or vacation at Disney World for a week kind of rich?"

Blake didn't smile, he said nothing.

"That joke getting old?" I asked.

But I knew it was something more.

"What's wrong? I asked slowly.

And as horrible as it sounds, though I knew what had happened, I still hoped that maybe someone in his life had died – preferably Neil. I'm not proud of that thought, but it's truly what streaked through my mind in the brief second between me asking Blake what was wrong, and him opening his mouth to speak.

"Did you think I wouldn't find out?"

I chose my next word very carefully. It would be insulting to ask what and to play dumb. It would be stupid to just blurt out the truth. So, I said just one word.

"Shit."

"Neil's an asshole. A shithead through and through" His voice was flat and low. "So you had to know he'd tell me. Hell, I'm surprised he waited. But I get it. He's a successful businessman so I guess he must be able to charm some people. I see it as being a douche bag. But some people must see it as charm. What do you see it as Katie?"

I said nothing. I didn't even move. I just stood statue still, biting on the tip of my thumb, and looking at my love. His hands were trembling but other than that, he seemed amazingly calm. Almost cold. Maybe it was his training to be an attorney. But he almost seemed too calm. In a scary way.

"But I don't blame you for maybe thinking he wouldn't tell me. I blame you for not being honest with me. But that's not my first question I need answered. The first question is: How the hell could you BANG HIM!?"

He screamed out the question so loud that it caused my ears to crackle. His voice bounced off the walls and hit me from my all sides. Still, I said nothing. For what seemed like hours, we just stood in the middle of my living room looking at each other. By the ticking of the clock, I knew it was less than a minute. But it felt like forever.

"Nothing? You've got nothing to say to me?"

"What do you want me to say?" I asked.

"Holy shit Katie!" he yelled. "What do you want to say to me?"

"I'm sorry," I shrugged. "I hate Neil and I hate that I slept with him and I hate myself for it. And I'm sorry."

The tears were streaming down both sides of my face. And the corners of my mouth were pulling downward, beyond my control. But I wasn't quite crying. Not really.

"That's all you got?" Blake asked.

"I'm sorry."

I wanted to say more. I knew I had to. But I couldn't find the right words.

Should I try to explain Neil wasn't the first older man I'd been involved with? Would that make it seem better or worse? But that was the old Katie anyway. I'd changed so much in the last couple of weeks. The new Katie would never cheapen herself.

Or do I tell him that I tried to explain it all to him dozens of times, but I didn't want him to be hurt? And besides I never slept with Neil after we met.

Would it matter what I said?

Blake shook his head violently and walked past me toward the door. I grabbed his arm and he ripped it from my hand.

"Please wait," I said.

"Why? What difference does it make? You're not saying anything because there are no words that can make this better. You slept with my mom's husband." He laughed loudly and put both his hands against his head. "God. Do you hear how horrible those words are? You slept with my mom's husband."

"Just give me a second," I begged. "Just a couple seconds to gather my thoughts."

"What? You don't a have a script all set in your mind? You weren't prepared for this? You didn't think this day would come? What was your plan Katie, to just have a fling with me and keep me in the dark and then when I left brag at the bar that you scored with a son and stepfather combo?"

I shook my head and sat down on the arm of the couch.

"Please. Just be quiet for a second."

He opened his mouth but he stopped. Maybe he saw the desperation plastered across my face. I put my hand on my stomach and for a frantic couple of seconds, I thought I might be sick all over the floor. But I sucked in a deep breath and tried to gather myself. I had to say something. I had to explain myself, even though I knew there was no explanation. I didn't deserve to keep Blake. I deserved every horrible thing he could say to me, and I deserved to lose him.

"Listen, Blake. I'm not sure I have any excuses here. I should have told you. And I shouldn't have ever gotten involved with Neil in the first place. But I do need you to understand that I never meant to hurt you. And I hate all of this. I hate myself for ever getting involved with Neil."

I pushed myself off the arm of the couch and walked closer to him. I realized that all I really could tell him was the truth.

"I haven't made good choices with men in my life. You're the first good choice I've ever made. So, I have been with some pretty big scumbags and yes, I've been with older men besides Neil. In college I had an affair with three of my professors. I hate myself for it. I hated myself while I was doing it. But it happened. And that's the truth. But please, that's not me. It's a distant part of me, but it's not who I am. The real me is the girl you love."

"Loved," he said sharply.

I ignored the word.

"And when I started to get to know Neil, he was charming and rich and took me to nice restaurants and hotels. He made me feel special and that felt good. You know? But I didn't know he was your stepdad until I saw him at the reunion at your house. Before then, he always just said that his wife had 3 boys who were brats. I always just assumed they were children. And by the time I knew the truth, I was already determined to break it off with him anyway. But I had no idea how to tell you."

"Did you ever sleep with him after we got serious?"

It was a fair question.

"No," I shook my head. "Of course not. I never slept with him after I met you. I never saw him in that way after I met you. Never. And I told him it was over. I told him that day."

"And that's why you were in his office when Kendra collapsed? You weren't in there laughing about me or having a quickie while I wasn't looking."

I wrinkled my nose and frowned. "Of course not. He called me back into his office and tried to kiss me but I wouldn't let him. I told him it was over."

"And what did he say?"

"He said if I ended it with him he'd make me pay. He'd tell you and make me pay in some other stupid way too."

"Like what?"

"I have no idea."

"He was probably just bluffing. Or he could get you fired from the bar," he shrugged.

"Yeah. I thought of that. Doesn't matter to me anyway. What matters is losing you."

Blake walked over to my refrigerator and opened the door. He bent down and reached inside.

"You want a beer?" he called over his shoulder.

"Please."

He twisted the cap off both bottles and held one out to me. I walked into the kitchen and grabbed it from him. He leaned against the counter and took a long pull, downing half the bottle in two swallows. I took one sip from mine and waited for him to speak. I prayed the worst was over. If so, it hadn't been bad at all.

But it wasn't finished.

"Did you know he was married when you started the affair?"

"Yes."

"And you knew his wife had kids?"

"Yes."

"Shit."

He stared at the floor and shook his head. Then he looked at me, drank another swallow of beer, and shifted his gaze back down to the floor.

My mind was finally beginning to work again. I sifted back through what I'd said and tried to make sure I'd told him everything. As much as it hurt to tell him, it also felt good. It was like ripping the scab off an infected cut and dumping peroxide all over it.

"What else?" I said softly. "What else do you want to know?"

"I think I already know too much."

"Well ask away. Please ask me. I'll answer anything."

He just took another swallow of beer and shook his head.

"I'm so sorry. I'm sorry for having all my affairs with older, married men, but I'm most sorry for getting involved with Neil."

"Were your professors married men too. Kids?"

"One had a girlfriend and one of them was married with one kid," I answered truthfully.

"But you knew Neil was married to my mom, right?"

"I knew he was married. But I didn't know she was your mom."

"But you knew she was some kid's mom, right? Before you even got involved with him?"

"Yeah."

He slammed back the last of his beer and put it down on the counter. His hands were still shaking.

"Shit," he whispered. "Neil." He shook his head from side to side. "Son-of-a-bitch."

"I'm sorry. I should have told you. But I didn't know how. And I didn't want to mess this up. I've never had anything like this. I've never met anyone that makes me feel like you do. And I didn't want to mess it up."

"And you never even kissed him after we started dating?"

"No," I shook my head.

"He said he kissed you in the office the night of my birthday dinner."

I thought about that night. I could feel Neil's disgusting tongue on my lips, and I could smell the garlic on his breath. But I did not kiss him back.

"No," I said simply. "I didn't kiss him that night or even once after we started dating."

Blake cocked his head and looked at me sideways. He probably noticed how carefully I'd chosen my words.

"Are you lying to me?"

"No."

"But you did lie to me but everything else?"

"I didn't lie."

"Our whole relationship was a lie," Blake said. "Don't you see that?"

He was getting loud again. I could see the anger seeping back into his eyes.

"It's all bullshit. This," he said pointing at me and then himself, "and everything I thought we were. It's bullshit."

"No it's not," I protested. "It's real. All of it. I mean, what happened with Neil is in the past and was in the past once I realized I was falling for you."

"Was that before you took off your clothes and tricked me into screwing you?"

"Don't do that," I said slowly. "Do not cheapen anything that we had."

I could take him attacking me and blaming me and all the rest. But I wouldn't allow him to attack anything that we had. It was too precious - the most valuable thing I'd ever had in my life. Ever.

"You cheapened all of it. It was all crap. Just a fantasy. It wasn't real. Don't you see that?"

"No. No, it wasn't. It was the best thing that ever happened to me."

I hated my voice for breaking on the word *ever*. That word was a hinge that nearly swung me into a crying fit. But I fought to keep it down and mostly succeeded.

"But it was all built on lies," he said sharply.

There wasn't just anger in his eyes anymore. There was hatred too. I saw it when he looked directly at me. I'd never seen him look that way, especially when he looked at me. I didn't know he was capable of such an emotion. But I'd seen it enough from other people. And I knew what it was. At that moment, the man I loved with all my heart, the man who'd changed me and made me believe life could be good, hated me.

"It wasn't a lie. I would never disrespect what we had by calling-."

"You'd never disrespect us?" he shouted back. "Everything you did was-."

"It happened before I knew you!" I shouted back. "Can't you get that? I would have never done it if-."

"I don't get it! And I never will, you slept with Neil! And you slept with me! Aww, he had his hands on you and his dick in you and ah shit." He put both his hands over his eyes and mushed his mouth in such a way that the most beautiful face I'd ever seen actually looked pitiful. "Shit," he said again.

My heart was racing in my chest, but when I saw Blake that way, it broke.

"I'm sorry," I whispered. I moved cautiously toward him. I put my hand on his shoulder and when he didn't shy away, I wrapped my arms around his waist. "I'm sorry. I'm so sorry," I whispered over and over.

He put his arms around me and squeezed tight. I could smell that same fragrance of musk and cinnamon. I felt the heat of his skin radiating through his tee shirt. That awesome comfort spread throughout me. But there was also a chill woven into it. Our embrace wasn't the same, it wasn't the perfection that it had been, but it was still close. Just close enough to make it nearly unbearable.

"I can't get that vision out of my mind," he said softly.

"What?"

"The vision of you naked and him beside you, with his hands on you."

"I'm sorry."

He put his hands on each side of my face and kissed me on the forehead. Then he took in a long pull of air.

"And that's what it all comes down to. That vision. I'll never get over it Katie. Never."

He kept one hand on my face, his hand flat against my check and his thumb under my chin. I looked up at him. He looked so vulnerable and fragile. Yet, there was still a strength underlying everything. It was impossible for him to lose that. And, though I know it was a wildly inappropriate thought at that time, the way he looked and the way he touched my face – like it was the last time he'd ever touch me – it made me want him more than ever. But I stayed still, with my arms wrapped around him and my head tipped back, looking up into his eyes.

"I'm going to miss looking into those eyes," he whispered.

"Then don't let it end."

I put my head against his chest and listened to his heartbeat. I savored the sound and I vowed to always remember it. And to remember the way his body felt against mine. I would remember it all, forever.

I hated the thought of going back to a life without Blake in it. My life was now divided by a river of sorrow. On one side was my life before Blake, and on the other side was my life after meeting Blake. On one side darkness and on the other side bright light. I couldn't go back into the darkness. I wouldn't be thrown back over the water to a life without Blake.

A tear slipped out of my left eye and slid down the length of my chin. Blake drew in a staggered breath and sniffed. He squeezed me tighter and I hugged him as tight as I could. Another tear slid down my cheek. But then I realized its line began on my temple, so it couldn't have come from my eyes.

My whole world was crumbling. Everything. And what made it all worse – a million times worse – was that Blake's world was crumbling too. It was coloring his eyes and painted all over his face. Our mouths were mere inches apart and I had to force my lips to stay away from his. My heart had not yet fully comprehended what was happening and it screamed out for a kiss. And the ignorance of my heart also made my skin yearn to be naked and against his bare skin.

But my mind knew. It didn't want to know, but it did. It clawed for some solution: Maybe go back in time and never start with Neil. Maybe tell Blake that night after the party and hope he understood. Maybe go back and tell Neil I would keep things going with him so he'd never tell Blake the truth.

They were all impossibilities. There were no solutions. The precious gift we shared had been blown-up and there was no putting it back together.

"What choice did I have?" I whispered.

There was a long pause.

"Sometimes one bad decision can take away all good choices," Blake finally whispered back. "I just wish you'd chosen honesty. You know how important honesty is to me. I told you."

And he did tell me. I was a fool not to consider that more.

"Would it have mattered?" I asked.

"It would have saved us a lot of time and heartache."

"I'd choose being with you if I had the choice to make again. I wouldn't trade the time we shared for anything. Including avoiding this moment. I wouldn't trade it."

And the truth was, I wouldn't trade it. Maybe the right thing was to tell Blake as soon as I knew his stepfather was Neil. Maybe it would have saved him and saved us both. But it also would have deprived us of ever knowing and experiencing such a powerful love. It would have meant that I'd never realize that there was such bright light and utter darkness in the world. Instead of having a dark and a light side, my entire life would still be gray. And I would never choose that either.

See? There were no good choices. Blake was absolutely right about that.

"I would trade it," he said to me. "It was just wasted time."

"Not to me."

He let go of me then and walked halfway to the door.

"Is your mom okay?" I asked. "Does she know?"

He turned back to me with a sad smile.

"That's the kicker," Blake said. "Neil called me outside by the pool and told me the news. At first I thought he was full of shit. But then he showed me some texts that you sent him a couple months ago and I was shocked. And then he told me to go in and ask my mom if I still didn't believe him. So I did. And she knew about the whole thing," Blake sort of coughed and laughed at the same time. He rubbed the back of his neck. "She told me I needed to grow up and become an adult. That Neil was good to her and gave her everything she wanted and needed. What did she care if he had other women on the side as long as he never brought anything nasty home to her? That's my mom."

Other women? I'd never even considered that I wasn't the only one. But I should have known. Did he cheat on me while cheating on his wife? Was I just one of many? I doubted it. But I didn't really know. And though the thought of being cheated on while being a part of cheating made me hate myself a little more, it really didn't matter. I truly had no feelings for Neil. Not anymore.

"I'm sorry," I said for what felt like the hundredth time.

"Me too," Blake said, and then he walked to the door and put his hand on the knob.

I wanted to stop him. I wanted to run and tackle him and beg him to stay. I knew it would only make things worse. But I had to say something.

"Don't go, Blake, please. Please just stay and talk a little while longer. Please."

"So that's that," he said still facing away from me. "I'm done with my mom, finally. I'm a slow learner when it comes to her, but I think I'm finally done. She left my dad and three little boys for this life. This life with a cheating, asshole husband who somehow manages to seduce beautiful young women. That's the life she chose over me. But that's who my mom is and always was. That's who Neil is too. That's how they are and always were. I guess I knew it all along. I just had no idea that's how you were too."

I picked up my beer and took a sip. I walked toward him and stopped just a few feet away. There was only a yard stick of space between us, but it might as well have been a canyon.

"That's not true," I said softly. "I need you to understand that may have been a little bit of how I was then, but it's not how I am now. Please understand the difference between who I am right now and who I was then. I know I haven't known you that long but you've changed me. Everything. The way I think and the way I feel and the way I see myself. And even if you walk out that door, that isn't going to change. The girl who screwed Neil is long gone. The girl who fell in love with you, the girl who needs you, is right here."

"And which girl was it that didn't tell me about the affair? Which one was it that slept with me while knowing she also slept with my stepdad? Is there a third girl too?"

"It's all me. But I'm just trying to tell you, that the girl who was willing to cheapen herself in exchange for attention and a good meal, is long gone. She met you and changed into a better person. And I'm standing before you now begging you to understand that I would give anything and everything to have never even known Neil. Because that would mean that we were just hanging out right now and you were spending the night with me and we still had a bright future."

Finally, he turned around and faced me one last time. "It's all bullshit now."

"But it doesn't have to be."

"It doesn't? You tell me how I'm supposed to ever see your naked body or touch your skin and not remember that Neil saw it and touched it first?"

"Because the girl he knew isn't the girl you know."

He seemed to consider that for a few seconds. But then he shook his head.

"So, I'm leaving for Chicago tomorrow. I called and accepted and they told me to come as soon as possible. The sooner I can start the better. So, I'm taking a little puddle jumper to Wilmington tomorrow. I'll stay at a hotel tonight since I'm certainly not ever going back to my mom's house. And then my flight leaves tomorrow at seven ten in the evening. That all makes sense, right?"

"I guess," I shrugged.

"And this," he said pointing back and forth at each of us, "is just a mess. And always has been."

The air stuck in my throat.

"Not to me," I whispered. "But I guess one man's mess is another woman's paradise. Huh?"

He smiled a broken smile. "I guess so."

"And if I go to the airport tomorrow. If I try to stop you once you've had some time to calm down a little? What then?"

"Don't do that," he said. He turned away from me and opened the door. "Don't do that, please. It will just make things even more of a mess. And it will just make it hurt all the more."

And that was it. I opened my mouth to say more, but I couldn't find the right words. I said nothing. I just watched him leave, as if I was viewing it all on a huge movie screen. I watched him until he disappeared, and then I stared at the door forever.

I put the bottle of beer to my lips and drank it all down, still just staring down at the door at the bottom of the stairs, seeing the vision of Blake leaving over and over again.

He's gone. Oh God. I will never see him again. Oh no, no, no! Oh please no!

Then it felt like I split open from my crotch all the way up to my neck. Everything inside of me spilled out onto the floor.

And I lost it.

Chapter Twenty-Two - Then

"I'm so sorry."

"I'm sorry too."

"For what?" he asked me.

"For sleeping with Neil. For not telling you. That was wrong."

"It's fine," Blake said to me. He was smiling wide. "I don't care. It's all okay."

We were floating on a boat in the middle of the ocean. Stars spread over so close that we could almost touch them. The moon was big and bright directly over our heads, shining down like a spotlight on Blake's face.

"Just say you'll never leave me," I whispered to him.

He kissed me on the neck, sending a chill all the way down the right side of my body. Then he pulled me close to him and squeezed tight.

"I'll never leave you. Never."

And then I soared fast out of the dream – like falling except the exact opposite. And when I awoke, for a few desperate seconds, reality nearly choked the life out of me.

Blake was gone.

Gone. Gone. Gone.

I barely slept that night. I mostly just lay in my bed staring at the ceiling. A few times I managed to drift off. But it was never pleasant. It was like sinking down into quicksand. And then I'd dream of Blake for a few minutes, being so grateful that all my sadness and worry was gone. So grateful that everything with him wasn't ruined. And then I'd wake and realize nothing had changed. And only seven more minutes of the endless night had passed.

I got up a little after five in the morning. I threw on a sweatshirt and a pair of old jeans. I walked out my door and down the steps. I thought maybe an early morning walk would do some good. But I only made it as far as the curb in front of my building. I sat down with my feet in the street. The coolness of the cement chilled my butt and spread up into my lower back. It gave me a strange comfort - if only for a few seconds. I looked up at the dark sky and then I put my elbows on my knees and my head in my hands.

Blake's smiling face kept flashing into my mind. His dimples were so glorious. And I could feel his ripped stomach pressing against mine and his breath on my neck. His taste was still on my tongue and his scent was in my nose. He was still with me and I knew he always would be. I didn't know if that was good or bad. I didn't know if the memories were making things better or worse. And I didn't care. I only knew it all hurt like hell.

What was Blake doing at that moment? Was he sleeping? Was he sitting and thinking of me? Had he already begun to move forward and plan his life in Chicago without me? Or was he as torn apart as me? I thought about calling him. But I knew I had no right. He'd made his intentions clear and I was going to respect that.

Eventually the night did turn to day and the street started to get busier. All over people were waking up and going about their day. They had no idea about the earthquake that changed my life the night before. They didn't care. Nothing had changed in their lives. I was alone in my misery. Absolutely alone. While most of the rest of the world was getting ready for and going about their day.

Of course, that included Neil. I knew he was climbing out of bed and getting ready for his day, happy as a pig in shit. He had to know that I hated him, and that Blake did too. But he didn't care. It was never about him caring for me. It was about control. He loved having possession of a twenty-three-year-old who looked good next to him. And when he couldn't control me anymore, he made me pay.

He made Blake pay too.

I'm sure it was a two for one in Neil's mind. And he probably hoped Steven would turn against him too. Then it would kill three birds with one stone. He got his revenge on me, and he'd finally gotten rid of all of his wife's *little brats*. Neil was smart enough to know that this whole thing would not only turn Blake against him, but it would also turn Blake against his own mother. And he was right. Blake was indeed done with his mom too. And that was all my fault, wasn't it? Yes, it was. But it was also Neil's fault.

And I knew Neil expected me to curl into a little ball and roll away. It's what the Katie of a few weeks ago would have done. I would have either begged him to take me back or I would have taken a few days to be a mess and then got up, dusted myself off, and gone out to find a replacement to Neil as soon as possible. That might be another older man, or a guy more my age who would put up with my bullshit and allow me to continue to stumble and trip through my mess of a life. I'd be with a guy who liked seeing me that way, because then I was easier to control. No, not just easier to control, but begging to be controlled.

I wasn't that girl anymore.

Enough of the bullshit. Enough of being a scared little girl who ran, tripped, fell, picked herself up, and did it all over again.

Enough.

Blake was gone. And that hurt. Like cut your nose off with a razor and then plunge your face into a sink full of alcohol kind of hurt. And that pain was going to stay for a long time. Because Blake was gone. Gone for good.

But that didn't mean I had to revert back to the girl from before I ever met Blake. It didn't mean I had to allow myself to be thrown back over that river running through my life, back into the darkness. It wouldn't be easy, but I would move forward.

I had choices and my health. And that was all I needed.

But before I did anything else, I had a little business to tie up.

I got off the curb and stretched my arms to the sky. I ached everywhere, inside and out. The heat of the day was already starting and sweat was running down my back. So, I pulled off my sweatshirt and went back inside to shower. I had about an hour until Neil would be at his office. And in about an hour and a half, I'd be paying him a visit.

∞∞∞∞∞∞

Neil's office was in a large three story brick office building almost in the exact center of town. A credit union occupied the bottom floor, an architectural firm was on the second, and Neil's business was on the third. I pushed my way through the heavy glass doors and smiled big at the two security guards who were sitting at the front desk. I gave them a seventy-five percent chance of escorting me out of the building in about five minutes.

I stepped into the elevator and checked myself in the mirror. I was wearing a pair of jeans and a button-up with the top three buttons undone. Though I didn't feel like it, I'd done my hair and put on make-up. I needed to in order to look good for this face to face with Neil. I had to make him regret losing me. And the practice of doing something I didn't want to do would come in handy. I had a feeling that my life was about to be filled with days of not wanting to get out of bed and not wanting to move forward. But I had to make myself keep moving.

The ding of the elevator told me the fight was on. When the doors slid open I walked right past the receptionist and down the hall toward Neil's office. I'd only been there one time but I remembered the way. It was take a right and then a straight shot to his secretary's desk. Neil's corner office was just to the right of her desk.

"May I help you?" his secretary asked with far too happy a smile on her face.

"I'm here to see Neil please."

"Do you have an appointment?"

"No," I said. "Just tell him Katie is here."

The adrenaline was pumping through my veins. It felt good. The fatigue and the sadness were gone. I knew they would come back, but before they did I was going to ride the wave as long as possible. But to keep it going, I'd have to keep feeding the beast that craved high drama in order to keep the adrenaline flowing in my blood. That was fine with me. I was in a shit-storm-raising, drama-causing mood.

"I'm sorry, he's on a phone conference right now," his secretary said far too cheerfully.

"Oh shit," I said under my breath.

I wasn't about to wait. I spun around and blasted through the door. His secretary was calling after me but I didn't care. Neil wasn't at his desk. He was across the room next to a leather couch, looking out the large picture window talking into his wireless headset. He turned and looked surprised to see me for all of a half a second, and then he smiled and raised one finger toward me.

I wasn't going to wait.

"Hang up," I said to him.

"Miss, you need to wait. Miss you can't just do this," Neil's secretary called out.

Neil tipped his head to the side and frowned at me. Then he raised his eyebrows high and extended his index finger back up in the air. He needed one more minute.

I answered his finger with a finger of my own and strode over to his desk. He turned his back to me and started babbling into his head set. I grabbed his phone, picked up the receiver, and slammed it down. Neil went right on talking. I did it again and still it didn't disconnect his call. So, I started hitting buttons on the phone. Still nothing happened.

What the hell? How do you disconnect a freaking phone call?

I wasn't about to wait or play games. So, I picked up the phone, yanked the cord out of the outlet, and threw it against the wall. Neil spun around when he heard the crash but he still kept on talking. Then he actually turned back away from me again.

What the hell? How did that not work? And what the hell was so great outside that he'd rather look out the window then look at me?

"Miss, you need to leave right now," the secretary was still babbling.

She was standing in the doorway with one hand on her hip and the other against her forehead.

The only possible way Neil could still be on his conference was if it was running through his laptop. So, I slammed the top shut. And when that didn't immediately disconnect him, I picked up the laptop and threw it at the wall. But the cords caught and it only made it as far as the side of the desk. So, I bent down and picked it up to throw it again.

"Hey!" Neil yelled from behind me.

Apparently, I'd finally managed to end his call. But I wasn't done with the laptop anyway. I picked it up and ripped out the power cord. Then I raised the laptop over my head and chucked it as hard as I could at the wall. It hit and bounced back against the floor. A large piece of plastic went skidding away from it and hit the side of my foot. Where it had hit the wall, there was now a hole about the size of a quarter.

There's a two for one asshole.

"Hey! Holy shit Katie," Neil yelled.

"I'm calling the police," his secretary yelped.

I turned and pointed at her. "Good idea, go ahead and call the police. And we can all sit and have a conversation about how your boss likes to screw young women in every way possible." Before I said the words I only had one meaning in mind for that sentence, but as the words flew out, I realized his secretary might find a slightly different meaning that wasn't intended, but was equally true. I didn't stop going though. "And we can talk about how your boss has such a little dick and how he has no idea how to use it. Or do you already know?" I looked her up and down. "How old are you. Late thirties? Maybe early forties? Nah, you're too old for him. I'm sure you are just his secretary."

Her jaw hung open and she stammered over several words before regaining full control of her tongue. "I am calling the police."

"It's okay Martha," Neil said raising his hand in her direction. "It's fine. Katie here is just a little unstable and going through a tough time. No need to call the police or security. Not yet," he said shooting me a warning glare. "Just shut the door and give us a minute. Okay?"

"Are you sure?" his secretary asked.

"Yes," Neil nodded. "This will only take a few minutes. Five at the most."

"Okay." She closed the door as she left.

"Holy shit Katie. I didn't know you had it in you," Neil laughed. "Holy shit. That was an important call too."

"Is this funny to you? Do I look amused?"

"No," he said. "You most certainly do not look amused." He walked toward me. "But I've never seen you look hotter."

He reached up to caress my cheek but I slapped his forearm. The clap was so loud that his secretary had to have heard it through the door.

"Don't you ever touch me again. Ever. We are through. How dare you try to ruin my life, asshole."

He shrugged his shoulders and casually strolled around his desk and sat down in his fat leather chair. None of what I'd done seemed to matter to him. He was so nonchalant about it. But that was okay. It just made me angrier and that anger sent more adrenaline into my blood.

I grabbed a framed picture of him shaking hands with former President Bill Clinton and hurled it down on the floor. Broken glass exploded in every direction.

"That frames replaceable," Neal said casually. "So is the phone and the laptop. It might take a day or so, but I can easily replace all of it. And you're replaceable too. Very easily. In fact, I don't even have to wait a day for your replacement. I already found her and she's going with me to the hotel I originally reserved for us."

That was it. My entire world was suddenly washed in red.

I grabbed the glass paperweight off his deck and threw it against the wall. It hit and actually stuck in the dry wall. Then I grabbed his desk pad and threw it over into his lap. I slapped my hand flat against his desk and swiped my arm to the left and then to the right. Papers and folders went flying in every direction. But I wasn't done.

I stormed over to the couch and hefted the huge fake plant that sat next to it. The glass pot was heavier than I expected but I still managed to pick it up over my shoulder and shot put it at the window. And that's when everything slowed down and I started to think again.

I watched the plant getting ever closer to the window and I saw the next hour or so of my life playing out. The pot crashes through the window and sails down the three floors. If I'm lucky it just crashes on the sidewalk below. If I'm unlucky it hits a car and does some nasty damage. If I'm really unlucky it hits a person and causes some serious injuries. No matter what. The result was not going to be good. And Neil, or his secretary, would call the police and I'd be going to jail.

But it was too late to take it back. The planter drew within inches of the window and I flinched just before it made contact. My eyes were shut when it actually hit. I expected to hear shattering glass followed by more shattering glass and maybe a car horn going off or people screaming. But I heard none of it. There was a whack followed by a thump and that was it. I opened one eye and then the other. Somehow, mercifully, the planter had simply hit the window and bounced off without even cracking the glass.

"Are you done throwing your little hissy fit?" Neil asked me.

The adrenaline that was just so plentiful suddenly hit empty and I was left breathless and exhausted. I bent down and put my hands on my knees, trying to catch my breath.

"Go screw yourself," I gasped, shooting a death glare at him.

"I think we both know I don't have to resort to that."

"You're seriously the biggest prick ever."

He smacked his lips and followed it with a tsk-tsk. "A woman scorned."

I straightened up and looked at him. I used both hands to smooth down my hair that was flying in a thousand different directions. Then I straightened my shirt and took a deep breath.

"I can't believe you told Blake."

"I warned you."

"But I still can't believe you would do that."

"You want to sit for a minute." He pointed at one of the two chairs that sat on the other side of his desk. "You look exhausted."

"No thanks. I'll stand."

Screw him. I needed to sit but I wouldn't give him the satisfaction. And yes, I knew I was cutting off my nose to spite my face. But with all the damage I'd already done to my face, who could really tell? And what did it matter anyway?

"I didn't get this far in life by always being nice," Neil explained to me like I was an eight-year-old child "I'm nice when it suits me and I'm not nice when it suits me. Unfortunately, you made the mistake of believing that somehow I would never turn on you. You foolishly believed I was always going to be that nice guy. But what you didn't understand, and might never understand, is that men are complicated beings. We only show you what we have to show you. And that's all. All you ever saw of me was what I showed you and that wasn't even a fraction of who I am. Not even close."

He was trying to hurt me. And he was trying to trivialize and belittle me too. Though I was tired and heartbroken, I could still recognize it for what it was.

But it was sad if men truly didn't reveal all of themselves. From what I knew most men didn't. But Blake did. Blake gave me all of himself and didn't hold anything back. I almost told Neil that he was wrong, and I almost used Blake as an example. But Neil wasn't worthy of knowing anything about me and Blake.

Still, I wasn't about to let his words go without challenge.

"And that's what's unfortunate about you," I said. "You're completely wrong about people. You only let people see a fraction of you because the rest of you is disgusting. It's rotten and messed up. But don't think for one second that you're the same as everyone else. That's just you. Most people do share themselves. They let others know them fully. It's a shame that you and your pathetic life is so shallow."

He threw his hands up and spread them out almost like he was attempting to fly.

"Does all of this look pathetic to you?"

"No," I answered honestly. My voice was low but strong. "Just you. And no matter what you surround yourself with, no matter who you're next to, you'll always be pathetic."

I turned and started for the door. That was a perfect note to end it on. It was drop the mic and walk away perfect. But before I made the door, Neil stopped me.

"Sorry about you losing your job too," he called to me.

I spun around. Obviously there was a lot about me he didn't know too (including what my relationship – past relationship – with Blake was like). What did he know about my job? Not much. I was quitting it anyway. I could care less if he told Buzz to fire me. Of course, I still had the problem of Buzz stalking me. But again, Neil had no idea about any of that.

Now the problem of Buzz actually got easier since Neil was going to make him fire me. Now I didn't have to quit. Of course, that wouldn't stop Buzz from stalking me. But that was another reason to move forward, out of Dulcet and into a better life. Even though any life without Blake didn't seem like it could be anything other than miserable. I had to at least believe it was possible to improve and grow.

"So what? You're going to make Buzz fire me? Big deal, I can go anywhere and bartend."

"Sure you can go anywhere, but that won't help Buzz."

"What's that supposed to mean?" I asked.

Did Neil know Buzz had some kind of creepy crush on me? Was he somehow a part of it?

"There is no bar anymore."

"What?"

"I'm kicking Buzz out. I'm going to gut it and turn it into a pizza joint. A friend of mine wants to buy it. Though to be fair, it's not directly your fault. I mean, Buzz is more than six months late on rent. And my buddy has been trying to buy it for a few months now. I just let Buzz go and kept telling my friend maybe. So, kicking him out is not as much of a punishment as it is a withdrawl of a favor. Albeit a favor you didn't know I was giving you."

He looked so smug. I considered jumping over his desk and bitch slapping him. But I just stood by the door, glaring at him.

"That doesn't bother me," I lied. "He's been renting that place from you for what, twelve years?"

"Fourteen."

"That's loyalty for you. But Buzz and I don't exactly get along anyway."

"Really?"

"Not lately. I was about to quit working for him anyway," I said confidently. I wasn't lying about that.

"That would explain why the little talk he had with you didn't work."

I was getting sick of this game. Neil was really good at it, and I was really bad.

He'd say something and throw me off with confusion. Then I'd basically have to play the fool and ask him to explain what the hell he meant. It gave him all the power. But I couldn't stop playing.

What the hell did he mean by *the little talk Buzz had with me* not working? Was he talking about Buzz asking me to break-up with Blake? Did Neil know about that?

"What're you talking about? My little talk with Buzz? What talk?"

"The other night. I told him he could save his bar if he convinced you to break-up with Blake. But I made it clear he couldn't tell you I put him up to it."

"Who the hell are you?" I asked. My cheeks grew red-hot and tears welled in my eyes from the anger that boiled inside of me. "Better yet, what the hell are you?"

"Oh come on Katie I warned you."

"But I thought Buzz liked me. I mean, he's been sending me texts. And I assumed-."

"Texts?" Neil interrupted. "He's been sending you texts. What kind of texts?"

"Never mind," I shook my head. I had to get out of there fast or I might seriously try to kill him. "It's not important."

Now a huge smile came across his face. "You mean the texts I was sending you?"

What the hell? He wasn't serious.

"Like the threatening texts? You said that wasn't you."

"Well I lied. That was me."

I balled my hands into fists and dug my fingernails into my palms so hard that I was sure I broke the skin.

"You're a psycho. Stay out of my life. Forever."

I opened the door and started to walk out. But I stopped. I sucked in a deep breath and walked three steps back toward him.

"Understand one thing. You have won this battle like you win so many battles. But they all don't mean a thing. You will lose the war. Because you're married to a woman who obviously doesn't love you. You have a string of affairs with women who don't even like you. They like your money and the food and the hotels. You are just a vehicle for all of them - nothing more than a really talented event planner. And you have no kids and each day that passes you are getting closer to death. And soon you will wake-up and your health will be failing and your dick will be limp and the only people who will be around you will be the ones you pay to be around you. But what do you care? That's no different than now, is it? Right Neil? The only people who are around you are those that you pay to be around you. Think about it. It's true," I laughed. "And soon you will be choking on your last breath and you'll look back on your pathetic life and realize it was all nothing. And you were nothing. And you leave behind nothing. Nothing but money that your widow will gladly spend wining and dining other real men before they even put you in the ground."

I kept my eyes on him just long enough to see the pain flicker in his eyes. I'd hurt him. At least a little. It would have to be enough.

Then I turned and walked to the elevator.

"Have a nice rest of your empty life," I called over my shoulder.

"Not a problem.," he yelled after me. "I will. Right after I file a police report about you trashing my office, Then I'll be through with you for good."

I hit the down button on the elevator. The doors slid open immediately. *Thank God for small favors.* And when the door closed, I kicked the elevator wall. A stabbing pain jumped from my foot all the way up to my hip. That wasn't smart. But I didn't care. I kicked the wall again. And then again and again. I think the elevator stopped on the second floor. I vaguely remember seeing a shocked couple out of the corner of my eye. They were waiting to go down but they didn't even try to get on with me. I just kept on kicking that wall until the doors slid open on the first floor. And then I limped away from the elevator, away from the building, and away from Neil.

Forever.

Chapter Twenty-Three - Then

On the ride home from Neil's office, I went by the bar and noticed Buzz's old pick-up truck sitting by the front door. A large *CLOSED* sign already hung over the bar's sign out front. I had to speak with Buzz and tell him how sorry I was and make sure he was okay. So, I pulled into the driveway and parked next to his truck. Buzz was behind the bar lining all the liquor bottles in a row on the bar top.

"Hey there," I said taking a seat on a bar stool.

"Hey Katie," he smiled at me. "Can I get you a drink?"

"Oh God no," I replied. "I'm not feeling so hot right now. I haven't hardly slept in over a day."

"Coffee then?"

"I'd love a cup."

He went back in his office for a couple minutes. He came back with a white mug filled with coffee and three twenty dollar bills.

"Here's the coffee," he said setting the mug in front of me. He put the money down next to the mug. "And here's some of what I owe you for the final twenty hours you worked. I'll try to get the rest to you before I go to Florida."

"Florida?"

"Yeah, I'll be heading out in a couple weeks. As soon as I get everything wrapped up here."

He sat down on the stool next to me and took in a long, weary breath.

"I don't want this money. It's fine. I'm sure you need it more than me."

"Don't disrespect me. The money is yours. You worked for it and that's the end of it."

I grabbed the thin stack of bills, folded them in half, and stuffed them in my pocket.

"Thank you," I said softly. I took a sip of the coffee. It was hot and strong, almost to the point of tasting burned. I looked at Buzz and tipped my head to the side. "And I'm really sorry about what Neil did to you."

Buzz shrugged his shoulders. "It's okay. I'll be fine. My brother owns a bar down in the Keys and he says he could use some help managing the place. So, I figure I'll head down there and help him out."

"But you love it here in Dulcet."

"I do," he agreed. "I was born and raised here. My daddy worked his entire life on the water and his dream was to own a bar of his own in town. But he died suddenly when he was fifty-two and never got the chance. So, I made sure I lived both of our dreams for the two of us."

Now Buzz was back to the sweet old man I'd known for years. How did I ever see him as a stalker or a creep? It's funny how one wrong thought or a misconstrued conversation can change a person's entire perception of someone else. I felt horrible that I allowed myself to believe Buzz was the one sending me the threatening messages and notes.

"I'm sorry," I said.

"Stop saying that," he told me. "You're gonna make me feel sorry for myself."

I sipped my coffee and licked my lips. "It just sucks that you have to give up your dream."

"Dreams do die hard, Katie. And I'm not going to let this one go. I was able to live it for a while and now I'll just reshape it on my way down to Florida. So eventually that will be living my dream too."

"Just like that?"

He smiled and rubbed his five o'clock shadow, which had turned into more of a three-day shadow.

"Nope, not just like that. I did a lot of drinking and spent a lot of sleepless nights while Neil was threatening to take the bar away. I've never liked that asshole, by the way. And I'm sorry if I ever acted inappropriately toward you while I was drunk. I can be an asshole too."

"That's okay," I said.

"But it was my fault for losing the bar. When business started to slow down, I didn't know what to do. I've never been a great money manager. And one month I couldn't pay rent, and that was my fault. Then one month turned into two and three and so on. It's all my fault."

He looked down at his hands for a while. He looked small and old sitting beside me. I wanted to hug him but I settled for just throwing my arm around his shoulder.

"I thought it was my fault," I said softly.

"Hell no," he rumbled. "You were the only reason Neil let me keep the bar so long. And I'm sorry that I tried to get you to break-up with that young man. I don't know him, but I know Neil hates him so he must be a pretty decent guy. And I know you seem a lot different since you met him."

"Different how?" I asked.

"More confident. Happier. I never understood how someone with so much to live for settled for being with Neil. But hopefully everything will work out for you and Brian."

"It's Blake," I smiled. "And we broke-up last night. Neil told him everything about us having an affair and everything."

"Well get him back," Buzz said.

And he said it so matter-of-factly that I almost believed it might be possible.

I shook my head. "I can't. I shouldn't. It would only make everything more of a mess. Besides he's at a hotel somewhere and then he's going to Chicago this evening." I shook my head and pinched my lips together. "It wouldn't have ever worked anyway."

"So go to the airport then. Or every hotel within a thirty-mile radius."

"Yeah right," I laughed.

"I'm serious. He's worth it, right?"

Of course he was worth it. Buzz was right about that, but he didn't understand everything. He couldn't. I'd do anything to get Blake back. But nothing would work. And deep down I knew Blake was right anyway. Me being with Neil, and Blake knowing about it, would forever be between us. It was a black mark, a deep ugly scar, on our relationship that would never go away. I had to face up to that. The choices I had made before I ever knew a guy as awesome as Blake existed, would forever keep me away from Blake. And though I doubted it, I had to believe that maybe, somehow there was another guy living who was at least close to being as great as Blake. And maybe that guy would almost make me feel as good as Blake made me feel. Maybe. It didn't seem possible, but I had to believe. I had to try to have faith. It was all I had left.

I had to just take the pain of the heartache, and try to move forward in a positive direction. That is what I had to do. Worry about myself, not about me and Blake.

"Well, it's a shame," Buzz said patting my hand. "And I need to get back to getting this place in ship-shape." He slid off his stool and walked toward his office. "But it's not too late Katie. It's never too late, despite what you might think," he called over his shoulder.

"You need some help with anything?"

"Nope. You go on home and get some sleep. You look like shit. No offense."

I laughed. Then I finished the last couple of swallows of my coffee and stepped off the stool.

"Hey Buzz," I called to him.

"Yeah?"

He appeared in the doorway of his office holding a large box against his stomach and chest.

"Did you mean what you said about your dream? About how you can just reshape it and it will still be your dream."

"Of course. It's my dream. Why the hell shouldn't I be allowed to reshape it and still call it my dream? Dreams don't have to be exact and precise. They're dreams not science experiments."

I loved that. And it had never even occurred to me. Although it made perfect sense. Dreams don't have to be precise and exact. I just always believed they did, but I was wrong. As great as those words sounded, they also paralyzed me. There was just so much weight to them. They meant anything was possible. And I could do anything with my life. And they also meant, that maybe relationships that are far from perfect, can still fulfill dreams.

Chapter Twenty-Four - Then

I went back to my apartment and decided to lie down for just a few minutes. I closed my eyes and was out cold. After what could have been ten minutes or ten hours, I awoke to my cell phone buzzing on the table next to me. I looked at the time and the caller ID. I'd been sleeping almost four hours and the number was from an area code I didn't recognize. I pressed *talk* and expected to hear Neil's voice on the other end.

So help me, if he's still messing with me I'll kill him.

"Hello?"

"Katie?"

"Yeah. Ken?"

"Hey."

It was Kendra. I sat up and rubbed the back of my sore neck.

"Hey. How are you?"

"I'm okay. Having a better day today. How are you?"

"A little tired but I'm okay too," I lied. "But how is rehab. How are you?"

"Okay," she said. "But listen, for the first four weeks I only get one phone call a week for five minutes so I need to make this quick."

"Okay."

"Tell Mom I love her and Chris too. Tell them I'm doing well, okay?"

"Okay."

"And tell them I'm really going to do it this time. I really wanna be done with the drinking. I just need to take it a day at a time and I'm going to do it this time. Tell them, okay? And thank Chris again for me."

"I will."

"And I wanted to thank you again too."

"For what?"

"For talking to Chris for me."

"You're welcome," I said. "But I'm just glad you're doing well. You get better. That's the thanks I need."

"I'm going to, I promise."

Something in her voice made her sound lighter. She sounded like she may finally be about to get the monkey off her back. She was hopeful, and almost confident. Maybe she really could make it this time.

"Good," I said to her.

"So how is Stephen? Have you seen him?"

"Not lately. He went back to Virginia a few days ago."

"Is he okay?"

"Yeah," I assured her. "He's fine. You just worry about yourself."

"And what about Blake. Did he choose Chicago or Virginia?"

"Chicago."

"Oh," she said. "Well, are you going too? Because if you don't then you should come out here and live with me. Maybe you can bring Blake with you too. At least for a visit, right?"

"Blake and I broke-up."

"What?" she asked with obvious surprise. "But you guys are so good together."

"Yeah," I agreed.

"What happened?"

"It's a long story. A messy long story. But I don't want to go into now."

"Well make-up with him. Get him back. He's good for you and you're good for him. You guys make a great couple."

"It's really not that easy."

"Yeah, but you deserve to be happy, and he obviously makes you happy. So get him back. He's worth it and so are you."

I thought of what Buzz had said to me a few hours earlier. It was just about the same.

"That seems to be the consensus," I told her.

"Well then just do it. And then – Oh crap," Kendra interrupted herself. "They are giving me the one-minute sign and I called you for a reason. Part of me getting better is being honest about everything and admitting important secrets about my addiction. And I have kind of a weird one to tell you."

My heart started beating a little faster. What secret could she be talking about?

"So that day I collapsed at Stephen's reunion, I had drugs in my system."

I knew it. Oh God Ken, what else are you addicted to? Please make this rehab work or you're going to die.

"But it wasn't really my fault," Kendra continued. "That morning I took a walk and I decided to rest for a couple minutes and then out of nowhere suddenly Marty was beside me."

"Marty? Marty your asshole boyfriend?"

"My ex-boyfriend," she corrected.

"Right. Your ex," I agreed.

"He was acting all weird and he handed me a canteen of water and told me to drink it."

"So you drank it?" I blurted. "Why the hell would you do that?"

"Because he told me to," she answered simply. "Old habits die hard."

I didn't understand it, but I knew it made sense to her. And that was enough for me to accept it as a reason, or at least an excuse.

"There must have been something in the water," she continued. "I mean I know there was. Because I didn't take any drugs."

An alarm went off deep in my mind, but I ignored it.

I remembered sitting on that hospital bed beside Kendra when she told me she had to get out of Dulcet. I remembered how scared and desperate she seemed. It all made sense now. She was terrified of Marty.

"Do you think he tried to kill you?"

"I don't know. I can't say for sure. But he's a psycho, Katie. Like serial killer crazy. That's one of the reasons I wanted to come here. To get away from him. And I should have told you before I left. He was there in Dulcet."

I shivered as a chill rolled down my back.

"Is he still?" I asked.

"I have no idea. Probably not. But I had to tell you about the whole thing. I'm sorry, but I didn't drink and I didn't take the drugs willingly. But I need this help I'm getting here. Okay? I need this so badly. But I didn't let you down, not really, okay?"

"Okay."

"And I'm over my time. So, I love you. Tell Mom I'll call her next week. Love you."

"Love you too."

The phone clicked in my ear. I set my cell phone down and stretched my back and neck. It was great to hear from Kendra, and a huge relief to hear she was doing well. And there was something in her voice that gave me so much hope for her. What was it? Optimism? Confidence? Both? Yes, for the first time in a long time, I felt as if Kendra was really going to beat her addiction. I knew it.

I stared down at the floor and thought about Blake. I thought about what Buzz had said, and about what Kendra said too. They made it sound like I should do anything to get Blake back. But they didn't understand. What ruined me and Blake was an all-time deal breaker. It was the atom bomb of weapons that destroyed relationships.

It made me sick to admit it. It made me want to scream until my voice was dead. It made me want to jump in the middle of the ocean and sink down and never come back up. But Blake and I were done forever.

But at least Kendra was getting better and at least I'd gotten rid of Neil.

So it was the best of times and the worst of times for me. But I really needed a shower. So, I went to my bedroom, grabbed a change of clothes and went into the bathroom.

Poor Kendra. All this time everyone was thinking that she fell off the wagon and drank and took drugs. But none of it was her fault. Granted, she was stupid to drink anything Marty gave her, but stupidity didn't mean she deserved to die.

Did he mean to kill her? He must've, right?

Again, a warning alarm blared deep inside my head. But I was sure it didn't mean anything. I was just tired and stressed and unbelievably sad.

But Marty had been in Dulcet and Kendra said he was a psycho. Did I need to be scared about that? I didn't think so. He was probably long gone. And besides, he had no idea where to find me.

I shampooed my hair and washed my entire body. Then I let the water hit my face for a while. The warmth soothed me and allowed the fatigue to really take hold.

And then I was struck with a memory of Blake: He was walking along the beach, mere seconds after he saved my life. And I ran into his arms and then we made love right there on the beach. I felt him on me and in me and all around me. I smelled the sand and rainwater in his hair, I tasted the salt water on his skin.

I would never see him again. I'd never be in his arms again. And I'd never make love with him again. Never… ever… again.

I put my head against the side of the shower and balanced myself with both hands. The thought of *never* made me want to puke. And for several desperate seconds. I fought to keep Buzz's coffee from coming up. I wretched once – doubled over, mouth wide open, staring at the tub drain - and then let loose with a couple whimpers. I stayed that way for a long time, allowing the pain to ebb and flow.

And then I thought that maybe I should try to get him back. Maybe there was still a chance.

In the movies I would go to the airport and stop him just before he got on the plane. He'd turn to me and show those glorious dimples and I'd run into his arms as the credits started to roll. But after the credits rolled, the truth would still be there. I had an affair with his stepdad.

I could probably figure out a way to get past that. I meant it when I told Blake that the girl who had the affair was not the same person I am now. That girl was sad and lonely and weak. That girl slowly went away after I first met Blake. And now I was a different person. So, I could probably get past the affair and forget about it.

But it was a bigger deal for Blake. That was obvious. And the chances of him getting past it were slim to none.

It was a huge deal for him. And rightfully so.

So, no, I wasn't going to go after him. Why create a big messy scene and just make things worse? Why rip both of our wounds wide open and pour pounds of salt into them?

No, I couldn't go after him. I wouldn't. (Although, just the chance of getting him back did cause a spark of hope to flicker in my heart.)

But I couldn't and I wouldn't.

I got out of the shower and dried my hair. Then I put it back in a ponytail and got dressed. Another pang of desperation hit me as I walked out of the bathroom. Blake was gone and I was all alone. He was gone forever. It didn't seem possible. It couldn't be real. But it was. And I had to deal with it.

I gave myself a couple minutes to feel the hurt. I leaned against the bathroom door jam and took a few seconds to cry. I put my face in a bath towel to catch my tears. And then I saw him lying next to me naked, I felt the heat of his skin, I heard his whisper in the dark.

I missed him so much. I thought I might actually die from the heartache.

That's when I heard the soft knock at the door. It couldn't be him, could it?

Yet, my heart had hope. Maybe Blake had decided to come back. Maybe, despite everything, he'd decided he couldn't live without me either.

I threw the towel on the bathroom counter and splashed cold water on my face. My cheeks were still too red, but there was no real evidence that I'd been crying. I straightened-up, drew in a deep breath, and checked my hair. Then I walked for the door.

Stay calm. It might not be him. It probably isn't.

But it could be. Blake. My love. Might be waiting right on the other side of the door.

Just before I got to the door, I noticed yet another sheet of paper on the floor.

I picked it up and read it:

I'm here.

It's time.

Neil. That bastard.

Why the hell was he still harassing me? Hadn't I already done enough damage to his office? Hadn't he already done enough damage to my life?

I swung the door open, ready to give him a piece of my mind.

But it wasn't Neil.

It wasn't Blake either.

And then, in a split second, everything clicked into place:

Neil confessed to writing the texts, but never said anything about leaving notes. Marty was back in town and Kendra said he was a psycho.

All those messages that had been slid under my door and left on my car, they were from Marty.

I looked up into his eyes, and I saw how blank they looked. The alarm that had been far away in the back of my mind came racing forward. It was suddenly so loud that I heard nothing else. I couldn't even hear what he was saying. But I read his lips. They formed the words: Are you ready to die?

I grabbed the door and tried to slam it shut. Then I'd lock it, grab my cell phone, lock myself in the bathroom, and call nine-one-one. But before I could move the door more than two feet, Marty stepped forward and stopped it with his foot and shoulder. I let out a quick scream as I took off for the bathroom. He grabbed a fistful of my shirt and I jerked backward. But his grip wasn't strong enough and I broke free.

"Come 'ere!" he growled as I made it into the bathroom and slammed the door shut.

I locked the doorknob and suddenly realized I didn't have my phone. I looked around the bathroom for a weapon, anything I could use to defend myself. But all I saw was the window. Even though I was on the second floor, I could shimmy out and hang down and then drop to the ground. I might twist an ankle or break a leg but that was nothing compared to what would happen to me if I stayed in that bathroom.

I made it halfway to the window. Then the door crashed inward. I screamed without bothering to look back. I darted to the window and reached up for the latch to unlock it. I flicked the lock off, but when I reached for the bottom of the window, my arms got tangled in the blinds. That's when Marty grabbed me around the waist and pulled me back away from the window.

I screamed and kicked backward. I felt my heel make solid contact with the side of his knee and he yelled out in pain. He let go of me just long enough for me to scramble back to the window. But I had no time to try to get out. To try would be foolish. So, I turned and faced him. I had absolutely no time to gather my thoughts or to figure out how I might defend myself against this monster.

He lunged at me and swung his fist around in a big looping arc. I saw it coming and ducked down. It flew over my head and crashed through the window behind me. As he screamed out in pain, a huge shard of glass fell at my feet and I saw my chance to really hurt him. I reached down with my left hand to pick it up and jam it deep into his belly, or better yet, his neck. But that's when I felt his hand in my hair. Then my head flew to the left and carried the rest of my body with it. The side of my head bashed into the wall. A flash of light filled my vision, and then everything turned off.

Chapter Twenty-Five - Then

I'm wearing a white sundress dress that hugs my curves and stops just above my knees. I'm walking slowly through a field of sunflowers. The air smells wonderful. The sunlight on my shoulders is so warm and perfect.

I stop and Neil stands up in front of me. He is wearing a nice suit that's jet black. His tie is blood red.

He's just looking at me in my white dress and shaking his head. I know he's judging me. I can feel the disapproving weight of his eyes pushing against me. He doesn't think I should be wearing white. He doesn't think I should be allowed to stand in the sunlight. He prefers I wear darker colors and stay in the shadows. I used to agree with him, but not anymore.

And just like that he's gone and in his place stands Blake. He's smiling, showing me those gloriously hot dimples. And I know he approves of, and even admires, my white dress. He's fine with me standing in the sunlight too. And he will stand in the sunlight with me, and enjoy the comforting warmth.

I open my mouth to speak. To maybe say "hello" or maybe "I'm sorry". But before I get one word out, he's gone. He vanishes just like that – poof – into thin air. I wait for him to reappear but he doesn't. And maybe that's okay. Maybe I can stand in my white dress, in the middle of a sun-soaked sunflower field, and be happy anyway.

And then I feel something breathing on the back of my neck. Someone or something is right behind me. I turn to see and BAM! Marty opens his mouth as wide as a crocodile and roars at me.

I opened my eyes and saw nothing but blackness at first. And then slowly the black billowed to the edge of my vision. It stayed there, like black fog, as I looked around my living room. I was sitting on one of my kitchen chairs, my legs duct taped to the chair legs and my hands duct taped together and sitting in my lap. Marty was sitting on the couch about five feet in front of me.

"Have a nice nap?" he asked with a smile.

I blinked several times trying to clear my vision as well as stop my eyes from being so sensitive to the light. There was a dull throbbing pain on the left side of my head. A horrible stench – a sickening sweet shit smell – was in my nose. I wondered what the hell it could be before I realized the obvious – it was him. The skin on his hands and face had a layer of light black grime, but they were cleaner than his clothes.

"Wonder what I'm doing here?" he asked taking a sip from a nearly empty bottle of beer.

I didn't speak. I didn't want to say the wrong thing. And I feared how scared my voice would sound if I did talk. Because I was in a shitload of trouble. I could barely move and I was alone with this psycho who obviously wanted to do me harm.

What the hell is he going to do to me? Is he going to beat me up? Rape me? Kill me?

All three?

That thought turned my stomach. My mind crept a little too far and actually imagined the smell of his hot bitter breath, and the feel of his scaly skin.

I glanced over at the clock on the wall to my right – it was almost seven o'clock. The office downstairs had long since closed. Screaming probably would do me no good. But were they still there when Marty first showed up? Could they have heard my screams or the window breaking? It didn't seem like it. The police would've already showed up.

"So what, you've got nothing to say now? But you had so much to say when you talked Kendra out of loving me and into leaving me. So, what now bitch? Cat got yer tongue?"

Still I didn't speak. I looked down at my hands and they were jumping up and down in my lap. I looked at him and he saw them too.

He grinned wide, revealing two missing teeth from the top of the left side of his mouth. I pressed my hands hard into my legs, and they mostly stopped their bouncing.

"Are you scared Katie? Scared that I might hit you?"

He finished the beer and set it down on the coffee table, beside two other empties. He'd just been sitting there, drinking the beer Blake had bought, watching me. For all this time.

My throat felt like sandpaper as I swallowed down a mouth full of saliva.

"Are you going to hurt me?" I whispered.

"Of course," he said nonchalantly. "You caused me to lose Kendra. You stuck your nose in where it didn't belong. So now I'm going to take it out on you."

"But why? I had nothing to do with Kendra leaving you. I just gave her a ride from the bar that night. And she's in a better place now, getting well. Don't you want her to be well?"

"No. I want her with me. I love her. She makes me see the world as a better place, and I need that. Without her none of this bullshit life is worth the energy it takes to breathe. Don't you understand that? What I had with Kendra was special. It's probably a little like what you had with that asshole guy who sucker-punched me at the bar that night. I saw the two of you at the park and I saw him here visiting you. And I was going to kill him too. But I decided against it. So, you should thank me for that."

"His name is Blake," I said. "And he'll be here any minute."

He looked at me for more than a minute. Then he shook his head and clicked his tongue.

"You're lying to me. You're just like Kendra. You have this little tell on the side of your mouth When you're lying a crack appears in your cheek. Right there next to the corner of your lips."

Of course he was right. Right then Blake was probably waiting to board a plane at the airport. He was about to fly away from this town and fly away from me.

"So what's the plan then?" I asked cautiously.

"I haven't quite figured it out yet."

"Really?"

"I know I'm gonna kill ya. And I know I'm probably gonna kill myself. Maybe."

I tried to look calm. But my chin started bouncing and my hands went back to shaking violently too, despite pressing them into my legs as hard as I could. And when I pressed too hard, my shoulders started shaking too. So, I just let my hands do what they wanted. They bounced like popcorn in my lap.

My mind raced to try and find a solution to the problem. The tape on my hands was as tight as could be. It was crushing my wrists together and causing the tips of my fingers to tingle. There was no way I was going to get it loose. But it felt like the tape on my legs was loosening. I could pick my legs up ever so slightly and the tape would give a little bit. I did this several times while speaking to Marty.

I didn't really have any hope that I could talk him out of killing me. He was a psychopath and from what I'd seen from him and known of him, he was just plain a nasty dude. So, I doubted I could try to play on his conscience or try to find some kind of common ground we shared so that maybe he'd see I was worth not killing. But I had to try something.

"It's never too late to start over," I said.

"Start over? You mean my life or with Kendra?"

"Your life."

"Without Kendra I have no life."

"That's not true."

"I'm good for Kendra. If you weren't such a stupid and stuck-up bitch then you would know that."

I looked down at my hands and then back up at him.

"I think maybe you need to get yourself well and then maybe you will have a shot with Kendra."

"Then how about you tell me where she is."

"She's gone getting help."

"Well, she'll hear about this. She'll hear about me killing her sister and then myself, all because she left me."

"Listen, you can walk out of here right now and I won't tell anyone. In fact, I'll give you the keys to my car and you can just take it. Wherever you want. Okay?"

"Your shitty car?" he smiled. "That piece of crap wouldn't get me out of the state. Did you know I almost killed you that night you broke down on the side of the road?"

I'd been stranded by my car many times, but I knew what night he was talking about. It was the night he left the message on my car and then I broke down not far from the bar.

"I just happened to be walking down the street, away from the bar. You passed right by me. And then you broke down about a quarter of a mile up the road. I was going to just slit your throat and walk away. That would have been nice and clean. But far less dramatic. And then your boy showed up and I decided it was actually for the best. I think it's best if Kendra knows I was the one who killed her sis."

"And did you try to kill Kendra with whatever drug you gave her?"

"She told you about that? Wow, you girls sure do talk."

I kept working my legs up and down. The movements were so small that I doubted he could see what I was doing. But it was beginning to work. The tape was loosening.

"She told me. And she said it scared her."

"Yeah, well, I wasn't trying to kill her. I was hoping she'd pass out and I could just take her away somewhere with me. I was in the bushes waiting for her to just drop. But I guess the drug didn't work like I thought it would. And then that other prick came and picked her up."

"You almost killed her."

He shrugged his shoulders.

"We're all going to die eventually. Leaving this shitty world is actually a good thing. I know that now. I can't wait to be free of all this bullshit."

"Maybe you just need some help. I can drive you to the hospital or to a rehab facility. You can use my shower right now and clean up and then we can go buy you some new clothes and get you to a place where you can finally get some help."

"Get some help. There is no help for me. Kendra made me feel better. She was all that made me feel better. And you ruined all of that."

"You were hurting her. I couldn't allow her to be in an abusive relationship. It really had nothing to do with you. I just didn't want her to be hurt."

"I told her I was sorry for hitting her. I was always sorry. And she knew it. She understood. But you put other thoughts in her head. Did you threaten her and force her to leave with you? Did you force her to leave me?"

I could tell from the expectant look on his face that this was a very important question to him. And the answer was even more important. But I had no idea what kind of an answer he was looking for.

"She didn't want to leave with me."

"I knew it," he blurted slapping his hand hard against his leg.

"Not at first. But I convinced her."

"You confused her."

"Maybe," I whispered.

He was getting agitated and I wondered if that was why he hadn't already killed me. Did he think that maybe Kendra still wanted to be with him? Did he want to make sure before he killed me? Maybe. And if that was the case then maybe I still had a chance to talk him into sparing me.

"Yeah. Maybe I did confuse her. And maybe I was wrong about you."

His eyebrows rose on his forehead. "What do you mean?"

"Kendra does love you. I know she does. And I think you guys would make a great couple. But you both have to get sober. In fact, that's Kendra's plan. She went to Upstate New York to get sober and then she's going to find you and convince you to get well so the two of you can be together and happy."

He was listening closely to my words with a trace of a smile on his lips. His eyes were beginning to show a new light. So I kept on going.

"So, let's get you some help and forget all about this. You can still be with Kendra. You can. So, please, please don't give up. Don't give up on yourself and don't give up on Kendra. Please just take off the tape and let's start by getting you a shower and then into a good rehab facility."

"I can't afford it. Good rehabs are only for rich assholes."

"I can talk to my parents. They might help you pay."

As soon as I said that, I regretted it. What if he decided to kill me and then go to Mom and Chris's house? And that fear increased as Marty pulled himself off the couch and strolled into the kitchen. He started going through my drawers, leaving each one open as he went to the next. I feared what he might be looking for. And when he came back toward me holding an eight-inch butcher knife down at his side, my fears were confirmed.

"You stupid bitches," he mumbled. "Yer all the same. Liars."

The look in his eyes had changed. He now had the look of a killer. His eyes were glossed over with ice and the frame of his jaw was set in a way that can only be described as determined evil.

"You don't have to do this," I stammered. "Please. Please you don't have to do this."

Everything was suddenly moving at warp speed. Before I could get out another word, he was behind me yanking my hair down, exposing my neck. I raised my hands up to try to protect my throat. And just as he brought the knife around to slit my throat, I kicked my legs forward, hoping I'd loosened the tape enough to break free.

I hadn't. The tape held my legs to the chair.

But the force of my kicking thrusted me back into him. It must have surprised him. Because we both went tumbling down to the floor – me in the chair, and the chair on top of him.

I kicked my feet back and forth like I was trying to pedal an imaginary bike. And I flailed with my arms in all directions. Marty pushed the chair over and as I rolled, the tape on my right leg caught on the corner of my coffee table. That created enough space for me to pull my right leg free. I saw Marty coming at me and I kicked at him with my free leg. He caught my foot with his empty hand and twisted and spun me around. I flipped over and landed on my back, facing up at him. Marty charged at me and I kicked out with all my strength and planted my foot deep into his crotch.

He let out a deep whimper and doubled over. I kicked at him twice more, the first barely grazing the side of his head and the second landing firmly in the center of his face. I felt his nose smoosh beneath my foot. He tipped to the right and then fell down onto one knee. Blood poured down his face onto the front of his shirt.

If I had any chance to survive, I had to get my other leg free, and my hands too. So I bit at the tape around my wrists. And with my free foot, I pushed the tape around my left ankle down while trying to pull my left leg up and out. Marty got back to his feet just as my leg pulled free. I bit and ripped with my teeth, but the tape held strong. I'd have to try to get away with my hands still bound. I had no more time.

I rolled away from Marty as he clutched and waved at the air trying to grab me. The blow to his nose had blurred his vision. He couldn't see. At least for a few seconds.

I stood up and faced him. Could I make the door and unlock it before he got to me? Before his eyesight returned? I didn't think so. My only choice was to fight.

I grabbed the lamp off the end table with both hands and swung it at Marty. He managed to deflect it downward and away from himself. So, I swung it back up at him and nailed him on the side of his face. He screamed out in anger and pain. And then he sprung at me cutting down through the air with his knife. I swung the lamp again and hit his hand, sending the knife flying across the room. But he kept coming. One last time I tried to hit him with the lamp, but he was too close to me. He knocked the lamp from my grip and grabbed a hand full of my hair. The world spun around as my feet left the ground, and I crashed into the wall, right next to the door

Unlock it and get out! Then run! Run! Run!

But before I could even get to my feet, he was over me. He grabbed me around the neck and pulled me up to my feet. I could smell the alcohol and nicotine on his breath as the sickening warmth blew against my lips and nose. He leaned into me with all his strength, choking the life out of me.

I beat against his chest with my bound hands. And then I pressed up against his chin. But it did no good. He was too close for me to get any momentum behind any hitting or pushing that might actually affect him. My strength was leaving me anyways. I felt like a sick old lady.

And with my strength, my life was leaving me too.

I tried to suck in air but it was like everything above my neck was no longer a part of my body. My mouth hung wide open and would not breathe in. My eyes were popping out of their sockets and they would not shut. Explosions of light – a lot like bright yellow fireworks – popped in my vision and left behind shadows where the light had exploded.

I pushed against his chest. I clawed at his neck and face, raking lines in his flesh and collecting his skin beneath my fingernails. But it did no good. He only pressed harder and tighter.

I was dying.

This had become a theme with me lately. But this time, it was actually going to happen. I was going to die. And after the initial panic subsided, it really wasn't that bad. The pain slid to the back of my mind and I felt myself floating away. My eyes were watching Marty as he continued to apply more and more pressure against my neck. I refused to allow him to be the last sight I ever saw. So, I slid my eyelids closed. And there was Blake.

There was nothing but him. And me. And a powerful and perfect love.

I hardly noticed the door crashing in beside me. And I didn't feel the floor as I crashed down onto my side. I gulped so hard that I thought my chest would explode. I tried to suck in but no air entered my lungs. All that entered my body was the quick rush of panic and fear. That ran back into me like a runaway train. Another suck of air, and nothing. My chest felt like a heavy wooden chest that was closed. It was locked and wouldn't open. I sucked in again, and I coughed, and sucked and coughed a couple more times. Finally, air - precious air - found its way through my lungs.

I don't know if there was a fight raging beside me while I was struggling for air. I only know, that when I'd finally recovered enough to see more than six inches from face, I saw Marty lying on his back. He was completely still.

I sat up against the wall and tried to collect my thoughts. What the hell had just happened? When a hand touched my shoulder, I jumped and banged the back of my head against the wall. When a second hand came down on my other shoulder, I slapped it away.

I had to get out of there. I had to get to the airport. I had to see Blake.

Blake.

My Blake.

My life.

A face appeared in front of me and I tried to focus in on the features.

"Hey, Katie? It's okay. It's okay now," a voice called out to me from miles away.

I shook my head back and forth, trying to snap my senses back into place. But I still couldn't focus. I felt my hands drop away from each other as something cut them loose. Then someone peeled the tape off my wrists.

"It's alright. It's going to be alright."

The voice zoomed from a long way off and suddenly connected itself to the mouth that was moving mere inches from me.

"Bl-Blake?" I stammered. "My God, Blake."

I saw him right in front of me. I reached up and stroked his cheek with my hand. But something was wrong.

"Who's Blake?' the voice asked me.

Finally, I was able to focus on the face. It wasn't Blake. It was someone I knew. Yet I couldn't place it. The eyes though. The eyes were so familiar.

"I have to go," I said.

And I did have to go. If I didn't get out of that apartment, I was going to explode all over the walls.

I struggled to get to my feet. The man grabbed my arm, pulled me into a standing position, and held my waist until I was steady. Out of the corner of my eye I saw a bright red pool of blood slowly expanding around Marty's head. The world swirled again, but only for a few seconds.

"Just take it slow. Take it easy," the man said.

His eyes were so familiar and his voice too. Maybe it was a little rougher, but there was something about the rhythm of his words and the timber of his voice. It was painfully familiar.

"I have to go," I said.

Something in me had snapped and I had to get to Blake. I didn't have a choice and it didn't matter what he would say or do. I just had to get to the airport. I had to see Blake. And I had to stop him from going to Chicago. Hell, maybe I'd go to Chicago with him.

I bounced off the doorway and nearly fell down the stairs. But somehow, miraculously, I kept my balance long enough to make it all the way down the steps and outside.

I don't remember going to my car or starting it or even beginning the drive to the airport. I was so loopy that my mind would not work.

Yet, I somehow I managed to keep thinking the same two thoughts over and over:

    I had to get to Blake.

    And I loved him more than anything could ever be loved.

Chapter Twenty-Six - Now

"So you just got up and ran out of your apartment?' the detective asks me.

"Yes."

"You didn't think about calling for help? I mean, there was a man lying on your floor. You didn't feel the need to try to help him?"

"Marty?"

I can't even say his name without feeling sick to my stomach.

"Yes. And the man who helped you. You just ran away without even thanking him or finding out who he was?"

Looking at it now, it does seem odd that I ran out like that. But at the time, it's what I had to do. I wasn't thinking clearly, obviously. But that wasn't a crime, right? I mean, the detective wasn't actually going to try to get me for leaving the scene of an assault or something, was he?

"Yes," I answer.

I'm looking at the table, seeing myself running away from the apartment to my car. I'm seeing the man who helped me. His eyes were so familiar to me. Could it possibly have been who I think it might have been?

"Does that seem strange to you?"

"Yes it does," I answer honestly. "But I wasn't thinking clearly. And I was terrified. I just had to get out of there. I had to try to stop Blake from getting on the plane. I don't know. That's what my mind jumped to. It's what I had to do."

"Well," he shrugs his shoulders and forms an upside down smile with his lips. "You were under a lot of stress and everyone reacts differently. And you were knocked out too. And then your brain was deprived of oxygen while you were being strangled. So that had to make your mind a little foggy. And both of those things are why you had a tough time remembering everything when you first came in here. It also might be why you didn't recognize that man who helped you. You have no idea who he was?"

I have an idea who that man could be. But I don't want to think about it. It would be another heavy weight to add onto a mind that's already about to collapse.

I shake my head and look away from the table, up at the detective.

"Is Marty dead?" I ask.

Because even though I don't want to know the answer, I need to hear it.

"Yes."

And I feel a horrible, sickly relief. He's dead. He won't be bothering Kendra anymore. He won't get the chance to harass or harm anyone else, including my mom and Chris. He won't be stalking me either. That's good news.

But he was still a human being. He had hopes and dreams. He was once a wide-eyed child just like everyone else. He watched cartoons and sang nursery rhymes. And now he's dead. Gone. And I was there when it all happened.

I cup my hand over my mouth and nod my head.

"I'm sorry."

"And when you got to the airport?'

"His plane was long gone. I missed it. Blake's gone."

"And that's it? Nothing else to tell me?"

"That's it," I reply.

He stands up as I keep my eyes locked on his face. Although I don't want to be sure who killed Marty, I am tempted to ask him. Is he going to tell me?

"I'll be right back. I need to check on one other thing and then we'll get you out of here."

"You're letting me go?"

He nods and smiles. It's a warm, genuine smile. I think.

"I don't see any reason to keep you here. You didn't do anything wrong. Well, leaving the scene wasn't smart. But it's understandable. I just need to speak with my lieutenant and another detective. My lieutenant might want to make a phone call, to the DA maybe, but then I'm 99% sure you'll be free to go. Do you a place to stay tonight? You probably won't be able to get back in your apartment until at least tomorrow afternoon. We need to make sure we get it all processed."

"I'll find a place. That's no problem."

I'm thinking I may never go back there anyway.

The detective turns to leave but I stop him.

"Detective?" He turns back to me. "Can I ask you a question?"

"Sure."

"Was that man my father?"

He gives one single nod. "Yes it was."

My heart feels like it's about to jump out of my chest. I can't process that information fully. I can't process any of it. And suddenly I feel nothing. My mind is overloaded and hardly anything is getting in or coming out. In the next five minutes I may be completely insane. It's a real possibility.

"Are you okay?" the detective asks.

"Not really."

"It's all a lot."

He comes back to the table and puts his hand on my shoulder. I fight the urge to wrap my arms around him and squeeze with all my might. I need to hug and be hugged. I need to feel some connection to someone. Because I'm feeling myself drift away. I feel completely alone.

"I'll be right back," the detective tells me. And then he walks out.

Something shifts inside of me and suddenly I feel like I am slightly above my own body. I'm higher and about six inches to the right. It's the strangest sensation ever. I am no longer inside my own body. That's me, down there several inches away. I am something else, up here apart from myself. And it feels okay. It feels numb. So that's actually better than okay.

The door opens and the detective walks in. He slides a business card across the table.

"That's my card. If you have any questions at all, or any concerns, please don't hesitate to call me. And on the back I wrote the number of the County Mental Health Department. You can call them and set-up an appointment to speak with a counselor. And they have someone available to talk to twenty-four hours a day too."

Maybe I do need help. A lot of freaking help.

Or maybe I just need to get to Chicago as quickly as possible.

Blake's plane has probably landed by now. He's probably already beginning his new life. Is he missing me like I'm missing him? Or am I nothing more than a memory he wishes he could forget?

"Okay," I whisper at the detective.

The ocean isn't far away. I can drive there in about ten minutes. And I'm sure the waves are rolling to the shore and back away. I'm sure the water's cold, but it will still welcome me.

"Your father is here and he'd like to have a minute with you. Just a minute. If that's okay?"

I snap back into myself. I'm no longer me and something else slightly up and apart. I'm whole again.

"He's here?" I ask.

"Yes."

"Is he in trouble?"

"No. His story matches yours and he stayed and called the police. He's not in trouble either. In fact, he obviously saved your life. I actually knew your dad years ago. I used to work with him."

"Really?"

"Can I tell him it's okay to see you? It's completely up to you."

I don't know how to answer that question. I want to see my father. Of course I do. And yet, I don't want to see him ever again. I love him. I hate him. I want to hug him and I want to beat the hell out of him.

"Okay," I whisper.

Because why not? This is already the worst day of my life. It will never be topped, even if I live another seventy years. But I would be willing to bet a day like this would top the charts of just about anyone who ever lived. So, why not see my dad? This day can only get better, right?

I put my head down on the desk and close my eyes:

Blake is beside me holding my hand. He's on top of me with his hands in my hair. He is smiling showing his dimples as the sun sets over his shoulder.

The door opens and in he walks. I don't know what to do so I don't move. I just look him up and down, partially trying to commit him to memory and partially trying to remember old memories. He looks like he is about to cry and that makes me want to cry. I hate that.

"Hello Katie," he says to me.

And I do recognize his voice. But not in a way that I would ever match it to my father. It's more in a way that unleashes a warm comfort that travels up my spine. I hate that too.

I hate all of this and I'm already regretting telling the detective I wanted to see this man. This man who was once my daddy and then decided not to be.

"How are you?" he asks.

I laugh a quick laugh and pull on my ear lobe.

"I've been better," I say.

"They said you're okay though, right?"

"Well if they said it then I guess it's true."

"May I sit? Just for a minute?"

His voice is softened around the edges now. And he sounds so polite. But I still remember how his words were so brutal and sharp that they cut my mom down. I don't remember much, but I remember that. And he is still the man who left all of us. He left us when we needed him most.

"Just for a minute," I tell him. "I really want to get out of here."

He sits across from me and doesn't speak for several seconds. He just stares at my face. I stare back at him. It is so surreal. I have to keep reminding myself that I'm not looking at a picture or watching a movie. I'm not dreaming either. This is real. My father is sitting in front of me. And my father saved my life.

My dad took my life from me and now he saved it. But it could be argued: If Dad had never left and stayed away for so long, then I'm pretty sure I would have never been in that apartment. I'm even more sure that Kendra wouldn't have become an alcoholic, would never have been in rehab, and would never have met Martin. So, my dad was the reason I needed saving in the first place. Excuse me if I don't feel particularly grateful.

"You are a beautiful woman. You still have the same eyes as the little girl I knew."

His voice cracks on the last few words. He bites on the tip of his thumb.

I fight hard not to bite on the tip of my own thumb. And I swear, I'll never do it again. Not after seeing that it was his first.

"Thanks. I guess," I say to him.

"I'm sorry," he whispers to me. "I know I missed so many years of your life. And I know it wasn't easy on you or your sister or your mom. And there isn't a day that goes by that I don't regret it. And I know *sorry* doesn't make up for anything, but I want you to know that leaving you and your sister was the biggest mistake of my life."

His words should have zero effect on me. I know that. He is an asshole. But somehow they do mean something to me. Somehow I want to accept his apology.

"Why?" I ask. My voice is weak and thin.

"I was a drunk mess back then," he says. "I've always liked to drink and when some stuff happened while I was working as a cop, I couldn't deal with it. It messed with my mind. So I turned to drinking. And I became a raging alcoholic. I became someone I hated, and still hate. And that's why I left. It's not an excuse, I know that. But it is the reason."

His answer is a good one, but not good enough.

And it wasn't the right answer for the question either.

"I was asking why you're here now and why are you sorry."

"Oh," he says.

He stares down at the table, biting on the tip of his thumb. I wait patiently.

"You have to understand something," he finally answers. "I've been in a lot of dark places over the years and all I have is the truth, so I'm only going to tell you the truth. Even if hurts me or you. Okay?"

"We've all been in a lot of dark places. Some of us were put there by our own father."

"I know," he whispers.

"So why now? Why didn't you ever contact me or Kendra. Why didn't you come back to see us? I mean, one day you just leave and then I never see you again. Until now? Why?"

"I don't have a good excuse, or an excuse at all," he says softly. "The reason is that I was a mess and I convinced myself that you were all better off without me."

"That's bullshit."

"I know," he nods. "It is bullshit. But it is the real reason." He draws in a ragged breath and looks me straight in the eyes. He must see this as being important. "I am not a good man, Katie, but I am trying not to be a bad man either. I am just a man – a human being - who has done horrible things to those I love. And now I'm just trying to be a person who does good things. And I'm glad I saved you and even happier that I get to talk to you now. Those are good things. They don't wipe away the past. I wish I could take it all away. I wish I could change everything. But I can't. And I am so sorry for everything. But at least I'm able to do good, and hopefully that will make some kind of a difference."

I almost feel sorry for him. Almost.

The part about just being a human being, neither good nor bad, just a person who does good things, brushed against my heart and mind. Those words feel warm to me.

"But why are you sorry?" I ask.

"Why am I sorry? Because I love you and your sister and even your mom. But I especially love and miss you and your sister. And I never should have left you. If I had to do over again, I'd never leave. But I can't undo the past. You know?"

I nod. I know all about not being able to undo the past.

"And why did I come back? Well, I've been sober now for over five years. One thousand nine hundred and eleven days to be exact. And I had no intention of coming back here. I wanted to, but I figured you'd all have moved on and the last thing you needed was for me to come back into your life. But I'm very active with a halfway house for addicts up in Ohio, just outside of Cleveland. In fact, I work and volunteer there as a counselor. It's pretty much my life."

"So you traded kids for addicts," I interrupt him.

He frowns and looks down at the table.

"No. It's true I care about all the people I meet at the house, but I'd trade all my years with them for just five good minutes with you."

"Sorry," I say to him. "I'll be quiet. Finish your little story, and include the part about your showing up at my apartment out of nowhere."

"Yes, I'm getting to that." He tugs on his ear lobe (God help me) and sucks in a deep breath. "So, news travels fast with addicts and former addicts, and I heard about this friend of a friend of a friend who was down in North Carolina to try to get his old girlfriend back. And if that didn't work, he was going to kill her and her sister. And something about it made me sick. It made the hairs on the back of my neck stand up. When you're a cop for long enough you develop a sixth sense, a kind of hunch. And so I guess I had a hunch. So, long story short, I used my investigation background and found out the guy was Martin, and he was talking about you and Kendra."

"So why didn't you call me or Mom? Or call the police?"

"I did call the police and they said they'd keep an eye out for him and appreciated me calling. Which meant, they thought I was full of crap. And I didn't know. I mean, addicts like to talk a lot and ninety percent of what they say is bullshit. I didn't want to scare you or Kendra or your mom for no reason. So, I got in my car and drove down here. I figured it was time to see you. And honestly, it finally gave me an excuse to get back in your life."

"So how did you save me? I mean, how did you know he was in my apartment?"

"I finally caught up with him just last night. I didn't know if he meant you any harm so I was just gonna stay around him for a couple days and then maybe talk to him. But I lost track of him for about a half hour so I went right to your apartment and I saw the broken bathroom window. That alarmed me. But as I was looking at it, I heard you scream. So, I ran into your building and tried to knock down your door. It took what felt like a half hour but was probably just several seconds, but I was able to knock in the door. And that's when I saw him strangling you and I subdued him."

"You killed him," I whisper.

He nods once. "Yes, I killed him."

"You okay with that?"

"I don't know yet," he answers. "Probably not."

I actually feel sorry for him. How can I have empathy for this man?

He's my dad. And that will never change. As much as I hate it, that's a fact.

He pulls a sheet of paper from his shirt pocket and slides it across the table to me.

"That's my cell number and my office number up in Ohio. Call me anytime. I'd love to hear from you. And share it with Kendra if you can."

I don't say anything about Kendra. I just nod.

"How is she?"

"She's okay," I say. "Actually at a rehab facility out west. She's had it a bit rough too, ya know?"

He appears to be in great pain. "She an addict?"

"An alcoholic to be exact. I guess it runs in the genes. I got your eyes and she got your addiction. But don't worry, she got Mom's loyalty to family."

He goes from looking hurt to looking like he might actually break down in tears. But he manages to keep it together.

"I deserve that and a lot more. I know that. And it's okay to hate me Katie. It's okay."

"I don't hate you," I whisper. "And I'm sorry I just said that."

"It's okay."

I stand and slide his number into the pocket of my jeans. He rises from the chair and looks at me. He just stares at my face, shaking his head and smiling. But it's mostly a sad smile. And damn it, it breaks my heart.

"Thank you," I whisper. "For saving me."

"You're welcome Katie," he says. His voice sounds like a frog. "My pleasure. I know it sounds weird. But it really is my pleasure."

"I need to get out of here."

"Yes, okay. Please, call me sometime. We can talk, when we have more time and we're not in a place like this."

I don't think that will ever happen. As much as the little girl inside of me wants to have him back in in my life, the adult knows it's a bad idea. And if I've learned anything in the past few weeks, it's that I make horrible decisions when I listen to that little girl speaking like she's an adult.

But despite it all, I walk around the table and wrap my arms around my daddy. And he is my daddy. He hugs me back and the feeling it gives me proves it all. I remember this feeling. It's the feeling I cried about for years. It's the feeling I dreamed about ever since he left.

It's the feeling I'd been searching for in all the wrong places.

I am that little girl who sat on his lap while watching Scooby-Doo. He's the daddy whose finger I held while walking to the park. And we're the father and daughter who once played Candyland together and danced like crazy to New Kids on the Block.

We hug and I only cry a little. He cries too.

And suddenly it hits me. I am not that little girl anymore. I'm now an adult who has grown more in the last few weeks than I grew in the previous twenty years. I am strong. I am capable. And I am worthy. I don't need my father or any other man to prove that to me. Life can go on and I can get through all the bullshit on my own.

And hopefully, I can be happy again. Even without Blake.

"I love you," Daddy whispers to me.

And it hurts so much to hear that. But it also feels wonderful.

"I love you too," I say, because I do. "And I hate you too," I add, because I do.

"I know."

I step out of his arms and smile at him. "But I have your number. And maybe I'll call you, okay?"

"I'd love that. And maybe we can get together sometime. And maybe Kendra can join us. Maybe someday."

"Maybe," I say.

"Good bye Katie."

"Bye Daddy."

Chapter Twenty-Seven - Now

I walk out of the police station and around the side of building where they told me they'd left my car for me. The air outside is fresh and crisp. I feel like a little girl stepping out into air conditioning after spending hours in an airless, overheated closet. Darkness has fallen but the parking lot is pretty well lit. I look up to the sky and there are no stars and no moon. Of course there isn't. But I keep looking up anyway.

Strangely, there is a feather-like weightlessness in my head. And my lungs are gigantic and wide open. It's like I've been holding my breath ever since I was a little girl wondering where Daddy went and when he was coming home. I can finally breathe.

The dark clouds slide to the left and uncover the moon. It's big and bright and staring down at me. And I am thinking of Kendra. I picture her sitting on a beach in California, and she is smiling because she's happy. Happy in a way I haven't seen her since we were small children. I'm thinking of Chris too. Things with us will never be like they were. And that's a good thing. I'd always looked at him through the prism of what my father had taught me. But not anymore. Now I see him for what he is. A good man. And I'm thinking of Neil too. That asshole is behind me and that's where he'll forever stay. And I'm thinking of my mom (the one who was always my safe harbor) and my dad (the one who was the ocean tossing me about). I don't know what will happen in my future. But I know it will be better than my past.

All that has happened. It's too much to think about all at once. Everything tries to rush in together: me almost dying in the ocean, Kendra dying and being brought back to life, me slapping Chris across the face and then finally getting to know him, Buzz losing the bar, me losing myself for years, and the psycho Marty. If it all pushes into me at the same time, it will drive me crazy. But it's all behind me now. I have to remember that. And though it seems awfully heavy, I know I don't have to carry it anymore. I can just set it down and leave it be. But I can't and won't let go of everything.

Blake. I will never let go of him. Not in my heart or my mind.

How will I live without him? He is now nothing but the wall that divides me. My life will forever be broken in two: My life before we loved, and my life afterward.

But I will be okay. I have to believe that. And I think I do. I just need to get to the ocean and let it take me away. And then I can figure everything out from there.

Another cloud, this one darker and bigger than the other one, covers the moon again. So, I shift my eyes back down to Earth and I walk to my car.

I jump as a car horn blares across the parking lot. But I ignore it. It's probably just some stupid kid fooling around with his girlfriend or maybe a mother trying to get the attention of her daughter who's across the street over at the Chinese restaurant.

My mind keeps trying to jump back to Blake. It wants to run movie reels of all the times we spent together. It wants to look at albums filled with snapshots of him smiling and laughing and looking directly at me. Worst of all, it wants to imagine where he is right now and wonder if he's imagining me.

I unlock my car door and climb in as that horn blares again. I slide the key into the ignition and try to start the engine. It coughs and stops.

Come on, not now. Please. Just start.

I try again and it coughs, hiccups, burps, and stops. The horn blares again and this time it's closer to me. Headlights fill my car with yellow and the horn blasts from right behind me. I try to start the engine again, and it coughs, chokes, and rumbles to a start.

Thank God. Now to the ocean. Just get me to the ocean.

I nearly have a heart attack from the sudden rapping on my window. I turn my head to see who could possibly be bothering me. And my heart really does stop.

It can't be. For so many reasons, it can't be. I have lost it. I've gone crazy.

But if this is me being insane, then I have no problem with it. As long as he is here with me.

I turn off the engine and open my door. My mind is obviously playing tricks on me. It's not really his face that I saw. It's not him. When I get out of the car and stand up his beautiful face will morph into some stranger's face, and his perfect body will change into some slightly overweight forty-year-old man's body.

But as I stand up and look at him. He doesn't change. It is still him.

My heart drops into my stomach and then rebounds back into my chest where it kicks hard in my breast. I am suddenly cold and hot at the same time. This cannot be. It's too good to be true. And anything that seems too good to be true must be. Especially when it comes to my life.

And yet, this is real. This is true.

"Aren't you supposed to be in Chi-Chicago?" I stammer.

"I didn't get on the plane," he says. "I couldn't."

I lean back against my car and close my eyes tight. I pray that when I open them he's still in front of me. My heart slows for a moment, but picks up again when I think what all this means. Everything bad is gone. Finally gone. Everything good is right in front of me. And I am finally ready to accept all of it.

Dear God let this be real. Please don't let this be some horrible dream. Please make him still be here when I open my eyes.

And when I do, there he is. Blake. Just looking at me. Waiting.

"Looking kind of rough," I say to him because I don't know what else to say.

He grins, and there are those amazing dimples. The ones I didn't think I'd ever see again.

"You're looking a little rough around the edges too."

"Yeah, well I just got out of jail and was attacked earlier and I lost the love of my life. Plus, I didn't sleep at all last night."

"Yeah, well, I didn't sleep last night either."

"Did some hot chick keep you up all night?"

"As a matter of fact, yes."

"Wait. What?"

"That hot chick was you."

"Oh," I say with an embarrassed smile.

I bite on the tip of my thumb and look down at the pavement.

"Listen Katie," he says to me. "I want to apologize to you and ask for your forgiveness."

He doesn't need to apologize. He just needs to take me in his arms and tell me everything will be okay. I need him to surround me. I need to feel his body against mine.

"Don't say you're sorry," I tell him. "You didn't do anything wrong. It was me who-."

He raises up his hand in front of my mouth. "May I speak? I just need to get this out, okay?"

"Okay."

"I was sitting there on the plane already to go to Chicago and start an awesome career in corporate law and to make a lot of money in a city that's great. But I suddenly realized none of it meant anything to me. And I didn't care about being some hotshot lawyer or about making money. Hell, I have money. What I'd always wanted to do was help people. I want to help people who've maybe made a few mistakes in their lives but now need someone to help them get out of trouble and start a new life. And then I realized what a hypocrite I was being for running away from you. If complete strangers deserve a new start, then so does the love of my life.

"But that's not why I got off the plane, Katie. I got off because even helping people as a lawyer means nothing to me. I care about it, and I want to do it, but without you, it means absolutely nothing to me.

I know it sounds crazy. And I know you make my life a little messy. But I like that kind of messy. Before you, everything was neat and tidy. But now that I've fallen in love with you, when I'm with you I'm a bit of mess. But when I'm not with you, I'm an absolute dumpster fire. And I can't convince myself that potentially throwing away Chicago and forgiving and forgetting everything that Neil told me is absolutely the right thing to do, but I don't care. I just want to be with you. I have to be with you. You're all that matters. Without you, my life is nothing. And I know that sounds ridiculous and impossible and corny and-."

"And perfect," I add.

"And perfect," he agrees.

"But my past is still there. It will always be there."

"I don't care. I love you. And your past is what brought you to me. That's all that matters. It brought you to me." He steps in closer so his left foot is between my feet and his chest is against my breasts. "I love you," he whispers. "And I want to spend the rest of my life with you."

"But you're not sure it's the right thing?" I ask cautiously.

"I am sure that being with you is right. And I am one hundred percent positive that the only way I'll ever be happy is if I'm with you."

"And you're sure you're sure?"

"I've never been more sure about anything in my life. And I've always been sure about everything. Until I met you anyway," he chuckles.

I smile. "I love you. Don't ever leave me again, okay?"

He puts his arms around me and pulls me in. I'm nearly picked-up off my feet. I wrap my arms around him and the final shadows of all that was bad, finally run away; the light rushes in.

In his arms there is nothing but good. There is nothing but light. A light that's so perfect that I wish I could live in it for the rest of my life. And I think I just might.

Our mouths meet and we kiss. I just want to climb completely inside him right now. And as he kisses me even deeper, it feels like we are floating away, high into the sky. But we aren't. We stay right here in this parking lot kissing each other and feeling like there has never, ever been anything this good in the world.

I love this man. I freaking love this man so much!

"Are you okay? Did that asshole hurt you?" he whispers into my ear.

"Yeah. I'm fine. And no, he didn't really hurt me. Not much. But can we talk about all of that later?"

"Of course," he says. And then he squeezes me tighter.

Eventually we let go of each other and Blake grabs my hand. We walk back toward his Jeep. My eyes blink at the brightness of his headlights as we walk around the passenger side and he opens the door for me.

"So what now?" I ask him.

"Now we never leave each other."

That sounds perfect to me and it makes me grin. But it doesn't answer my question. I meant what are we going to do next? What is he going to do about his job and what the hell am I going to do? I know he'll make a good decision and I'm ready to finally move on with my life. No matter what happens, everything really will be okay. Better than okay actually.

But I don't know what comes next. Like right now.

"I mean, what about right now?" I clarify. "What's the next step?"

"Just get in the car and drive," he says taking my hand and helping me into the seat.

"Just get in the car and drive, huh?"

"Yeah. Maybe drive across the country and see Kendra and then maybe head up north to Seattle or down to San Diego. Just drive wherever we want. Just get in the car and drive."

That sounds absolutely perfect.

"What about my car?" I ask.

"Leave it behind. Let them have it."

"Really?"

"Yeah really."

"Just leave it and then off we go driving wherever we want for as long as we want?"

"That's the plan."

I leave one leg out of the car and just look at him with a huge grin on my face.

"What?' he says with a laugh.

I just shake my head.

"What?" he asks again.

"Just drive forever, huh?"

"If you want."

"So you're that kind of rich?" I ask. And then I put my other leg in the car.

"Yep," Blake grins. "I'm that kind of rich."

And then he looks at me with that perfect smile, showing his irresistible dimples. And he tips me a wink just before slamming the door shut and jogging around to the driver's side of his Jeep. He hops in next to me and shifts it into *Drive*. Then he grabs my hand in his and squeezes it tight. He slams on the gas so hard that I let out a little *whoop*.

And into the night we drive. Racing toward our future.

BEFORE WE LOVED

Chai Rose

b

About the Author

Chai Rose lives in New York with his family. Chai is a former high school and middle school English teacher. In his free-time he enjoys hanging out with his children, reading, writing, and watching movies.

Chai is also the author of the novella, *About the Fall*, and two short stories: "Our Reunion" and "Our Christmas Spirit".

Chai Rose

Also by Chai Rose

About the Fall
Our Reunion
Our Christmas Spirit

Please visit Chai online at:

chaiwriter.com

Made in the USA
Middletown, DE
14 July 2024

57266452R00188